ord Pierson Reforms

)

Lord Pierson Reforms

Donna Simpson

THORNDIKE
CHIVERS

This Large Print edition is published by Thorndike Press®, Waterville, Maine USA and by BBC Audiobooks, Ltd, Bath, England.

Published in 2005 in the U.S. by arrangement with Zebra Books, an imprint of Kensington Publishing Corp.

Published in 2005 in the U.K. by arrangement with Kensington Publishing Corp.

U.S. Hardcover 0-7862-7458-1   (Romance)
U.K. Hardcover 1-4056-3326-3   (Chivers Large Print)
U.K. Softcover 1-4056-3327-1   (Camden Large Print)

The text of this Large Print edition is unabridged.
Other aspects of the book may vary from the original edition.

Set in 16 pt. Plantin by Minnie B. Raven.

Printed in the United States on permanent paper.

British Library Cataloguing-in-Publication Data available

Library of Congress Cataloging-in-Publication Data

Simpson, Donna.
    Lord Pierson reforms / by Donna Simpson.
        p. cm. — (Thorndike Press large print romance)
    ISBN 0-7862-7458-1 (lg. print : hc : alk. paper)
    1. Large type books. I. Title. II. Thorndike Press
large print romance series.
    PR9199.3.S529L67 2005
    813′.54—dc22   2004029994

Lord Pierson Reforms

One

"You're a right heavy bloke, y'know that?" The pretty young Cyprian hefted her bulky burden and grunted to her friend, "Maisie, kin you carry a bit more o' th' load?"

"Bloody hell, no, Becky! He's a-gonna have to help, or we'll end in the bloody gutter." Maisie, a homely blonde girl, shoved her shoulder under the man's arm.

They stumbled down the foggy, gaslit London street, making their way through the sulfurous yellow miasma, dodging muddy puddles and avoiding the splashing of carriages that rumbled along the cobbles. A light rain started, the drops dotting the puddles left from the rain earlier that evening.

"Of all the filthy luck!" Becky moaned. "As if it ain't bad enough. Me best dress is already covered in muck . . . Now it's rainin', an' only gonna get worse."

Finally, their burden spoke up. "Ladies," he slurred. "S-sorry t' be such a bother, but I promise t' make it worth your while."

"Yer lucky it's us, yer nibs, and not one

o' those blokes who was eyein' ya wiv interest in the hell." That was Maisie, the homely one; she was kinder hearted than Becky, but also hoped for a sizable reward from their handsome burden.

Lord Pierson shook his head, scattering raindrops from his nose as he tried to clear the fog in his brainbox, which was more persistent than the London haze surrounding them. He *had* to clear his head, had to think, and find his way home. He would not be found in the gutter for all the gossipmongers to make sport of. His name was already synonymous with the degradation he had brought to an old and worthy name.

Not that he was the one who had harmed the name most. That honor fell to his esteemed pater, who had passed from the living world to the one beyond in an opium den. No, his only part in the shame had been to further the decline, debasing the Pierson title even more with his wastrel ways.

And yet, there were things he thought he would not descend to, for example, to be found face down in the gutter, drunk, and robbed of his stickpin and purse. And so he had chosen two of the more honest of the Bacchanal Club's fair "barques of frailty" and offered them a reward if they would see him safely home to Eleven Varden Square, his townhouse. Another hour spent drinking at the Bacchanal would have been his undoing for he suspected, from his advanced state of inebriation, that someone was spiking his gin with a narcotic.

Again, he shook his shaggy head and tried to cooperate with the girls helping him home, picking his feet up and plodding along the walk. He would make it, and then he wouldn't drink for a couple of days, he swore to himself.

Though he had sworn so before with little effect.

"We hafta cross here," he mumbled, pointing with one finger across the road. "And then turn." He snuffled, rubbing one wet sleeve across his running nose.

One of the girls grunted and sniffed, mumbling about the rain again, but he was concentrating fiercely on the way home and paid no attention. They continued their uneven progress as they crossed the cobbled street.

The deep rumble and clatter of wheels on cobblestone behind them announced another carriage coming, and Maisie and Becky tried to haul him to the relative safety of a gaslight standard — they were already in a better part of town, or there would not be gaslights — and he staggered, his boot heel catching on the gutter.

Damnation, but his legs would not work right!

"C'mon, ya great lout. Up t' the walk, now," Maisie said.

They made it up to the walk as the carriage approached, and Pierson, stumbling down on one knee, looked up. In the open window of the carriage was framed an angel, her silvery hair braided into a coronet around her oval fair-skinned face, her perfect lips parted slightly in a beautiful smile, jewels sparkling at her white throat. She was like a painting framed in the window, the lamplight glowing on her face creating the effect of radiance. He stared, preternaturally aware of her every movement even at such a distance, and as he gazed, open-mouthed, a wave of filthy water engulfed him and his companions.

Maisie and Becky swore in high-pitched screeches and shook their fists as the carriage driver rolled on, oblivious, the clop-clop-clop of the horses' hooves receding in the muffling fog.

But Pierson, mud and water streaming down his face and trickling down the front of his coat, stared after the carriage. He had just seen the face of an angel, like a seraphim, the one woman in the world for whom he could reform himself, if she would just deign to favor him with another radiant smile. Surely this was that elusive love-at-first-sight, for never had he felt this surge of hope, this delirium of optimism. He was engulfed in a wave of gratitude more than the torrent of filthy water, for he knew in his heart that in one moment his destiny had changed.

Who was she, the bright angel? And what could he do to make her see that she could make him a better man, the kind of man a woman such as she could be proud to call her own?

He stood, slowly, shaking off more of the fog of alcohol. He would find out who she was, or his name was not Dante Delacorte Pierson.

In the carriage, Amy Corbett gasped and tried to rise from her seat, but the carriage shuddered and she sat back down abruptly. "That poor man! James must go back and . . ."

She was stopped by her charge's gales of laughter.

"Did you see him, Amy?" Lady Rowena

Revington held her stomach and gasped out the words through fits of laughter. "Did you see that fellow, muck and filth in his eyes, his hair all streaming down and muddy, kneeling in the gutter! He was gaping like a . . . like a cod."

"Lady Rowena," Amy said, shocked reproach in her voice, as she twisted back around from looking behind them. Trying to set the matronly tone she considered appropriate for the chaperon of a duke's daughter, she primmed her mouth and said, "You should not laugh at that poor fellow. I have never seen anything so awful! We should go back, make sure he is all right and that his two companions are not . . ."

"His two whores, you mean," Lady Rowena said, wrinkling her nose in disgust.

"His . . . Oh, Lady Rowena," Amy said, her gloved hand muffling her words. "You should not say such awful . . ."

"*Oh, Lady Rowena,*" the young woman said in a strangled, prissy tone, imitating her chaperon. "Do not try to correct me, Amy," she said, in her normal voice. Her eyes lit up in merriment and she burst into laughter again, rocking back and forth. She wiped a tear from her eye with her Paisley shawl and continued, "I shall be laughing about this for days. You must admit it was a diverting sight when James splashed that drunken sot, while he knelt in the gutter, muck all over him, and those two *girls* swearing and shaking their fists . . . I would give a quarter's allowance to see that again! Truly, I would."

Amy lapsed into silence and stared in mortification at the beautiful young woman opposite her. The interior of the carriage was gloomy, the only light from the coach lanterns, but there was no concealing the glory of Lady Rowena's fair hair, glowing like pewter, silvery, with a light like the moon. The jewels sparked and twinkled at her ivory throat and her expensive gown hugged perfect curves. She was a most beautiful young lady. But for her to laugh at another human's plight in that way . . . What did it say about her heart?

And this was the girl for whom it was her duty to find and capture an unexceptionable bridegroom. Better than unexceptional: no one but an earl or a marquess at the very least would do for the daughter of a duke. She quailed at the thought. What did she know of the upper echelons of the aristocracy?

Well, she knew more now than she did just a few short months ago.

Looking back at the circumstances that had brought her to this difficult pass, Amy reflected that it was all a matter of chance. She had been extraordinarily happy in her previous position in Ireland, as governess to a brood of girls, the daughters of the Honorable Mr. Laurence Donegal and his wife, Mrs. Honoria Donegal. At twenty-four, and with no connections to the greater world or "good society," Amy felt fortunate in her post and loved the girls sincerely, especially the eldest, a vivacious and impetuous girl who had vowed never to marry. Miss Bridget Donegal, eighteen, and past all need of a governess except as a chaperon at village assemblies — Mrs. Donegal fancied herself ill much more often than she actually was and would not attend those small affairs — had told all who would listen that she had no intention of marrying, and had publicly announced that she and Amy would someday, when all the Donegal brood were past their need for a governess, take a house in the village and live on her inheritance. After that announcement Mrs. Donegal had spent a week in bed.

But an eighteen-year-old girl, spoilt and

doted upon, knows little about what she truly wants, and when a young English gentleman of impeccable birth and considerable property happened to visit the Donegal house, saw Bridget in some amateur theatrics, the mounting of which was Amy's great joy, he fell immediately in love with the "fair Ophelia," as her part styled her, winsome, lovely, and ethereal. He promptly — or at least within two days — had declared himself, been accepted, and the betrothal was announced and the banns read in church for the first time. Some people in the village declared it unseemly, the haste with which the young man had been accepted.

The Donegals might not have been so hasty if they were not sure he would abscond the moment he found out their daughter's true personality. But Bridget was no one's fool. The young man was handsome and rich, and she saw immediately that she was unlikely ever to have another offer so fine. Marriage to him promised a life of ease, travel, and fine society, a far cry from the spinster's existence she had imagined as the pinnacle of her ambition, when faced with the village lads as her only alternative. She abruptly abandoned all her announced plans and accepted him with an alacrity the young man chose to find flattering.

Amy still had grave doubts of them ever being truly happy, but she was only the governess, not Bridget's mother, and had nothing to say in the case. The girl was swiftly married, and somehow, Amy was sure neither how nor why, it was all attributed to her own superior common sense and powers of persuasion. Mrs. Donegal, proud of having a very proper young English lady as her governess — the Donegals, Protestant but still Irish down to the bone, were very conscious of their inferior status in English eyes — had taken the opportunity to trumpet the young lady's abilities far and wide. When the incredibly wealthy and powerful Duke of Sylverton happened, on his way to his estate in England from some business on the Irish coast, to briefly visit Mr. Donegal on horse purchasing business near Christmas time in 1818 — it was a visit that sent Mrs. Donegal again to bed, this time for two weeks, but only after the duke left — he heard about the eldest daughter's miraculously good match. It was unavoidable, since the wedding had just taken place and the happy couple had returned for a brief visit to her family before heading to the young man's home.

From that moment, Amy Corbett's fate was sealed, even though during the duke's visit she was ensconced in the nursery upstairs with the younger children. She was not privy to Mrs. Donegal and the duke's conversation, but from experience she could imagine the boasting about "Miss Corbett, our English governess," and how the lady would amplify and exaggerate Amy's part in Bridget's marriage. For some reason Mrs. Donegal felt it reflected well on them to have such a treasure in their employ.

Amy wished Mrs. Donegal had kept her compliments silent.

She glanced at Lady Rowena, who still chuckled over the poor man they had deluged, and then back out the window. Surely they were almost home? Or at least back to the duke's London residence, which was far too grand in Amy's unassuming view to ever feel like "home." It was like living in a museum, but not as cheerful. But she had never had much choice in the matter of where she would live next. The Donegals had received from the Duke of Sylverton an offer that was worded as a command. They would release Miss Corbett from her employment in their household so that the young lady

17

could work for him as chaperon to his lovely daughter Lady Rowena. Her duties would not be onerous, so they could, in good conscience, let her go.

Of course, they had not needed his reassurance of Amy's good treatment to see the necessity of releasing her immediately. No one who had ever met the duke would deny him anything. Even if his grand and elevated title did not awe them — and it did the Donegals — his manner, which was lofty and regal, would have. They let her go immediately, and she had no recourse but to become Lady Rowena's companion and chaperon for the approaching Season, with the understanding that the duke expected her to work the same kind of miracle with the duke's daughter that she had done with Bridget Donegal.

Leaning her head against the carriage window, Amy remembered the relief she felt meeting Lady Rowena for the first time. During her long voyage from Ireland and the travel to the duke's country mansion, she had worried that the duke's daughter would be some kind of fright or virago. But then, on reaching the manse, she had been escorted up the long winding staircase to Lady Rowena's bedchamber.

She felt immediate relief. Lady Rowena

was lovely, and though physical beauty didn't mean much to Amy in her evaluation of people, with it the girl combined a sweet and helpless gentle personality. The poor girl was ill, just recovering from the effects of a putrid throat and fever. She was wan and thin and grateful to anyone who talked to her and would sit with her. *Poor, poor girl,* Amy had thought, gazing down at the young woman wrapped closely in woolen shawls and covers. With a father like the duke, she mostly needed someone to intercede for her, perhaps, someone to make sure she was not hustled into an unhappy marriage against her wishes. She was certainly too weak and feeble to stand up herself to a man like the duke.

All of Amy's protective instincts were stirred. The duke only said his daughter was known in society as a pure and unsullied flower of English maidenhood. No one had a word to say against her in society, he claimed. She had begun to feel that this position might be even more enjoyable than her post at the Donegals' tumultuous and disorderly house.

Later, after they had traveled to London and she was ensconced in the ducal mansion, Amy found it to be the literal truth that Lady Rowena was everywhere proclaimed as the perfect picture of English purity and demureness, and she was puzzled by the duke's vehemence in attaching her as a chaperon to his daughter. Why, with such a sweet and gentle daughter, known throughout society as a paragon of English feminine virtue, had he needed to employ herself, most famous for making a match for a difficult young lady? Amy could not understand it, but did not dare ask the duke. She had been forced to accept the position for lack of any alternatives, but Lady Rowena's doting father had also offered, as an incentive, such a staggering sum to achieve the object, Lady Rowena's marriage to an acceptable suitor, that Amy had begun to dream of her heart's desire, to go home to the village of her birth down in Kent and buy a certain little cottage. She was a talented seamstress and if she was assured enough money to go on for a while, she knew she could make a living doing what she loved.

That had become her inspiration, and as she helped her charge recover her strength, she had felt her heart's desire as close as this one Season. Surely it would not be difficult to find a husband for such a little turtledove as Lady Rowena!

Reality came as a shock. Once fully recovered, Lady Rowena was, in truth — at least in the bosom of her limited family structure — a headstrong, determined, obstreperous, demanding termagant, as similar to Bridget Donegal as a stubborn mule was to an ewe lamb. Like her father, she was a Tartar, difficult and temperamental, and with such a low opinion of men that she had sworn never to marry. To the outside world she might appear the veriest lovely turtledove, but she was a hellcat.

And then the complete truth was revealed to Amy as she witnessed a raging argument between the duke and his daughter, the like of which Amy had never in all her years seen, or imagined. It appeared that His Grace had tried, with threats and intimidation, to force his child to choose a suitor and marry, but she was truly her father's daughter and she knew him far too well. He would neither carry out any of the horrible threats he made, nor would he ever force her to marry against her will.

And yet it was Amy's duty to find a gentleman and promote a match. It was her only hope of securing the promised reward, and she did not even want to think about what would happen should she fail. The duke had made it abundantly clear that failure was unthinkable.

So she was chaperon to a lady who had no intention of marrying, even though she was certainly willing to enslave any young man who came within her sphere. This was only the second week of the Season and already Lady Rowena had turned down the offers of a foreign prince and a duke's second son. Her father, as impetuous as his daughter, had hired Amy away from the Donegals without even asking if she had entree into society. The result was that Lady Rowena knew far more about society than her chaperon, and that situation could not be conducive to any reliance or respect between them.

If only she could have gone on being Lady Rowena's companion without the relentless pressure of finding her a husband and convincing her to marry, Amy could have lived with it. The girl was inconsiderate and obstreperous in private, but not completely unbearable. There were whole minutes when she was sweet-tempered and obliging.

It was the pressure from the duke that was wearing Amy down. He had seemed so accommodating and gentlemanly in their only interview. But as his daughter recovered her health and showed her true character, he too had revealed himself as demanding, unpredictable, choleric in the extreme, and virtually unapproachable. Amy's task, as stated by the duke, was to get Rowena married off before the end of the Season. How did one marry off a girl who did not ever want to marry? Bridget had been younger, just eighteen, and spoilt, but not impossible. Rowena was twenty-one, and had inherited from her father his temperament.

And what did Amy know about the kind of society inhabited by dukes and earls? By now the duke was virtually blaming her for not having any experience in elite society, and his unreasonableness was giving her nightmares of what would happen if she did not fulfill her part of their "understanding," as the duke insisted on calling it.

It seemed to be an impossible task.

She glanced through the dimness at the beautiful girl, whose head had now lolled back as she fell asleep against the squabs in the carriage. If only she was the wraithlike, gentle girl Amy had first met. Many men equated femininity with that kind of wan, helpless lethargy. But then, the problem was not in finding a man who wanted to marry Lady Rowena — there were many suitors for her hand — but in convincing Lady Rowena that she wanted to marry at all.

What was Amy going to do?

She had a very sound understanding of human nature, after years of observing people at their best . . . and their worst. If she didn't succeed in marrying Rowena off by the end of the Season, it would be deemed by the duke as *her* failure and he would blame her wholly, as unfair as that was. She wouldn't be able to get another position with that on her head, nor would she be able to go back to the Donegals, for they would never risk angering the duke.

What was she going to do?

Two

"Pay the girls, Rupert," Pierson said, staggering into his townhouse and sagging onto a bench in the hall. It felt so good to rest after that arduous crawl through the streets of London.

His valet, Rupert Charpentier — that name sounded so much better for a proper valet than the "Robert Carpenter" he had been born with — resplendent in a cast-off silk robe of Pierson's, held his candle high and looked the two girls over, but he merely said, "You are dripping on the carpet."

Maisie looked him up and down with an insolent gaze, stuck out her grimy hand, snapped her fingers and said, "You 'eard 'is nibs: Money!"

Rupert gave them a couple of shillings apiece, even though they demanded gold. They called him a couple of foul names as Pierson watched in foggy amusement, but then finally the viscount said, "Go on, give them more, Rupert, old man. They've been good girls and should be rewarded." He sat up a little straighter and shook his head. Droplets of scummy water showered the carpet and sprinkled the valet. "And besides, I think my fortunes are on the mend. I feel kindly toward the world tonight."

"You do not even look *of* this world tonight, my lord." The valet shook a stray drop from his bare hand and gave more money to the girls. They stuck their tongues out at him, he made a rude gesture, and they left. "Come, my lord, let's get you upstairs. You smell like the sewer, but I doubt we'll be able to do anything about that tonight, with you in this state."

"Where is Dorcaster?" Pierson said, as his valet pulled at his arm, trying to haul him to a standing position. Though the bench was hard, being a rococo monstrosity brought back from Germany by one of his more respectable ancestors, it still felt better than moving at the moment. He resisted.

Rupert released his arm and looked down at him thoughtfully. "Mr. Dorcaster said he could not remain as butler in a household that had no form nor dignity. He said he was leaving to work for a gentleman as deserved the name, and though he wished you well, he daily expected to hear your demise announced in the papers.

I am quoting him exactly, my lord."

Pierson put one hand over his heart. "Oh, the arrows! Pierced through the heart by a butler's disrespect!" He fell back giggling on the bench. Then he frowned. He gazed up at his valet. "Am I so very bad, Rupert? Am I beyond hope? Can a fellow as far gone as I reform?"

Rupert, his pale eyes steady on his employer, said, slowly, "Do you want to reform?"

Pierson, his mind clearing, looked down at himself. He was filthy and he stank. Nightly he haunted the hells and dens of the worst parts of London out of boredom and a restless desire for excitement. Granted, he met with many others of his own ilk, gentlemen of good social standing and low tastes. But most, like his friend the Marquess of Bainbridge, drank in moderation, gambled no more than they cared to lose and then left before the evening devolved into the kind of melee that had erupted that very night at the Bacchanal Club. So why could he not do the same? Why was he adrift in such a sea of squalor?

He had tried to stay home or visit the tamer entertainments considered suitable for a gentleman of his standing, but boredom and an irritated awareness of how unwelcome he was in better society always sent him back to the underbelly of London life.

"I do," he said, more to himself than Rupert. "I am heartily sick of myself and my life. But do I dare? Do I dare seek her out?"

"My lord, who do you mean?"

Pierson gazed up at his valet. His shaggy hair, the despair of Rupert, flopped in his eyes, clumps curling wetly against his forehead. "Her: The vision, the fair angel I saw this very evening and who holds out to me the possibility that there's more to life than this wretched existence. Somewhere, somehow, there is grace and beauty and sweetness." *Very good, old man,* Pierson thought, he was slurring only a little now. He gazed up at his valet. "Why do you work for me, Rupert, old boy?"

"Truthfully, my lord?" The valet again tried to pull the viscount to his feet, this time succeeding. They started out the dim hallway, through the dining room, toward the stairs.

"Of course, truthfully! Why do you work for me?"

They started up the gloomy, chilly stairs, stopping only occasionally for the viscount to catch his breath and once for him to

28

sneeze. When they got to the third floor landing, Pierson looked up and saw three pairs of eyes staring down at him from behind the railing. The housemaids, he thought, watching their master come home.

"Pretty maids all in a row," he giggled, and then abruptly stopped. He straightened as the girls retreated into the shadows with a collective gasp and murmur of nervous chatter. "What a bloody mess I am," he said, passing one filthy hand over his hair. Somehow, somewhere he had lost the very correct gloves he had started the evening wearing. That would make three pairs of gloves lost that week, as well as a miscellany of missing stickpins, a pocket watch, and even a ring. He looked up again into the shadows. "I am sorry, all of you," he called. "And if it is possible, I shall do better in future."

Rupert opened the master chamber's door and guided the viscount toward his bed. Pierson was sleepily aware of his boots being pulled off and his clothes being removed, none too gently. He slipped naked under the clean sheets and sighed, almost asleep.

As he drifted, he thought he heard his valet speak again.

"I have stayed, sir," Rupert murmured, "for the rare flashes of good breeding you display. And because I hoped this day would come. I *knew* this day would come."

"I still cannot forget that ridiculous man on the street and how he looked, filth all over him and his hair down in his face. What a wretch!"

Amy, pacing behind Lady Rowena's vanity table as the duke's daughter regally allowed her maid to braid her tresses for the night, stopped and glared at her charge's back. "I still don't think it is humorous. Poor fellow."

"He was drunk, and those two girls were his whores. Who knows what they were going to do once they got wherever they were going." Rowena's tone displayed her disgust.

Amy sighed, but did not bother remonstrating with Lady Rowena. The girl knew how she felt about such language, and she used it more as a result. Instead, Amy consulted the small book she held in her hands. "Tomorrow is Lady Bainbridge's literary tea, and then tomorrow evening is the ball at the Plimptons'. Wednesday evening, of course, is Almack's, and the day after that is the Venetian breakfast at Lord and Lady Sayres' . . . They reside in . . . Varden Square, I believe?"

"Do I care?" Rowena twisted her head and slapped at her maid's hand. "Jeanette, you pulled my hair! Be more careful." She gazed back into the mirror and met Amy's gaze in it above the candlelight. "And as to the other, I won't go to Lady Bainbridge's. I have heard she is the veriest old scold, and that her teas are the height of boredom."

"But we have to go! Lady Bainbridge was a friend of your mother's, I have heard, and she will expect that notice from you! She knows you are in London for the Season. It would be the height of ill manners not to show her that notice." Amy shocked, stared at the girl's back.

"I don't care. Make an excuse."

"I won't; Rowena, you *must* go!"

The young woman turned in her chair as Jeanette patted the last braid into place and retreated. Rowena fixed her cold gaze on Amy. "Never, *ever* do that again! Do not tell me what I will and will not do. I won't go."

"You will," Amy said, refusing to be cowed by Lady Rowena's obstreperous behavior. Ultimately it was the duke Amy must please, not his daughter. But she would rather not quarrel, and so, employing a cunning she seldom used, she continued, "You will, or you risk looking like an ungrateful wretch, and then Prince Verstadt — who will be there, for he never misses a literary experience and I know he has been invited — will learn of your ingratitude and ungraciousness and will be glad he has had an escape from your . . ." She took a deep breath. "From your clutches, instead of being heartbroken as he is now. Lady Frances Mortimer is just waiting for you to make a misstep so she can lay her nets for the prince."

A calculating expression crossed Rowena's fair face. "Lady Frances will not be there, will she? She may never learn of my absence."

Amy knelt at the girl's knee. "She may or may not be there, but Lady Harriet, Lady Bainbridge's daughter, will most certainly be there and she, I have heard, is Lady Frances's most particular friend."

"All right. We shall go. But only so I can pay my respects to Lady Bainbridge, for poor mama's sake." She turned back to the mirror.

Amy sighed and sent up a silent prayer of thanks to whatever divine power had directed her to Mrs. Bower, a chaperon of extraordinary ability, who had taken Amy under her wing and given her a few tips and much gossip about who was who, and who hated whom. Mrs. Bower also, without saying so, seemed to understand Amy's predicament with Lady Rowena and had subtly encouraged Amy to use such tactics as she had just employed. Until now Amy had hesitated to use what felt like manipulation, but it was a matter of survival. She must do what she could.

She gazed up at the girl, who was fussily primping one wayward curl, and wondered what had made her the way she was. "Lady Rowena," she said. "Do you know how fortunate a young lady you are? You know I am not one to flatter, but there is not another in London, I think, who unites your beauty, wealth, good health, and position."

"I know that," she said, with a self-satisfied smile.

"Then why do you insist on behaving like a spoiled child much of the time? It is not becoming in one with so many blessings."

"I do not act like a spoiled child," Rowena said, her face pinched into a frown.

There was a disbelieving snort from the maid who was tidying Rowena's washstand.

It was hard to believe, but it appeared that Lady Rowena truly did not fathom how her behavior appeared to others. Amy sighed and stood. "Good night, then, my lady. Sleep well."

"I always do," Rowena said, crossing the room, shrugging out of her dressing gown — the waiting maid caught it before it fell to the floor and then pulled her mistress' covers back — and climbed into the bed. Jeanette, the maid, very French but very dour, pulled the covers up for her.

Amy retreated to her own room, which was a grand suite just next to Rowena's. It was a beautiful room, with high molded ceilings and gilt carved wood panels on the walls. She drifted around the perimeter to the ornate wardrobe, removed her clothes and hung them away, donning her nightrail as she thought of the past few months, her descent from hope to despair, and then her slow ascent to the determination she now had. She could not fail in her quest. Somehow, some way she must convince Lady Rowena that what society said was true, a married lady had much more freedom than a single lady. Restrictions would vanish overnight and many things that had been closed to her would then be open, travel, more daring clothes, more freedom of movement.

Even though Lady Rowena must have known it was true, she sniffed at such reasoning, for she was having such fun as a sought after unmarried lady, how could marriage improve her lot? After all, when married she would be expected to pop out baby after baby, she said disdainfully, and everyone knew what that meant. She would be immured in some country estate, fat and haggard and with no company except servants, for her husband would no doubt come to London and make merry while she suffered.

Amy had been shocked by the forthrightness of her speech, but had not been able to counter such reasoning with any proof. And yet . . . children; didn't Lady Rowena want children? Perhaps, the duke's daughter said, but she was young and had years and years to worry about that.

Amy put out her candle and climbed into bed. If she was honest, she would say that if her own self-preservation was not involved, she would have advised her charge never to marry if she had those opinions, because there were already enough unhappy marriages and neglected children in the world.

She turned onto her side. What did *she*

truly want out of life? If she could just choose, would *she* choose marriage?

Moonlight filtered through the sheer curtains. The maid had neglected to draw the drapes in her room again, likely because she knew that Amy was not one to complain about such negligence. But she didn't really mind. Moonlight was lovely and shimmery, and gave a soft glow to the cavernous room.

She pondered the question. Marriage would make life easier in some ways, but there might be a whole new set of difficulties with a man to please, not the least of which was the necessity of being intimate with a gentleman one might not care for in that very personal way. No, on the whole she had relied on her own good sense up until now. If it wasn't for the unpredictable nature of the duke, she would be content in her current position. It was only uncertainty that made life unbearable, she thought, and her present situation was extremely uncertain.

She closed her eyes. Who was that poor gentleman in the gutter, she wondered, picturing him anew, turning her mind away from her own difficulties to a fellow inhabitant of the earth. In that one second she had not been able to get a very clear idea of what he looked like. He was kneeling, so she didn't know his height. His hair was likely brown, but with the darkness, the fog, the odd color of the gaslight, and the filth that was sprayed over him, it could have been blond.

But in his distress she found him an interesting subject. If she had been mistress she would have stopped the carriage and offered him aid, even if the ladies with him were, as Rowena conjectured, ladies of the evening. It reflected poorly on her own moral character, she feared, but she could not consider them as anything but other creatures on the earth, fellow travelers on the path of life, doing what they had to do to survive the vagaries of this world.

Life was hard, as she had discovered when her parents had died within days of each other from a wretched bout of typhus when she was only fifteen. She had been dejected and lonely, and if it hadn't been for her Aunt Marabelle, and that woman's extreme self-sacrifice in taking in a desolate, pitiable, and poor niece, she could have been one of those girls, with nowhere to go but the streets of London. Who knew?

"There but for the grace of God go I," she muttered, and it was almost an invocation. Sleep approached, creeping toward her in silent steps. Exhausted, she murmured a prayer for the girls and more especially for the gentleman in the gutter's well-being, and drifted off.

Just a few city squares away, Lord Dante Delacorte Pierson, eighth viscount of that title, awoke a couple of hours later from a dream in which his fair vision was stroking his brow and murmuring faint words of comfort. The fog of inebriation had completely worn off and he slipped out of bed and padded, naked, over to the window, pulling the heavy brocade drapes open and staring out over the rooftop of the neighboring townhouse. A faint shimmer showed in the east that dawn was coming.

His vision haunted him with longings he had never experienced before. Was it an illusion, his fleeting impression of exquisite goodness and purity, the fair Belladonna of his desires? All his life he had followed in his father's footsteps, not seeing any chance that he would ever be able to reclaim any respect for the Pierson name. Delacorte, his country estate, was heavily mortgaged to finance his life in London. He had hated the country for that very reason, that the old home of his remembrance only held reproach for him now that he was Pierson, of a long line of Piersons who had sacked and looted the land. He felt helpless in the face of such a long history of neglect. What could one man, one generation, do to right that ancient wrong?

But a woman such as his vision, with wisdom in her bright eyes and patience in her soothing touch, if he had her he could feel some hope of rebirth. And he wanted that renascence, that second chance. There would be something to work for in the hope of a child, a son, to carry on the old name. There would be a reason to make the name something, not to be ashamed of, but to be proud of. A wife and a son would give him the incentive he needed to stay away from gambling and the bottle.

So his first step must be to find and woo — if she were not already married, dread thought — the fair beauty of his adoration. And yet for some reason he felt sure that the lady he had seen was not married. He knew that she would change his life forever.

He padded back to bed and slipped under the covers. He would start on the morrow. It would give him some object, some way to occupy his time that would keep him from the gambling hells and drinking dens. He buried his head under the pillow against the insistent light of dawn and drifted back to sleep, contentment stealing through his exhausted body for the first time in many months.

Three

Pierson, with the restless energy of the newly sober, paced in the magnificent Bainbridge drawing room waiting for his friend to join him. Lady Bainbridge, clad in her usual attire of pearl gray half-mourning, sailed into the room but drew back to the doorway when she saw him.

"My lady, please don't leave," Pierson said, offering her a courteous bow.

Reluctantly the lady, her gray hair stiffly waved and topped by a lacy white cap, stepped inside the door again.

Pierson took a deep breath. The widowed marchioness had despised him for some years, believing him to be a bad influence on her son, the marquess. It was, in her opinion, that bad influence that kept her darling boy from following his mother's, grandmother's and aunts' inclination, which was that he find a wife to bear a slew of children to carry on the illustrious title of his forefathers. Never mind that that was hardly fair to Pierson, since Bainbridge had no desire to marry until he decided on his own; the ladies had decided Pierson was in the wrong and that was that. His despicable reputation gave them all the reason they needed, and many an afternoon visit had been spent commiserating with the unfortunate widow over her son's terrible judgment where friends were concerned.

Pierson had been apprised of all of this by Bainbridge himself, who had found it all too deliciously diverting. In essence, he did exactly as he pleased about his marital plans — that being nothing — and his friend received all of the blame for his inaction. The viscount had not minded so much before but, now he had a desire to mend his ways, that prolific gossip and entrenched society matron, Lady Bainbridge, was the best person to start with. If he could win her approval, he was on his way back to respectability. He had no illusions that it would be an effortless climb from rascality to respectability. "My lady, how are you on this lively . . . er, lovely spring day?" He tapped his fingers against his thigh nervously.

"I am fit, as always." She edged one step further into the room.

"And how is Lady Harriet?" Pierson asked, of the woman's daughter.

The marchioness drew herself up. "My daughter is well, I thank you. She is considering offers from a number of suitors at the present, among them Lord Newton-Shrewsbury."

Pierson's first instinct was to laugh, for he had heard Bainbridge despairing many a time over his sister's lack of suitors. Lady Harriet was not unattractive — though she was accounted plain by most — and she had a piercing intelligence and a horror of pretension. She was just as likely to rip a man to shreds over his lack of learning as she was to consider him a suitor. She openly derided the dandy, the Corinthian, the beau, and every other sort of London gentleman, including the one she had named the "faux-intellectual." Pierson rather liked her, but not enough to consider her anything more than an amusing sparring partner in debate. "Shrewsbury's a grand fellow. Make a good match for Lady Harriet."

"I think so," Lady Bainbridge said, thawing slightly at Pierson's acceptance of her conversational sally. She paced across the Turkey rug and adjusted a painted blue bowl on a table near the tall window overlooking the street below, so the porcelain ornament was more exactly in the center.

"If Harriet will only think so."

Bainbridge, cool, amused, and perfectly turned out, sauntered into the room just then. "Ah, Pierson, how are you this morning?" There was a secret glint of humor in the fellow's handsome countenance.

"I'm well."

Bainbridge chuckled.

"Truly," Pierson said, raising his eyebrows. He felt the need to express his new energy, his new life. "I'm better than well, I am . . . reborn."

Lady Bainbridge furrowed her brow and stared at Pierson while her son appeared skeptical.

"Really. Well, I received your note and I'm ready to undertake any mission you have in mind. Where am I and the *new* Lord Pierson going this morning?" Bainbridge said, a sardonic curl to his lip.

"To the studio of a sketch artist of my acquaintance. You do not believe me, about being 'reborn,' but I have much to tell you," Pierson said, with a warning glance and a faint movement of his head toward the older woman in the room. It was a sordid tale, especially the part about the Cyprians, the overindulgence in alcohol, and the long stagger home, and it was not a story he wished Lady Bainbridge to know of. It was a part of his old life.

"Then let us be off for parts unknown," Bainbridge said.

"Do not forget to come back for my literary tea this afternoon," Lady Bainbridge said to her son, waggling her knobby finger at him.

"Mother," he said, in answer, his tone polite but steely, "you know I do not attend such monstrosities. Let you and my sister revel in the bookish bellowings and erudite eruptions of amateur poets and bluestocking ladies."

Frostily, she said, "And what is so important that you will miss this?"

Pierson bowed. "I promise you he will be at no gambling den this afternoon, my lady."

She sniffed and glared at him with a hostile glint in her eyes. "I do not need your impertinence, Pierson, nor your worthless promises. Get you gone, both of you. The servants need to arrange this room for the tea."

"Phew," Pierson said, as they descended the steps to a brilliant spring day. He took a deep breath and coughed. "Your mother is the most frightening woman I know. It's the one thing I fear about marriage, wedding a kitten only to wake up with a hellcat."

"And it's what you will never be sure of, my friend," Bainbridge said, as they made way for a lady with a parasol, and then started their journey. "Why do you think I resist all the most determined efforts at matchmaking? I'm cynical about women as it is, but that sham they are all forced to perpetrate, that they are all sweet, virtuous, innocent, mild pictures of docility . . . that keeps me from any serious marital thoughts."

"Don't you think, then, that you can tell a woman's character from her countenance?" Pierson glanced curiously at his friend. "Many of the most learned philosophers of our day have determined that the physiognomy of a person does not lie."

"Not only does the face indeed prevaricate," Bainbridge said, curling his lip, "but the countenance lies only as much as a lady's behavior, and the same in reverse. And it is so much more reprehensible that behavior is a liar, for while a face is immutable, behavior is ours to determine. I do not believe you can tell a woman's character at all before marriage."

"And that," Pierson said, stopping and turning to face his friend, "is where you

46

and I part company." He had never considered it before, but his friend was the most determined cynical non-romantic in all of his acquaintance. Bainbridge had had his encounters with ladies of a certain stamp, but they had always been conducted with a cold-blooded nod to his own physical needs. In his own experience, Pierson found that though he had had as many liaisons with ladies of the evening as Bainbridge, he had always needed to be attracted by something other than a fair face or figure. Even girls of that receptive class, who traded money and jewels for their favors, differed widely in their cynicism in the exchange, or their soft-heartedness. He had always looked for something in their eyes, some tenderness of expression lingering even after all their jaded encounters. That was a rare find indeed among ladies of the evening.

But still, he had never been in love, nor had he imagined himself to be before now. Almost to himself he said, "I believe that I have been looking only for that lady whose countenance promises the sweetness I desire."

Bainbridge gazed at him steadily. "I heard what happened to you last night," he said, crossing his arms over his chest.

"How? What did you hear?" Pierson asked. A carriage rolled close and he moved back from the road, not wanting to get sprayed by mud. The streets were still not dry after the rain of the night before, but with the sun out and at full strength, it shouldn't take long. It was unusually warm for early March, actually, a brilliant early spring day. That had to be a good harbinger for his future, that he should awaken to such a start.

"Oh, much! My valet, Staynes, heard from the long-suffering Rupert." Bainbridge chuckled and cast a humorous glance at the nearby mud puddle. "They are friends, after a fashion. Rupert appealed to him for a receipt for muck removal — according to your valet your clothes from last evening smell of the gutter — and Staynes heard everything, about the harlots and the carriage and the spray of filth, and the odd way you behaved after. I suppose you must have muttered about the whole evening even as you slept, but were too far into your cups to remember. Rupert felt there was still something behind it all, your behavior and manner, but he was puzzled as to what it was. What's going on, Pierson?"

Pierson turned and began their walk

again, moving as if in a dream along the sunny street. "I saw a vision, my friend." Again, Pierson felt the surge of hope and the determination to seize hold and march forward to bliss. "I saw a vision, and I will never be the same again. I have found my fair infinity."

"Oh, Lord, a woman! Likely to be your fair extinction, you mean," Bainbridge muttered, following. "All right, first to a coffee house, and then, if we must, let's go on to this artist acquaintance of yours and you can tell me all about it."

The sun had passed its zenith and in the parlor of the Marquess of Bainbridge's townhouse a crowd milled waiting for enlightenment from the several writers and poets who had come for the free luncheon after their performance, mostly, Amy suspected, eyeing their hollowed cheeks and ravenous looks with alarm. Being a literary figure must not pay very well, even less than a chaperon or governess, she would guess. It was fortunate she had no aspirations in that direction.

The hostess, an imposing woman with a bust like a ship's figurehead, sailed toward them.

"Ancient harridan," Lady Rowena muttered under her breath, so only Amy could hear. Then she curtseyed demurely to the approaching lady.

"Lady Rowena," the older woman said, as she came closer. Her beady eyes held a speculative gleam. "I would know you anywhere. You look the very image of your beautiful mother! I regret that I did not see you last Season, but my husband's death . . . We were in mourning, of course. How delightful that you could grace my literary tea with your presence this afternoon."

"My lady," Rowena said, casting her gaze shyly down to the carpet, "I would not have missed this enchanting engagement for anything. It is a delight to meet you at last, my mother's one, true friend."

Amy cast one glance at her charge, impressed despite herself by the young lady's artful quaver and modest deception.

"Oh, we have met before, my child, but you were so young, just a babe."

The older woman reached out one gloved hand and caressed Rowena's cheek. Amy hoped that only she saw the duke's daughter flinch. Indeed it was such a slight movement no one else would be likely to discern it.

Lady Bainbridge went on, with a sigh, "I regret that I did not see your mother in the last years of her life, but my own dear husband was so very ill, we did not spend much time in London."

Amy watched Lady Bainbridge with curiosity. She had heard legends of the woman's iron will and harrying manner, but she saw nothing but gentility and mildness on her lined face. She and Rowena said everything that was polite to one another, and then the woman bustled off to her other guests as befit the hostess of the afternoon.

"She seems very pleasant," Amy said, watching her skillful passage around the room.

"Don't be cozened by her parlor face," Rowena murmured, darkly, as they nodded to acquaintances and moved through the crowd toward the seating area. "I have heard she is a legendary scold. It is why no one will marry her son, the marquess. No one could stand having her as a mother-in-law."

"My lady, that is hardly fair! You would not judge a man on his family, would you?"

"I do not judge men at all, since the subject has no interest for me."

Once again Amy wondered how to counter this inexplicable prejudice the young lady had against men. Glancing around the room, she saw many ladies with less to offer in the way of personal attractions engaging and holding young men's interest. Not that Rowena could not do the same, but she chose whom to dazzle carefully, making conquests when she wished with frightening ease. It was all very calculated.

Prince Verstadt was there after all, Amy noticed, in full military regalia, even though the war was so long over. Still, he had served in an English regiment and continued to hold his rank in the peacetime army. He was a generally pleasing young man, handsome, good-natured, intelligent. He was watching Lady Rowena with a sickly expression of longing on his pale countenance. He had been her first conquest of the Season, and had as quickly been discarded after he proposed. But still, even rejected, he remained in love with the beautiful Lady Rowena. That was her skill, to keep them on her string even after telling them she could not marry them. And all without earning a reputation as a jilt, more was the marvel!

He was moving toward them, on an angle that would halt them in their perambulation. Amy was not sure whether to warn her charge or not, and dithered so long, the young prince was upon them.

"Ladies," he said, with a deep bow, forcing them to pause. "I am indeed fortunate to find you here, since I wished to personally invite you to a reception at my cousin, the royal duke's, residence here in London."

As Lady Rowena's chaperon, Amy spoke for them both. "If you send us an invitation, sir, I will peruse our calendar and see if we are engaged for that day."

The young lady beside her had colored very nicely, her alabaster cheeks blushing to pink as she gazed down at her slippers, and the prince stared at her, lost in admiration.

Amy cleared her throat. "As I said, if you send us a written invitation, I will see if we are engaged for that evening!"

"Uh, yes, Miss Corbett, I will most certainly do that." He bowed deeply to them both and retreated, to sit across the room and stare, even when accosted by other guests.

"Poisonous royal toady," Rowena muttered under her breath, then smiled and nodded to an acquaintance who strolled arm in arm around the room with another young lady.

Amy sighed at her impossible task as they continued to make their way through the crowded room toward one set of chairs. This was ever Rowena's answer to everything, a murmured censure masked by a pleasing smile. "Whatever lady marries him will travel in exalted circles indeed, though," she reminded Rowena, "since he is connected to our own royal family."

"I am the daughter of a duke. I travel wherever I wish and meet whomever I wish," Lady Rowena said, her voice chilled by an unbecoming hauteur.

"But as a married lady you could . . ."

"Enough! I will not be badgered in company!"

Amy clutched her hands into fists and squeezed, a rare flare of temper surging to the forefront. Just once she would like to say what was on her mind, which was that Lady Rowena was a spoiled, rude, impossibly poisonous child, and that all of the men in England should consider themselves lucky that she did not compound her hideous faults of demeanor by marrying one of them and making him miserable for the rest of his days on earth. With a deep sigh, she relaxed, finding even that internal venting of her bile a release of sorts.

Just for a moment, as she and her charge took seats while the literary guests readied themselves for their reading, Amy let her mind wander. What would it be like to be so sought after, as Lady Rowena was?

She pictured herself, dressed in pink silk, the center of attention and with adoring gentlemen vying for her hand. With Prince Verstadt on one side offering her a lemonade, and Lord Norland on the other, plying her with a plate of sweets, she sat in perfect bliss, knowing that whichever gentleman she deigned to offer her hand to, he would enthusiastically accept it and strive to make her life an everlasting picnic.

How easy life would be! Her life had not been comfortable by any means; she had known early that her poor aunt could not support them both, so she had scrambled herself into the best education she could and had begun a governess job, one of several that led to the propitious moment when she found her way to the emerald green island and the Donegal's doorstep. She had been happy enough there, but it was still a paid position, and there was never a guarantee of it continuing. Perhaps her resolution, the night before, that independence was worth the struggle was a mere concession to the futility of wishing for anything more. For she had to admit how pleasant it would be never to have to worry again about the future. How lovely to have wealthy gentlemen tripping over themselves to gain her favor, as they did for Lady Rowena!

But a vision would interrupt even that happy dream, an apparition of a man in dark clothes, shaggy hair in his eyes, and muck streaming down him. Poor unknown gentleman! He had haunted her dreams all night. She hoped he had recovered from his drenching with no ill effects. Why could she not forget him though? Was it simply her own predilection for rescuing strays? As if a man could ever be a stray! Still, she would give much to know of his fate. Was he even now laying in feverish delirium, needing the soft touch and cooling effects of a lady's touch on his heated brow?

She roused herself from her daydream to the unusual sight of Lady Rowena smiling upon a gentleman who sat some distance away from them. He was well looking though not exceptional, but he was certainly attracted by the fair Lady Rowena, for his cheeks suffused with a dull brick red, his lips parted, his eyes glittering. As Amy watched, an uncertain smile trembled on his lips, and then the lady at his side claimed his attention. She was a plain but elegant lady, older than either Lady Rowena or Amy by some years, Amy guessed.

Amy glanced sideways at her charge and caught a secretive smile on Rowena's lips. What was this all about? If she had learned anything about the young lady in the first few weeks of the Season, it was that the duke's daughter did not dispense smiles without a return expected. She enjoyed conquest.

Spying Mrs. Bower, her mentor in the chaperoning of a *ton*-ish maiden, Amy determined to ask that lady who the gentleman was.

After some more droning poetry and a reading of a passage of Byron just to shock everyone, there was a break for a light repast. It was not strictly necessary at a reading, certainly, but Lady Bainbridge set her own standards of conduct, and she liked to feed people, showing how brilliant a pastry chef she had stolen from the household of the Prince Regent himself.

Amy, seeing Lady Rowena moving to sit with one of her few female friends, made her way to Mrs. Bower, who was chewing contentedly on a pastry, whipped cream clinging to her mustache. After their mutual affectionate greeting, Amy nodded toward the gentleman who had exchanged looks with Rowena earlier. "Who is that gentleman, Mrs. Bower, and what is his marital status?"

Mrs. Bower glared shortsightedly across the room and adjusted her lorgnette. "Mmf," she muttered, swallowing and licking the cream from her lips. She brushed crumbs from her fingers. "That, my dear, is Lord Newton-Shrewsbury; earl, well set-up, no vices, thirty-eight but in good health, widowed sister dependent upon him. Good prospect, but not on the block, my dear," she murmured, her words concealed by the chatter of the crowd near the refreshment table. She cleared her throat and continued. "Lady Bainbridge has marked him for her daughter, Lady Harriet — that is the gel he is sitting with — and woe betide any young lady who should interfere with her plans. You remember I mentioned Lady Harriet when we were speaking of her friend, Lady Frances Mortimer? So it is not worth it, my dear, to even consider him a possible suitor for Lady Rowena. Lady Bainbridge's favor is more important than *any* potential beau."

Amy felt a spurt of alarm. Why would

Lady Rowena be smiling at him? And he smiling back at her with such a look of warmth. Oh my. She felt a sharp presentiment she was learning to trust as the internal voice of self-preservation. She glanced at her charge, and saw, to her alarm, that Lady Rowena was glancing over at Lord Newton-Shrewsbury, and that he was, again, looking back!

She could do something about this, and would. She thanked her friend, who turned her attention back to her plate of pastries, and bustled over to Lady Rowena.

Detaching her from her friend, Amy took her aside. "My lady, of all the gentlemen in the room, please do not fix your interest on that man, the one who was just smiling at you."

A frozen look on her pretty face, Lady Rowena said, "I have not fixed my interest on anyone, Amy; I don't know what you are talking about, but I do know that you are being impertinent and vulgar."

Taking in a deep breath, Amy surged ahead, despite the young lady's forbidding tone. "You know very well what I mean. That gentleman in the blue jacket, who is sitting with the lady in the peach gown. The lady is our hostess' daughter, Lady Harriet."

"I knew that already."

"And that gentleman is her intended beau, Lord Newton-Shrewsbury."

The secretive smile teased Lady Rowena's perfectly shaped lips again. "I know that, too, Amy, so you have just wasted your breath."

Amy stood stock-still for a moment. If Lady Rowena knew all of that, then why was she deliberately . . . Oh! In that moment Amy came to understand just how much more difficult her task was going to be. The last puzzle piece of Lady Rowena's character slipped into place. Amy was chaperon to that most despised of feminine species, a determined, if very subtle, flirt and beau-thief.

Four

Bainbridge stood staring out the window of the garret while Pierson paced behind the artist.

"That's it, man, that is *it*," Pierson cried, clapping his hands together and gazing down at the drawing. He reached out to it and touched it with reverence. "You have captured that sweetness of expression, that moonlit hair, those lips, that angelic, demure and modest cast of features."

The marquess snorted and turned to stare at his friend. "I cannot believe that this is actually you. Have you been consorting with brownies? Have they left a changeling in your place? You sound absurd."

Pierson colored crimson as he looked up from the artist's rendering of his fair obsession. The artist, a lanky young man with dull eyes, gazed with little interest at the two peers.

Perhaps Bainbridge was not the ideal companion for this task. Stung into a defensive retort, Pierson said, "You are just loath to be left alone in your misogyny, my friend."

"I am not a misogynist," Bainbridge retorted. "I adore women, all kinds of women, even my sister . . . even my *mother*. But I do not believe in their ineffable sweetness, nor that they are any different from men in their needs, frustrations, furies, aggravations, and tempers. I think we mistake them, adore them from afar, place them on a rickety pedestal and then blame them when it crumbles and they tumble into the dirt. I will not marry until I find a woman honest about those baser feelings and urges."

Pierson pulled the sketch away from the artist's charcoal-smudged hands and held it up to the light of the garret window. A coldhearted fellow like Bainbridge would never understand how he longed to surrender to this image of innocence and rectitude he held before him, how he felt that if he could just give his life over to her, she could fashion it into something pure and fine with her delicate hands. The marquess wasn't capable of the kind of renascence he was experiencing, but he wouldn't insult his friend with the cold, hard truth. "I think you are talking utter nonsense just to hear yourself talk as usual, my friend." He gazed at the picture and sighed deeply. "Behold the face of the perfect lady, and the one I will marry."

"That is she?" Bainbridge said, staring at it without admiration. "*That* is your paragon? She looks like the epitome of a milk-and-water miss, no spirit, no fire, no independence. What would anyone want with a woman like that?"

Pierson held the sketch to his breast and glared at the marquess. "You wouldn't know an angel if you trod on her wings!" he exclaimed.

"I think if I ever found such an angel, I would *want* to tread on her wings!"

"That is where you and I are different." Pierson stared down at the sketch and traced the line of her chin with one finger. "I think a lady's place in a man's life is to inspire him, to give him a reason to follow a straight and true path, to work toward some better life. Just think of the artists who have slaved over great works, just for the love of a woman. Great writers have written tomes of poetry devoted to love and inspired by a woman. For *her* I would do that; for *her* I will change my life." He waved the drawing in front of his friend's face. "But instead of poetry or art, my homage to her will be to turn Delacorte into something worthy, a home to be proud of. I will toil with my own hands until they are rough and brown, making a better life for her and our children."

Bainbridge frowned at him, his gray eyes dark with some strong emotion. "I have never seen you like this, Pierson. And yet I should have known this was in you; I always felt like you were waiting for something, but maybe it was *someone*. You are a romantic at heart, aren't you, my friend? All of that, just for a woman."

They stood in silence for a few minutes, two friends peering at each other across an abyss comprised of lack of understanding. Pierson didn't regret his grand speech, but knew that, to someone of Bainbridge's stolid deportment, it likely sounded flowery and excessive. He couldn't help it; it was just how he felt and it flowed out of him like water from a pump, and so he didn't try to explain himself any further. He and the marquess had known each other long enough that he should not have to.

Bainbridge finally ventured, "Perhaps we will agree to disagree on this. If this lady will inspire you to reduce your drinking, stop gambling money you can't afford, and reclaim your inheritance, then I will think her the paragon you describe."

"I will ignore your slurs on my character since it is all too accurate an account of my failings," Pierson said. He hesitated, but then continued, "If you really feel that way, Bain, will you help me find out who she is? I will be unable to continue with any of my intentions until I find that out, for I am completely captivated and in her thrall. She was young, perhaps twenty, and lovely, of very good *ton,* I should say, judging from the jewels at her throat and the quality of the carriage. I think there was a coat of arms on the carriage, but there was so much mud I could not see the elements."

"I will help you."

"Thank you, old friend," Pierson said, choosing to ignore the reluctant tone in his friend's voice, and they clasped hands warmly. "I feel myself at some fork in the road." He tried to clarify his feelings, his strong belief that the young lady he had seen the night before represented something more than some meaningless infatuation. There had to be a way to make even Bainbridge see that this was not some passing fancy, but a new course he was setting himself on, the new road to a new life. "If I can only find the right path, I may be able to reclaim some of this wretched life and turn it to a good purpose, Bain. But I know myself well; I have been purposeless so far in my life. I need something . . . *someone* to work for, someone to inspire me."

Bainbridge shrugged but shook his good friend's hand. "I will not pretend to understand, my friend, but I will help in any way I can."

The two men left the studio after Pierson handsomely rewarded the artist. The sketch was rolled up and the viscount carried it under his arm. "Do you think it would be safe to go back to your house?" he asked his friend.

Bainbridge chuckled. "If you mean, will that hideous invention, the 'literary tea,' be over, I would say yes. But why would you want to go to my house? You have always had a horror of my mother. I was startled to see you two talking this morning."

"It is time I got over that ridiculous . . . uh, aversion. Your mother is . . . is a wonderful woman."

"Don't choke on those words, Pierson."

"But she is! And she knows everyone in society; she could help me find my fair destiny."

"Ah, I see your purpose. All right. We'll go."

Just twenty minutes later they strolled up

to the Bainbridge house as a carriage with an ornate coat of arms was pulling away from the curb in front.

"I hope that was the last of them," Bainbridge muttered.

They entered and doffed their hats, gloves, and sticks. The rotund, gloomy butler took the items and disappeared.

"Hallo, Harriet," Bainbridge said to his sister as he ambled into the parlor. "Well, Mother, how did your day go?"

Lady Bainbridge was reclining on a sofa, a damp cloth to her forehead.

"Don't ask," Lady Harriet said, smiling up at her brother from the divan. "Hello, Pierson. Haven't seen you in an age."

Lady Bainbridge stood, tossing the cloth away and pulling herself up to her full height. "It is an *outrage,* what happened here this afternoon. I cannot believe you are taking this so lightly, Harriet. He was your beau, after all."

"What, let another one slip away?" Bainbridge said, with a casual caress of his sister's simple coiffure.

"Oh, I didn't let this one slip away," she said, a sly smile on her face as she caught her brother's hand and squeezed it. "This one had help."

"He was . . . was *stolen!*" Lady Bainbridge spat the last word out.

"What, you mean someone packed him up under their arm and carried him away? I know we've missed some silver lately, but I did not know anyone could lift a beau."

Pierson, chuckling at his friend's witticism, said, "I understand why the fashion is beginning for ladies to wear such voluminous capes, if they are pilfering more than extra cream cakes and silver forks."

Lady Harriet broke into giggles, but obscured them with a cough.

"We are speaking of a serious subject, the deliberate theft of a gentleman admirer by another lady." Lady Bainbridge gave Pierson a quelling look. "And her mother was my dearest friend! It is that daughter of the late Duchess of Sylverton, Lady Rowena. One simpering look at Lord Newton-Shrewsbury and he fell completely under her spell and abandoned Harriet."

"Mother, you make me sound like a parcel left behind by accident on a park bench." Harriet's tone was acidic. "I was no more than friends with Norman and he knows it. He is free to wander where he may."

"But I had great hopes of this one, and

then that hussy cast her sheep's eyes at him and . . ."

"I would say if the fellow was so easily conquered he was not deserving of your daughter's favor, my lady," Pierson said. He earned a warm look of regard from the marchioness for that remark, but Lady Harriet just flushed and bit her lip.

"I suppose you are right, Pierson," the marchioness said, with the back of her hand against her forehead, "but I am overset, nonetheless."

"I have a favor to ask, my lady, that may take your mind off . . ."

"Not now, Pierson," she said and started toward the door. "I am too upset. I had even hoped, before meeting Lady Rowena, that she might be right for . . ." She glanced at her son and stopped. "I am going to my room for a while," she announced. "I will come downstairs for dinner, but not before."

She sailed from the room.

Lady Harriet burst into laughter, her color returning to normal. "Lord, you should have seen Shrewsbury, Bainbridge. He went positively white, and once I gave him permission, he beetled over to Lady Rowena and never left her side all afternoon, even when her chaperon — poor

69

thing, I did feel for her — tried to separate them."

"If that means the fellow won't be haunting my parlor, I say I am glad," her brother said, lounging around the room.

"Bain!" Lady Harriet said, with a mock expression of shock. "Did you not like Norman? Did you not think him my ideal beau?"

"I think the man is the ideal idiot. And I think mother is doing it up a bit brown when she blames the poor girl. I have seen Lady Rowena at a few balls already this year, and she seems a perfectly demure young lady, remarkably beautiful but not in any way a heartless flirt."

"Oh, I don't say she flirted with him, Bain; I saw nothing of the sort, and her manner at the tea was everything that could be considered modest. I think that Norman was just becoming frightened by mother's repeated hints that it was time and past that he should be making his offer for my most valued hand in more solid terms. And really, anyone looking at Lady Rowena and comparing her to my own aging person would be smitten by her immediately."

Pierson laughed, once again entertained by the lady's determined lack of conceit.

She was a good sort, was Bain's sister, the kind of lady a fellow would like for a sister. He regretted that he had no siblings and thought how different his life would be if he had had family, as Bain did. It would have given him that purpose he had always lacked. If a man had a sister and mother to care for, then he could not, in all conscience, act the wastrel. "Lady Harriet, any man so ungallant as to desert you in favor of *any* other lady must be considered wanting in wits."

"What a gallant speech, my lord," Lady Harriet said archly, but her cheeks colored faintly once more. She hesitated a moment, but then patted the seat of the divan next to her.

The viscount sat down beside her and unrolled his sketch. "Perhaps you can help me. You are much in society. Do you recognize this lady?"

Lady Harriet gazed at it, silent for a long minute, then shook her head. "I don't think so. There is something familiar about the eyes and the shape of the chin, but I suppose she could be one of a hundred girls. It is not a very good sketch. Who is she?"

"My future," Pierson said, fervently, staring at it. Again he felt that sureness in his veins, that quickening. "She is my future."

Amy faced the facts as they trundled back to the ducal residence from the afternoon tea. Lady Rowena was not only determined to remain single, she was equally as determined to enslave every man who came within her sphere, chaining their hearts securely to her petticoats. She already had a pretty string of them following her wherever she went, and yet she had managed to do it all without one word of reproach staining her name or reputation.

The young lady was humming a happy tune and staring out the carriage window as they passed a park. Amy examined her. Every benefit known to womanhood — wealth, indulgence, status — united in her life with her beauty and health. She was the most fortunate of young women, and yet she would squander all of those gifts on a hollow pursuit of every beau she met.

"Why are you staring at me so ferociously, Amy?" Lady Rowena said with a pert smile. "Have I agitated you in some way?"

Hesitating a moment, Amy then said, "No, I am not agitated. Disappointed."

"Disappointed? I have disappointed you?"

Amy nodded.

Haughtily, the lady said, "It is not your place to be disappointed in anything I do or say."

"Of course, you're right," Amy said, and turned her face away.

There was silence, except for the rattle of the carriage and clop of hooves. It was late afternoon, almost evening, and they would be returning home only to change for the evening's entertainment, a supper and a ball. The sun was already starting to set, casting a golden glow on the brick walls of the houses and making the park greenery a fierce shade of chartreuse.

"Why would you be disappointed in me?" Lady Rowena finally said, the words rushed.

Amy thought for a moment, wondering why her charge was even asking when she so clearly flouted her chaperon's authority and disdained her opinion. So, to be truthful or not? Would it gain her anything to tell the truth, or would the lady have one of her famous tantrums? And did Amy really care?

Her livelihood was at stake, no matter what she said. The duke's only concern was that his daughter be engaged or married by the end of the Season. Amy did not see that happening, not with Lady Rowena's determined detestation of men and resolve never to marry.

So it really didn't matter what she said. The next couple of months she would have to use planning what to do when the end came and the duke sacked her, leaving her with nothing, no wage, no position, and no recommendation. But in the meantime she could be honest.

"I am disappointed that, with so much," she said, turning her gaze to Lady Rowena and examining the girl's fair countenance, "with such beauty and wealth and spirit, you would stoop to deliberately turn your wiles on the beaux of other women."

The girl tossed her head. "I don't do it deliberately," she said. "Men just are attracted to me; I cannot help that."

"I believed that at first," Amy said, examining Rowena's profile. "But after today, I don't. I watched that performance with Lord Newton-Shrewsbury. It is a game with you, I think." She saw that she had hit her mark when the girl colored faintly. "It is a game, to see if you can attract even a man with another interest. It's one thing to deliberately ensnare a fellow with no thought to any serious end. When he has no attachments the worst you will do is hurt *him*. But when you do what you did today, you hurt another lady as well. And why? For hollow triumph? I feel sorry for you if that gives you some feeling of superiority. I truly pity you from the bottom of my heart."

"How absurd you are," Lady Rowena said, attempting to make light of the conversation. "You make it sound as if I am some . . . some Siren, luring men to their destruction. If their interest was so fixed on another object, I couldn't, with just a look, attract them away, could I? Why, that would make me a *very* powerful lady indeed."

"Powerful?" Amy frowned and thought, was that what this was about? Was Rowena one of those women who relished power over men? "No, that doesn't make you powerful. Men, poor creatures, are very swayed by beauty. I would think it power indeed if you were plain and poor. *Then* it would be a feat to attract a gentleman's attention. But you have everything, including wealth and position. And you are uncommonly beautiful, Rowena; I think you are very aware of it, so it makes your actions . . ." She steeled herself and took a deep breath. "It makes your actions pathetic."

"Now you have gone too far, Amy," Lady Rowena said in a resentful tone, as the carriage rolled to a stop outside the ducal manse. "You have insulted me, and I won't forget it."

Amy sighed and shrugged as a footman opened the carriage door and took Lady Rowena's hand. So her charge was now furious with her. Since Rowena was generally unpredictable as to her moods, and even the smallest thing could set her off, Amy did not think she would suffer more materially than she did any day of the week. So be it; let her be furious. After all, how much worse could things get?

Five

"I don't know, Pierson, it's been three days and no one seems to recognize your fair incognita."

The two men were strolling down a commercial street on the way to a club on St. James's. The weather was fine, a brilliant day with a soft breeze and the promise of a lovely spring to come. For the last couple of days they had been visiting every club and entertainment the viscount was still welcome at, asking anyone they encountered if they recognized the now-smudgy drawing of Pierson's ladylove.

"I know, I know," Pierson said, only too aware that it was unlikely he would ever find the girl of his dreams, especially since his black reputation barred him from all the most likely places for her to be. He had lived up to his name's reputation for years now, whoring, gambling, and drinking deep. And it wasn't just that. He had engaged in antics — usually when he was well into his cups — that could only be described as unruly.

From the beginning his quirky sense of humor and impulsive nature had gotten him in trouble. He once dressed a Cyprian up in fine clothes and took her to a ball as his fiancée. That had earned him censure and had seen him barred from most polite homes.

He had stripped off most of his clothes down to less than unmentionables and fallen asleep in Hyde Park. For months he had been the object of derision among the men and censure among the ladies.

So then he had, dressed in a domino, arrived at a masked ball with a filched invitation and danced with the hostess, then whispered a sly invitation to go upstairs to the private chambers for a "tumble and a tickle." She had agreed, to his astonishment, and then been furious when she found out who he was. It seemed that the invitation he had arrived with was that of her very own illicit lover. That had resulted in a ban of a more subtle sort, and many in polite society gave him the cut direct after that.

But inevitably being the jester and clown had worn thin. He had devolved, in recent years, since being cut off from decent society, into a drunken pariah. It was boring and often lonely. He had chosen a late day to repair the damage, and an illusive object as his inspiration. His success was doubtful, and yet it was what he wanted more than he had ever wanted anything.

Pierson didn't feel much like talking, so the walk was silent. Why was he so obsessed with finding this lady when the common sense corner of his brain told him that he could have no idea what she was truly like? He had assigned virtues and qualities to her just based on a quick glimpse, and surely that was not realistic. He knew that, and yet he could not get over the feeling that his life was about to change, that *he* was about to change. And that *she* was to be the catalyst.

He certainly could not go on any longer the way he was. His estate was depleted, and the last demand for money sent to his steward had been returned with a note from his ancient housekeeper that Mr. Lincoln had disappeared with the estate staff's quarterly pay and had not been heard of for weeks. He had depended upon his land steward for ten years, and yet now that man had absconded?

In truth, if he faced the cold hard facts, he should be home that very moment sorting it out instead of staying on in London when there was no money to support his style of living. He was in dun territory, but since that was nothing new, it did not worry him as much as it ought.

Even if he did go to his estate, where to start? How to retrench and rebuild an estate that was decaying at an alarming rate? Was it even possible to save it now?

He looked back with some bitter anger at the last ten years since his father had died, leaving him, at eighteen, with no knowledge of how to go on and nobody reliable to guide him, even. He had trusted Lincoln, and it now appeared that that trust had been misplaced. If only he had been content to live on his inherited estate and take the first steps needed on the long road to recover the worth of his inheritance! But he had been eighteen, and Mr. Lincoln had advised him just to go to London and enjoy himself while he looked after all the "drudgery" as he called it. It had not taken much persuasion, and he had his father's example before him to model himself after.

The years had passed swiftly, and he had seen little reason to go where there were no warm family memories to welcome him, and where the decay was like a constant reproach. So he had spent the off-season hunting with the few friends he still had, visiting country house parties where even a pariah, if he was titled, was welcome, and finding, in other words, every way of keeping his mind off his birthright, Delacorte, his country estate. He visited there seldom, and when he did, stayed only a couple of days at a time. The place was depressing to the spirit.

And that was the quandary he found himself in. Every time he started thinking about the estate, he felt the urgent need for a drink. And then, when he drank, he gambled. He was currently, like most men of his age and class, living on credit, but would soon need to start selling off the family's meager collection of jewels to repay some of his living expenses, and he had sworn some years before that he would never do that. His heir was a cousin, a boy of eleven whom he never saw, but as things stood he would hand at least some of the remaining Pierson estate over to the new heir intact if he should shuffle off the mortal coil early and without an heir of his own body.

An heir, he thought, a tiny wellspring of hope burbling in his heart. What an incentive to work hard and recover his estate that would be! A child, a *boy* child. Perhaps a son with silvery blond hair and an alabaster brow.

He shook his head, a little disgusted with himself and the futility of hope. He might just as well face facts. He was never going to find the lady, and even if he did, what did he have to offer her? Years of toil and heartache without respite; drudgery and travail, living with little hope but to make some headway every year on regaining Delacorte's once legendary beauty. Perhaps fate was merely teasing him, showing him a glimpse of what he could never have. Perhaps it was too late for him.

With that gloomy thought, he said to his friend, "You know, Bain, old man, I am beginning to think that I will never find my . . ." He stopped in the middle of the walkway and gaped.

Bainbridge stared at him with alarm. "Pierson, what is it? You look as if you have just seen a ghost!"

"That is she . . . That is my fair angel." Pierson gazed at a carriage from which two ladies were just descending.

"Which one? And how can you tell?"

"The blonde goddess, idiot, in the pale green dress." She was there, just across the street, his seraph, the archetype of all that was good and pure, all that was most unlike himself.

"*She?*" Bainbridge, his gray eyes wide,

stared at the young lady then slewed his glance back to his friend. He grasped Pierson's arm and said, "Good God, man, she is the one? That is Sylverton's spawn, the beauteous Lady Rowena Revington. You remember the other day, the literary tea, the girl who supposedly stole away Shrewsbury, m'sister's . . ."

Pierson heard words coming from Bainbridge but could assign no meaning to them. "I cannot believe I have seen her again. Cannot believe . . ." Suddenly speechless, he took one step toward the street.

"If you had ever bothered to set foot in a respectable family's drawing room and behaved yourself long enough to be welcome, you would have known who she was immediately. She is wealthy, beautiful, a paragon of purity and virtue, untouched, unsullied . . . and unwed. Unbetrothed even, apparently." Bainbridge shook his head. "The complete aristocratic innocent, according to reports. The flawless diamond of every London Season since her first, three years ago. And *that* is who you choose to fall in 'love at first sight' with?"

"How does that happen," Pierson asked, in awe, gazing across the street at the two ladies, "that she remains unwed?"

Bainbridge shrugged. He frowned and stared at Lady Rowena, who was fussing with her gown, which had become tangled with the step of the carriage. "I don't know. It's odd; she's been asked enough. She's just never said yes. But even the fellows she has turned down are still head over ears in love with her, even if they've selected another bride."

"So, she really is perfect?"

" 'Fraid so, old man," Bainbridge answered. "She is *apparently* boringly, stultifyingly, perfectly innocent and pure."

"That's what I was afraid of."

"So Lady Rowena is your fair vision, eh? I would never have guessed it from the picture. Ought to fire that artist. Lady Rowena is much more beautiful than the sketch shows."

"Yes, I can see that now. I can very well see that." And how would he ever approach someone so perfect and lovely? How could he even stand in her radiant presence?

Amy followed in her charge's wake, descending from the carriage. Lady Rowena had been on a tear all morning, in as foul a mood as she ever got into. In truth, their relation had not returned to any semblance ·

of their former understanding since Amy had called her behavior pathetic, and it was possible that it never would. Lady Rowena tolerated her, it seemed, because she could not go anywhere without her for fear of looking fast or immodest. Some ladies did so, calling carriages for themselves, asserting their independence, but the *Times* had printed many articles decrying such behavior and bewailing the crumbling of good society in the wake of such conduct. Lady Rowena was always, in public, resolutely ladylike.

Amy could not really blame Lady Rowena for her ire. No one besides her father had ever spoken to her that way. Lady Rowena was the daughter of a duke and therefore one of the foremost ladies in the land. Amy had sorely overstepped her bounds, and she knew her position was only secure because her charge needed a chaperon to maintain her freedom of movement. If there had been any other choice, Amy would have been sent packing.

She disliked being at odds with Rowena, who could be tolerable company when in a good humor, but Amy could see no way back to her good graces short of apologizing, and even though her disposition was mild, she could not lie, and to apologize for saying what she felt was the truth would be a lie.

So she was caught in an untenable position, one that could not continue indefinitely, but to which there seemed no ready solution.

Once Rowena had fussed her gown into tidiness, they began their ascent up to the dressmaker's shop. The proprietor bustled out to the steps. He knew they were coming and liked to be seen on his front step with the daughter of the great and powerful Duke of Sylverton.

That was when the placid morning split open into confusion.

Amy had noticed a pretty gray and white cat creeping up the stairs behind them, and thought maybe it was the shop owner's cat. If so, she would be happy to sit with it and pet it while Rowena had her latest dresses fitted.

It brushed past Amy and rubbed up against Rowena's leg. She shrieked in alarm, while Amy cried that it was only a cat. But Rowena kicked out at it and screamed. The shopkeeper grabbed a broom from beside the door and started swatting at the cat, who, frightened, made a dash for the shelter of Lady Rowena's skirts, which caused her to scream even louder.

Pierson, in conversation with Bainbridge, heard the first shriek, and was aghast to see the shopkeeper beating at Lady Rowena's legs with the broom. A cat cowered there, and he could see immediately that the poor thing was frightened for its life. What on earth was the shopkeeper doing?

He dashed across the street and bounded up the steps, snatching the cat out from under the lady's skirts with one hand while trying to catch the broom in the other. He succeeded only after the shopkeeper accidentally smacked him on the ear with it.

"Cease, idiot, you are beating the poor thing to death, and the lady, too!" Pierson shouted, as he hugged the cowering cat. It clung to him, digging its claws into his shoulder. He settled it quickly and turned to the two ladies. "My lady, your poor pet. I hope this imbecile has not caused it any harm."

"But it's not . . ."

He gazed raptly at her, holding the cat out, and saw her lovely face relax into a beatific smile.

"Thank you, sir . . . poor puss!" She

turned to the shopkeeper with a pretty pout on her face. "What were you thinking, Mr. Lance, to beat poor puss that way?"

He stammered and finally said, "I'm so sorry, my lady, but I didn't know the creature was yours. I th-thought it was one I have seen skulking around the alleyway for a few days now, trying to get in."

"Why, can't you see how beautiful it is?" Pierson said, reaching out and stroking its fluffy head, feeling almost dizzy with joy, as the motion forced him nearer the lovely Lady Rowena. "Such a clean and lovely creature could not possibly be a stray."

Mr. Lance quickly retreated into the shop with a deep bow and a murmured request that the ladies enter when they so desired.

Pierson bowed and said, "Excuse me, my lady, you must forgive me, but in this unusual circumstance I feel it may be considered appropriate if I introduce myself. I am Viscount Pierson, and this," he said, waving his hand toward his friend, who approached the group, "is the marquess, Lord Bainbridge."

Lady Rowena handed the cat over to her companion and curtseyed prettily, giving him her hand. "I am Lady Rowena

Revington and this is my companion, Miss Amy Corbett. Thank you, my lord, for rescuing poor . . . poor puss."

Amy, wide-eyed, watched the exchange, gladly taking the cat, which was being rather strangled in Rowena's iron grip. The viscount's friend was grinning, his gray eyes dancing with some hidden merriment, but the viscount was clearly smitten by Lady Rowena's beauty, as what man was not? There was something almost familiar about the fellow, Amy thought, examining him. He was of medium height, dark brown hair swept back from a high forehead, and he had the most intriguing golden brown eyes she had ever seen. His voice was husky and she loved the sound of it, as he spoke to Lady Rowena.

She stroked the cat in her arms and watched his face. Perhaps she had seen him at one of the balls they had attended, but she didn't think so, for she would remember him in that circumstance, she was sure. He had completely misread the situation of course, but it was a testament to his soft heart that he dashed over like that to rescue what he thought was Rowena's pet. Of course, in truth, Rowena had almost tripped on the cat and had been shrieking at it in annoyance when the shopkeeper, mindful that the lady was an excellent customer, began to beat at the cat to shoo it away from her feet.

It must have looked very different from across the street, and she wondered if that was what Lord Pierson's friend was so merry about; had he guessed the truth? She met his gaze and he raised his eyebrows and stared down at the cat in her arms.

"The cat appears happier in your arms than in my lady's," he murmured, leaning toward her.

Amy thought it politic to remain silent.

Conversation had ground to a halt, with Lord Pierson staring in rapt fascination at Lady Rowena and the lady blushing and staring in modest confusion down at the stone step.

Lord Bainbridge cleared his throat. "I think we should let the ladies get on with their task, Pierson," he said, finally.

"Uh, yes," he said. "Uh, my lady, I crave a proper introduction; this was too hasty and too indecorous. Will I see you at the Livington ball tonight, that we may be properly introduced?"

"Oh, no, my lord," she murmured, her voice sweet and low toned. "My father would never countenance the Livington ball, for it is a masquerade, and the family is not one . . . not one we visit. But we do go to the Parkinson ball. Will we, mayhap, see you there?"

Pierson swallowed. Amy watched him and wondered at his hesitation.

"If it is at all possible, I will be there."

With a demure curtsey, Rowena swept into the shop, with Amy trailing behind.

Six

Once inside the cluttered shop, Rowena clapped her hands together and gave a happy little hop, her skirt flouncing prettily. "Lord Pierson! Oh, this is too rich! How Papa would *storm* if he knew about this!"

"Why?" Amy asked, taking a chair near the door and stroking the purring cat as it settled on her lap.

The younger lady paced to the window and looked out, watching the men retreat, Amy guessed, though that was hardly lady-like.

"Because," Rowena said, as she whirled, her pale green skirts belling out around her with her graceful movement. "Lord Pierson is the most renowned rogue and rake in the London *ton*. He has been whispered about among my acquaintance — those few who have seen him, for he is not welcome in most houses — as having an unconquerable heart. Many a young lady has tried to entice him into love, only to be rebuffed. He is accounted dark and dangerous!" She clasped her hands to her heart in a dramatic pose.

Amy frowned down at the floor and rubbed at a minuscule spot with the toe of her shoe. "Dark and dangerous? That makes little sense, my lady. If he is so renowned as a rake and is not welcome in most houses, then how have young ladies been in his company to make the attempt to entice him into love? That doesn't make any sense to me. And truly, he does not seem so dark, or so very dangerous to me."

Lady Rowena waved her hands, pushing away Amy's objections. "If that is so, my dear Amy," she crowed, her tone gay, "that he appeared so lacking in menace, it is because he looked most taken with *me!* The man positively stared as if he wished to collapse at my feet in adoration!"

Amy could not deny that allegation, though she would have liked to for some reason. It was too true. He was smitten, as what man was not when faced with Lady Rowena's spectacular beauty? As for Pierson's fearsome reputation, it must be a mistake. It was clear he was good and kind and compassionate, to rescue a cat! And, though she set little store in appearance, he was quite the most handsome man she had ever in her life seen, with those brilliant gold eyes. She felt as if she had seen him before, knew him from some other occasion. And yet that was impossible.

"I hope he comes to the Parkinson ball. Won't Olivia," Rowena said, naming her best friend, "be pea green with envy, that I have captured the attention of the most notorious rake of the *ton!*"

Amy felt a spurt of something too close to jealous anger that Lady Rowena should take so lightly the regard of every man she came close to. All of them fell at her feet like ripe pears, unable to resist the power of her beauty. And yet she cast them aside, and would likely do the same to Pierson once assured of his undying devotion.

As Mr. Lance bustled forward and sent Lady Rowena away with his seamstress for a fitting, Amy curled up in the hard chair cradling the cat and thought about the man she had only seen for a moment, but who had affected her heart in such a very strange way. She felt a stirring of emotion, an unfamiliar quiver in her untouched heart. She had for so long concentrated solely on self-preservation. Even now, she knew that any moment she could be tossed out of the duke's home if he had an impulse to do so, or if Rowena convinced him to. And yet, instead of planning her precarious future, should that happen, she was mooning like a green girl over the charms of a handsome stranger.

The cat stretched and purred, luxuriously happy in Amy's arms. She stroked its silky head and sighed. She must eradicate such strange longings as her admiration for Lord Pierson from her breast, before they took root and led to the kind of dissatisfaction with her lot that had been the downfall of many a woman in her position. It seemed to her, in her experience, that somebody who had to make her own way in the world had better look at life in the cold, hard light of reality. No lady's companion or chaperon ever found a fairy-tale prince to rescue her, least of all a nonentity like herself.

And that was that.

To dream of a happily-ever-after ending, or of some knight, in shining armor or otherwise, rescuing her from her life of struggle, could only lead to discontent and restlessness, and she was far too sensible to let herself be afflicted with such thoughts. So she would bid her mind's image of the too-handsome Lord Pierson to be gone, like so much smoke, wafting away on the spring breeze.

She stroked the richly purring cat and cuddled it closer, burying her fingers in its soft fur. "You are the closest thing to a boon companion I shall have, I think, Puss," she whispered, "and I'll be satisfied with that. We will make our own way in the world, no matter what. I know I can rely on myself, and no one else."

"So, Pierson, are you going to remind Lady Rowena of where she saw you first?" Bainbridge said with suppressed laughter in his voice, as they walked on toward their destination.

"No!" Pierson shuddered in revulsion at the memory. "Of course not, simpleton, I'm just happy she doesn't remember me from that night or I would die of shame on the spot. I'll tell her that story when we are married ten years, and not a moment before." Pierson dashed across a street between carriages, and Bainbridge followed him.

"And how do you propose to capture your fair one, now that you have met her?" the marquess asked, gasping and out of breath. He stopped and put one hand against the stone corner of a building. "I must take up fencing again; I have quite fallen out of sporting shape, I think." He breathed deeply and slowly recovered. "Anyway, you are not welcome in most ballrooms, nor drawing rooms, nor parlors, and certainly not at the Parkinson ball, where m'lady will be tonight. There were a couple of incidents if you remember, that put you on a list I am sure someone keeps, of gentlemen not welcome in polite homes. In the last ten years you have created a fearsome reputation, my friend, and now must defeat it."

Gloomily, Pierson shrugged and scuffed his boot on the paving stones. "How well I know it. I think the gallop through Lady Decker's Venetian breakfast three years ago was the topper to all of my previous revels. I was quite drunk, and don't remember anything but Rupert being summoned to take me home and his disgust with me. I know I have a number of obstacles to surmount in my quest for the hand of the fair Lady Rowena. My black reputation is only one of them, though. I must have a plan for reclaiming my estate, as well as my name. But one thing at a time. Once assured of her devotion, then I can ask her to wait for a year, to give me time to bring Delacorte up to some condition worthy of receiving a bride."

Bainbridge squared his shoulders, having caught his breath, and gazed at him steadily. "You're serious, aren't you?"

"Deadly serious, my friend. And you must help me. Your character in this city is very good . . ."

"Only because I have taken great care never to blacken it. It is through assiduous care on my part. I would never dishonor my family name as you have." Bainbridge began to walk again, and they turned the corner onto St. James's.

Pierson grimaced. Sometimes Bain was a priggish devil. He would wish just once that the fellow would do something wild and unpredictable, but knew better than ever to think it. "I know, I know, through care on your part. But it is *so* good, you could squander a little of it, letting your reflected glow rub off on me, couldn't you? If you helped me get into the Parkinson ball tonight and were to begin to put it about that I am a changed man, some of the matrons *may* believe you." Pierson stopped at the bottom of the steps up to their club and watched his friend, an appealing expression on his face. "Please, Bain, it's important to me."

"Perhaps I could do something," Bainbridge said, doubt in his voice, "but Lady Rowena's sire is the Duke of Sylverton. That man's temper is estimated as one shade darker than old Nick's. An invitation to a ball is one thing, but do you honestly think he will allow you anywhere near to her?"

"But he won't be there, at the Parkinson's, will he? I have heard he never attends frivolities. And the companion, she seemed a mild enough girl."

"Oh, you even noticed there was someone other than Lady Rowena there?" Bainbridge said. "I'm surprised. Yes, she doesn't look old enough to be a chaperon, but that is what I must conclude she is. I have seen the pair together at every ball Lady Rowena has attended this Season. She must have replaced the squinty old dragon the young lady was apparently afflicted with last year."

"Well, you see then," Pierson said, as they climbed the steps and entered the hushed, smoky enclave of their gentlemen's club, the one place in which the viscount had taken great care never to blot his copy book. "You charm the companion, and I shall sweep Lady Rowena off her feet, and I will attain my heart's desire."

"Don't misunderstand me, old man, but you *do* intend only honor to the young lady, do you not?"

Pierson drew up at those words. He

stared at Bainbridge and in disgust said, "How can you even say that, Bain?" Realizing his voice was too loud for the quiet club, he lowered his tone and said, furious, "I should call you out for that slur! When have I *ever* been a debaucher of innocents?"

"Never, my friend," the marquess said, clapping his hand on the viscount's shoulder. "Calm yourself; I apologize. But since you do not go about in good society, you may not be aware of how black your reputation really is. I am afraid you are something of a legend among the young ladies, more for what you are rumored to have done than any of your actual dissipations. Don't know how these rumors start, but they are rampant. Your name is a byword among the chaperons and a thrill to the maidens."

"I know it will be an uphill battle," Pierson said. "But armed with your help, I shall make the charge."

"Feel like I'm at Waterloo, with such martial language."

They strolled together into the largest of the reading rooms, a wood paneled haven with ironed papers folded neatly on tables for the members' perusal.

"I'm well aware that this will be a

battle," Pierson answered, his tone grim. "But I'm prepared, and watchful for opportunity. If I can only attract her, attach her, show her how very much she means to me, then the rest will follow, I'm sure of it."

"Why this one? Why Lady Rowena?" Bainbridge said, watching his friend's face.

They chose two chairs separated by a table and a discreet waiter asked their preference. The marquess asked for brandy, but Pierson took a deep breath and said, "Nothing for me."

There was silence for a moment as the waiter retreated, and then Pierson tried to answer his friend's question. "Why Lady Rowena? I'm not sure, but when I saw her face, I just knew. I knew because I wanted to be better for her. I wanted to change my ways . . . for her. I wanted to reclaim my inheritance. All for her."

Bainbridge sat back in his chair, steepled his fingers before his face and said, "I must say, I am worried for you. I have hoped something would happen to inspire you to make a change, but my concern is, what if you are not successful in your suit? Her father is devilishly difficult. And then, by an enormous leap of the imagination, if you *do* manage to attach the lady, and the father *is* amenable — and all that is improbable in the extreme, not to be discouraging — what if she is not what you think? After all that effort, what if she turns out to be some insipid, spoiled, idiotic child?"

Pierson, shocked, said, "Don't even suggest that! What could she be that would be less than what she appears? You saw her today; she is an angel, demure, sweet-natured, modest . . ."

"Yes, a veritable angel," Bainbridge said as the waiter brought his brandy. "I'm sure she is all that is heavenly."

"You're being sarcastic, Bain, but I swear, one can see it in her eyes, hear it in her voice."

"But remember my mother's condemnation of her, Pierson. What if she should be right, and the girl is not at all what she seems, but is a beau-thief and flirt?"

"Do you believe that? If I remember, even your sister — and Lady Harriet must be judged impartial in this instance since it was her beau who was supposedly stolen — contends there was no thievery on the lady's part, just a preference on Shrewsbury's. And who could blame the man?" Pensively, Pierson added, "She has the look of heaven about her."

"She certainly appears to be a modest,

lovely, perfectly innocent young maiden."

"And what more does a man need? A wife should come to one largely unformed, my friend, for we men are so set in our ways a lady will need to adjust herself to our eccentricities. So it is better if she is young and willing to be molded." Pierson nodded at his own logic and stretched in the chair. "Yes, all I ask is a sweetness of disposition and mildness of temper, and together we'll make our marriage work."

Bain snorted, guffawed and then roared with laughter.

"What is wrong with you?" Pierson asked. Bainbridge was acting most strangely, for he had certainly said nothing to inspire such a fit of laughter.

"There's nothing wrong with me, but really, old man, you have the oddest ideas of marriage! Where did they come from?"

"I . . . I don't know. But it is what society says, is it not? Young ladies are untaught for that very reason. If a man is to be the head of the household, then he must take a wife who will look to him for instruction and molding."

"Trust me, my friend, if you had witnessed marriage first hand, as I did with my mother and father, you would have seen no such relationship as you describe.

Unformed! You make a young lady sound as if she is a lump of clay. Do you not think that women have thoughts and ideas and opinions?"

"I had thought that was the philosophy behind keeping them largely untaught. Then what do you think of Lady Rowena? She seems so . . . so untouched."

Bainbridge rubbed the arm of the chair. "I don't know. I cannot credit my mother's opinion, that she is a flirt and a beau-thief, and yet there seems something more to her than just a blank slate. Don't think ladies are untaught, Pierson. First, untaught does not mean unlearned; just look at Harriet. A more opinionated lady there never has been. I was a decent student in the languages, but truly, she reads widely and knows more Italian and French than I do, and almost as much Greek and Latin. I should be ashamed I suppose, but really, keeping up with my witty and far-too-intelligent sister would have been impossible. And then, Pierson, they *are* taught . . . taught how to attract a husband. Dangerous information in the wrong hands." He fell silent, but then said, "What think you of the companion?"

Pierson shrugged, struggling to recall her face. "She is . . . young?"

"True, very good. I'm surprised you even noticed that much, your gaze was so fixed on the fair Rowena. She is also remarkably pretty for a chaperon, if that is what she is. I'm interested enough to find out more about Miss Corbett. My mother may know something. Or better, Harriet. As you noted, she is more even in her judgments than Mother."

"So," Pierson said, impatient with his friend's deviation from the object of his interest. Who would notice the chaperon when faced with Lady Rowena? "Can you procure for me an invitation to the Parkinson ball?"

Bainbridge nodded slowly. "I will. It should not pose too much of a problem, actually, since Lord Parkinson is my godfather. But I rely on you to behave and not disgrace me."

"Count on me." Pierson launched himself out of his chair. "Excellent. Then I am off. I have much to do, including letting poor Rupert do all of the things I have not allowed, such as a proper haircut."

"You are forsaking the sheepdog look?"

"I am," Pierson said, with a sudden grin, tugging on one long, loose curl that drooped down on his forehead. "And," he said, more soberly, "I am going to write to my solicitor and ask him to take the search for the absconded Mr. Lincoln in hand. It's possible that there will be some money to recover for my poor serving staff at Delacorte."

"I heartily approve," Bainbridge said, rising too. "If you need any advice, ever, my land agent will be happy to consult with you."

"I appreciate the offer, Bain." He clapped his friend on the shoulder. "Send me a note about tonight, then."

Bainbridge sat back down in the club chair after his friend left and remained for a while just sipping brandy and staring into the distance. Pierson's affairs were in such a tangle and his estate in such a bad way that even the marquess was not sure how he could ever recover. He had been lucky in his own life that his paternal line had always been exquisitely careful of the Bainbridge name and holdings. If he had had Pierson's life he might have ended up just the same, drinking himself into a stupor every night at the sheer hopelessness of it.

But Pierson was not only impulsive and good-hearted at the core, he was also an optimist. If there was any way to recover the estate, Pierson was likely the one who could do it, given the right helpmeet and encouragement. If he should marry wrong, though, it would be the end of any hope for order and recovery in his life, just as if he should marry the right lady, it could well be the making of him. Bainbridge did not subscribe to the notion that one should interfere in a friend's life for his own good, but surely in this one case it behooved him to be sure that Lady Rowena Revington was all she appeared to be.

But what if she wasn't? What then?

He wouldn't worry about that for now. He would handle that problem if it cropped up. For surely Lady Rowena, daughter of a duke and well-raised young lady of the *ton,* could not be so disastrous a match for Pierson? After all, she was certain to be well-dowered, and money never was amiss. The real fear was she was not truly interested in Pierson the way he was in her.

But judging from the blush on her face and the looks she had cast him, there was the beginning of a preference there. He would keep his eye on things, though, for sure. Friends looked out for friends.

Seven

Amy, her stomach quivering with anticipation, stood outside the duke's library and patted her hair down. She had been summoned to His Grace's presence, an event that occurred about every other day, but she still had not become accustomed to it. He was a duke, after all, and she had never in her life expected to have to deal with such a lofty creature as that. Added to the natural intimidation one would feel in the presence of such a man was the dismay engendered by the Duke of Sylverton's haughty and imperious manner and infamous temper.

She pushed the heavy door and it swung open effortlessly, just as everything worked in this perfectly managed household. Everything except the relationship between the fearsome duke and his headstrong daughter.

The library was enormous and dark and now, with the sun setting outside, the curtains were drawn, making the interior even more gloomy. At one end of the room the walls were entirely covered with calf-bound, gilt-edged books, oak bookshelves reaching up so far she could not see the highest shelf in the dim light. At the other end was the duke's massive desk, so big that one could waltz on the surface. Lining the walls were glass-fronted bookcases and a folio table, with maps spread out and weighted with polished brass cannons and other military decorations. The duke had been involved, from a government standpoint, in the war, now over for almost four years, and one had the sense from his library's decoration that he mourned the end of the war, rather than celebrated it.

She walked down the long open area, her feet silent on the lush carpet. On the desk facing her — pointed directly at her, in fact — was a military cannon replica larger than the brass one on the folio table. Mounted on the wall behind the desk was a selection of edge weapons and firearms, a valuable collection, she had been told, and a lethal one. She approached the desk but the duke, his head bent over his work, either did not know she was there or chose to ignore her.

Amy remembered just three months before, meeting him for the first time. She had been frightened, but at first the duke had been so kindly, almost patriarchal. He had complimented her pretty manners, told her about his poor daughter, so ill right then, and that she needed a chaperon just for the Season. Amy had demurred that she was not really "in" society and had never participated in the London Season, but looking back, she didn't think the duke had been listening, for he then started questioning her about Bridget Donegal.

Yes, Amy had admitted, Miss Donegal had oft stated her intention of never marrying, and yes, she had been quite adamant on the subject. Was she a weak character, he asked? No, Bridget was generally accounted to be a very intelligent, strong-minded young lady. Pressed even closer, she admitted that yes, Bridget had a reputation as a termagant.

Had she ever refused an offer of marriage? Yes, she had, Amy stated, but was about to add that the offers she had previously received had not really done honor to her standing in the community, since the Donegals were the foremost family of their small Irish town. That accounted, in Amy's opinion, for Bridget's quick about-face when presented with the startlingly handsome — and very wealthy — young Englishman who was now her husband.

But the duke had cut her off, saying that was all neither here nor there.

From there he had dazzled her with an offer so rich, that even if she had not been compelled to accept for lack of any other position, she would have likely accepted.

His transformation into the irritable, acrimonious, irascible man she now dealt with had occurred after Rowena's recovery. Amy soon found that she had on her hands a father and daughter so much alike that there was no hope of peace in the ducal manse.

"Your Grace?" she said finally, tiring of standing to attention and awaiting his pleasure.

He looked up. "What is it?"

"You asked Martinson to tell me to see you?"

"Ah, yes, that is correct."

He didn't ask her to sit. He never asked her to sit. He glared up at her over his spectacles. "Ball tonight?"

"The Parkinsons, Your Grace."

"How is it going? Any potential beaux?"

Amy thought of Lord Pierson and the look in his golden eyes when he gazed at Rowena. "Well, yes, there are many gentlemen interested in Lady Rowena. Everywhere she is acknowledged as the foremost diamond of this Season and every other."

"But is she interested in any of them?"

"Ye-es," Amy said, reluctantly, again thinking of Lord Pierson. Lady Rowena had done nothing but talk of him all afternoon, and was closely planning her toilette that very moment with her maid.

"Good. It is just March. You have almost three months to accomplish your task. Should be easy. I expect a son-in-law by June."

And he looked back down at his work, that being all the dismissal she would get from the duke. Taking a deep breath, she gave a smart salute and whirled on her heel.

As she exited she heard him say, behind her, "I saw that, Miss Corbett. Your impertinence has been noted."

She leaned against the door as she closed it behind her and said, "Infuriating man!"

It echoed loudly. A footman, polishing a sword-wielding armored knight in the great hall, gazed at her in surprise and she shrugged.

Returning to her room, she knelt on the floor by her bed and petted Puss, as the foundling cat had been named. Though the housekeeper had raised a fuss and put her nose in the air, claiming that cats were dirty creatures and spread disease, on this one item Amy had been adamant. Puss was staying. She would keep her in her own room, but Puss was staying.

In the end, the housekeeper herself had been the one to bring a dish of milk, and to coo over the young cat's pretty manners. Amy felt herself blessed that the duke's staff had readily accepted her, due mostly, she thought to the desperate failings of the last two chaperons. As a result they had been unusually kind to someone in her difficult position, neither servant nor family, but inhabiting a dreary nether world in between. Of her treatment at the hands of the ducal staff she could not complain, if only she could say as much for her employer and her charge.

"What am I going to do, Puss? If Lady Rowena does not deign to marry by the end of the Season, the Duke will not only dismiss me, I'm certain he will ensure that I never receive another position. He has, I'm afraid, a resentful temper, and will make sure no other family of any consequence will ever hire me."

The cat purred and stretched, too full of chicken and milk to care.

"How I wish I could be like you and never worry as long as my belly is full. But

I have been too close to destitution." Amy laid her head against the cat's side and felt the vibration of its purring. It was soothing, but nothing could relieve her anxiety for the future. She had been, in her life, very close to penury on several occasions. So far another position had always come right at the moment she needed it, but this time, she feared, there would be no miraculous intervention. Once the duke had vented his ire, no one would dare help her.

She plucked at the figured pattern on her bedspread. Her Aunt Marabelle would welcome her with open arms, but that poor woman was sixty and mired in poverty herself. She would never turn away her brother's only child, but to take her in was to suffer herself, for a pittance split between two was not enough to subsist on.

No. She would make it on her own. And no spoiled heiress was going to destroy her life. Amy stood and paced to the window, gazing out over the walled gardens of the neighboring London homes. The sun was setting and reflecting golden off mellow stone.

She had to hold onto the knowledge of how very fortunate she was in her life. Just gazing over the roofs reminded her of that, for her view included chimneys, puffs of smoke emanating, and that reminded her of all the little chimney sweeps, tiny boys and girls of six and seven, driven to do their work by pins prodding their callused feet. And the sound of a maid moving out in the hall reminded her that those poor girls worked from sun up to sun down with little respite, and still considered themselves more fortunate than the scullery maids and pot boys, who slept on the floor under the work tables in the kitchen at night, not afforded even the luxury of a bed.

Turning her back on the window, she gazed at her beautiful room. Puss looked up at her sleepily and mewed.

Amy straightened her shoulders and spine. All there was to do was find Lady Rowena a husband to her taste, one that she could not resist. He must be titled, elegant, handsome, witty, and willing to be completely captivated by Rowena's beauty, so much so he would not look beneath the surface to the hellcat underneath. And then, the girl must be convinced to marry him. That was the most difficult task of all.

Hitherto she had been willing to give that quest up as impossible. And yet, there must still be hope! She would not be so spineless as to give up without even trying. Rowena might be determined, but determination faced with desperation *must* give way, and Amy was desperate. If she succeeded, the duke had promised her such a bountiful wage as would set her up for a good long time, and even allow her to help her Aunt Marabelle. In Lord Pierson she had seen sufficient dazzlement to promise that he might be amenable to a swift courtship, and if it pained her just a little to think of the viscount wed to Rowena, it was just a passing qualm, surely. Lady Rowena was intrigued by his reputation in the *ton,* and that was a problem as well. Would the duke allow her to marry such a man, if he could be enticed into making an offer?

Or could it possibly be that he would be so happy to be rid of his daughter that he would welcome any suitor, even one with a reputation as a rake?

"I need some knowledgeable advice, Puss, from someone who will advise me. I will not give up this fight." She would go to her mentor, Mrs. Bower, and ask some questions. She would start her campaign that very night.

"What do you think, Rupert?" Lord Pierson stood in front of the mirror in his suite and gazed at his elegant reflection.

"I have never seen you look so . . . presentable, my lord."

"Presentable? Is that the best you can say?"

"If you will allow me, my lord." The valet faced his employer and poked and prodded his neckcloth into more precise folds, then flicked a minute speck of dust from his jacket and finally knelt and buffed one spot on his black leather ballroom shoes. When he stood it was with a restrained smile on his face. "My lord, you are now perfect."

"Glad to hear it, Rupert." The strain of three days of sobriety was making him fanciful, Pierson feared, for when he looked into the mirror and saw his perfect reflection accompanied by that of his valet, he would have sworn he saw a tear in Rupert's eye, sparkling in the candlelight. But when he turned, he knew it must be a trick of the light. "Have you received a note from Lord Bainbridge yet?" he asked.

Smiling, the valet whipped a scrap of paper out of his sleeve. "This came while you were in your bath, my lord."

Taking in a deep breath, knowing this determined whether he would see his fair angel that night, Pierson opened it. It was brief, and very "Bainbridge." *Success. See you there. B.*

"Now it is up to me," Pierson murmured. "Now it is all up to me. I must haul out and dust off my company manners, Rupert, in order to make an impression on a young lady. Do you think I can do it?"

"Of course, my lord. You can do anything you set your mind to."

Pierson met his valet's gaze in the mirror. "I have the idea that you intend by that praise more than I even asked. However, that is not for tonight. If I am to make my reformation, I must start somewhere, and I will start where my heart leads, to the Parkinson ball."

It had been some time since he had graced the ballroom of a respectable member of society. His usual haunts were highly disreputable. The only balls he was invited to were those with risqué undertones, held by fringe members of the *ton* who looked to any title to bring cachet to their gathering.

But to court a society belle of Lady Rowena Revington's standing, he needed to frequent the higher-toned balls, held by the cream of society. As his carriage approached and queued outside the Parkinson London house, he remembered that

118

brief moment nights before, the first time he saw Lady Rowena's face gazing out of her carriage. He was not a complete idiot. He had wondered if it was just the effect of his drunkenness and misery that had made him vulnerable to her perfection. But seeing her again, her shy smile, her retiring manner, her gentle demeanor, he knew he was right. She was all a man could hope for in a future wife, and more.

He hadn't cared for anything or anyone for such a very long time that he felt fragile, like glass under pressure, and yet he was going to put himself in the way of being shattered. Could she learn to care for him? Her manner toward him had been, in front of the shop earlier that day, as encouraging as a young lady's could be. Could he coax that flicker of warmth into a flame?

Urgency coursed through him, a dread fear that her heart was already claimed, or would be if he did not make an immediate impression. He could not believe his luck that she was not already betrothed.

His coach pulled ahead and stopped at the foot of the steps up to the Parkinson residence. He descended from the carriage and gazed up at the house, the windows ablaze with light, a thousand candles glowing.

"There is my future," he said out loud, as his conveyance pulled away and another disgorged its passengers behind him.

"Then go to it, man, and don't just stand there."

"Bain!" Pierson cried as he turned.

And indeed it was his friend accompanied by his sister, Lady Harriet.

"And the lovely Lady Harriet," he continued, bowing over her gloved hand. "My lady, you are sure to be the most enchanting of ladies at the ball tonight."

"Would that you were sincere, my lord," the lady said, archly, her cheeks glowing pink.

They ascended the steps together, but Lady Harriet was claimed by friends immediately, so Bainbridge and Pierson strolled in, greeted the host — who looked askance at the viscount but nodded politely enough at his greeting — and entered the fray.

They ambled around the perimeter of the rapidly filling ballroom, the chatter of a hundred voices at once making every conversation private.

"It has been an age since I met with such polite society, and yet I see many of the same faces as I would at a ball of a lesser sort," Pierson said, bemused. "There is

Lady Merkley; I saw her at the Villeneuve fête just last week on the arm of that foreign prince, the notorious one who is reputed to have a legion of lovers."

"But tonight she is with her husband, the earl. That is their agreement, I have heard, that she be circumspect and parade with her lovers only at places like the Villeneuve affair, and he will do the same."

"How cynical is our world," Pierson said, watching the lady, who was now all that was demure and matronly on the arm of her husband, when at the fête she had disappeared with the foreign prince for, it was rumored, two hours. And her behavior even before that vanishing act had been lacking in discretion, to say the least, not to mention how scandalous her revealing gown had been. But this night, at the Parkinson's eminently proper ball, she was attired in a gloriously respectable gown. "And what frauds so many are, pretending to be chaste and decorous in public while consorting in private with the denizens of the most depraved entertainments."

Bainbridge shrugged. "And what is wrong with that? It is what will allow people to forget about your . . . ah, adventures, if you comport yourself with propriety from now on in public. You can disport in whatever manner you choose in private, just don't ride your horse through any more Venetian breakfasts, or at least not those of the *ton*."

"I see. My fault, then, was not truly in what I did, but just that I did it so publicly."

"Exactly."

Pierson snorted in disgust. It truly was deceitful in his opinion, the way society was so very blind to its own failings, but who was he to cavil at it? It was to his advantage that his peers were so very willing to turn a blind eye to shortcomings kept private. "I suppose I ought to be grateful, and I will not disappoint you, Bain. I appreciate your aid in this."

"I would do much more for you, my friend."

Pierson threw him a thankful look, but then his attention was claimed. "There she is," he whispered.

Lady Rowena Revington's arrival was an event. She was trailed by her companion, and the moment she had greeted her host and hostess, she was surrounded by a sea of black coats; Pierson swore at himself, thinking all her dances would be claimed by the time he got to her, was properly introduced and asked for a place on her dance card. He should have thought of that, should have realized how it would be with a lady of such spectacular beauty.

She was gowned in white, just like many of the ladies, but her white dress frothed around her like seafoam, adorned by palest pink rosebuds and rich gold trim. The skirt was cut away to reveal an underskirt of gold tissue with her family's ducal shield embroidered on it in silver thread. Her silvery hair was dressed high off her white forehead, and a jeweled tiara nestled in the coronet of intricate braids.

It was impossible to ignore her spectacular figure, slim and lithe, yet womanly. Her white arms were clad in long white silk gloves and her exquisite throat was circled by diamonds, as befit a young lady in her third Season.

In that second Pierson became sure that any warmth he sensed toward him earlier that day must have been an habitual sweetness of disposition, because she was worthy of a royal prince, and he was very far down the peerage from her esteemed father. And yet —

And yet he must try. He must at least approach her, and if he was very fortunate say a word to her.

Accompanied by his friend, he made his

way across the crowded ballroom, and was soon at her side. His heart pounding as if he had just ridden the Derby, he saw her turn toward him.

Eight

It was he! Amy, standing just beside and a little behind Rowena, gazed at Lord Pierson, drinking in his masculine perfection, the sweep of his strong jaw, his dark hair, cut and tamed into a fashionable crop, and his black evening attire perfectly pressed. He was so close she could catch his scent, spicy and masculine, and feel his warmth. He was staring at Rowena, who had not seen him yet, and there was a yearning expression in his golden eyes that broke Amy's heart.

Oh, that she should ever see a man such as he look at her like that!

But she would be sensible. She had met many men in the last few weeks, and almost without exception, though they were courtly and polite — almost obsequious — to Rowena, to her they were just passing courteous, or even oblivious. Lord Pierson would most likely never know her name, even long after she could enumerate the freckles that dotted the skin just below each of his gorgeous golden eyes.

In the normal course of events, gentlemen would attempt to charm Amy too, for as Rowena's chaperon she ostensibly held the power of deciding who the young lady could or could not dance with, and controlled the itinerary she would follow for her daily visits and perambulations. And yet even though Rowena kept up that fiction in public, referring offers of riding or walking or visiting to Amy, gentlemen seemed to sense Amy's powerlessness to affect her charge's preferences and benignly ignored her. In truth, Amy had swiftly found that Rowena would simply make up her own mind about engagements, quite willing to break an appointment if it suited her and then blame it on some caprice of her chaperon or father. So, as chaperon, Amy had found it best to keep plans deliberately vague, merely saying she would send an answer the next day by post or messenger.

Seeing Lord Pierson again, feeling that instant surge of attraction that was surely based solely on his handsome appearance, she took comfort in the knowledge that his treatment of her would likely end any tender feeling she had toward him. She had, in the past weeks, met many London "gentlemen," and for the most part they seemed to be vain, selfish, and witless; they were crude sometimes, rude often, and on most occasions employed what little wit they possessed to the detriment of others. To all that they added an air of doing a favor by bestowing their presence. That sat poorly with Amy, as she was sure it would to anyone with a modicum of spirit. But since Rowena never saw anything that occurred beyond her perfect nose, she never appeared to notice their slights toward her chaperon.

Rowena turned just then and found Lord Pierson at her elbow. She colored prettily and curtseyed, then looked around, wide-eyed.

The marquess drew forward the host of the ball, Lord Parkinson, and a proper introduction was quickly effected, after which the man was pulled away by his wife to see to some other guests just arriving.

"My lord, what a pleasure to see you here." Lady Rowena was at her most gracious.

"I am ecstatic to see you, my lady," he said, his face aglow with pleasure. "You remember Lord Bainbridge from this morning?"

Amy watched as her charge greeted the marquess with a nod of acknowledgment. That young man, with a cynical lift to his brows, stepped back after the greeting and watched his friend and the lady converse, her replying to his question about a free dance, which she — what a miracle! — still had, and not just any dance, but the dinner dance.

"Miss Corbett, and how are *you* tonight?"

She was surprised by the marquess' notice of her and so her tone was one of astonishment. "I am very well, I thank you, my lord." She looked up into Lord Bainbridge's eyes to find their silvery depths alight with mischief.

"And how is her ladyship's cat? Did it recover from its . . . experience?"

Amy bit her lip to keep from laughing. Did he know the truth? Is that why there was such humor in his voice and a sly smile on his lips? After Lady Rowena's fitting at Mr. Lance's shop, when they returned to the duke's carriage to go home, Rowena had gazed with disgust at the purring creature in Amy's arms.

"What are you doing with that filthy animal?" she had asked, her lip curled in a sneer.

Amy explained that since the viscount had thought it was Lady Rowena's, it seemed they were now the owners of it.

Rowena had made an exclamation of disgust and pulled her skirts close to her. "I suppose you're right. Just keep the beast out of my way or . . . or I swear I will kick it again."

Amy knew that Rowena was not especially mean or vicious, and she actually seemed rather to have a fear of cats; perhaps it was some ingrained dread that she could not control.

But the marquess could not know any of that. "Puss is fine, my lord," Amy said, evasively, in answer to Lord Bainbridge's question.

"Good, since for a moment on that shop step it truly appeared as though her ladyship was trying to *kick* the cat. Very disturbing. Until I learned the truth, of course, that the poor thing is actually her own dear pet, and all due to the perspicacity of my friend, the viscount."

"Of course," Amy said primly, avoiding the marquess' piercing gaze. "Actually, though," she added, "Puss is more my cat. It is a foundling." That much was truthful, anyway.

Just then the music started, and Lady Rowena's first partner claimed her for the dance. The viscount, his gaze lingering on the lady as she departed, finally turned with a sigh to his friend.

When he saw Amy, he immediately said, "How rude of me, miss, not to have greeted you properly." He took her hand and bowed low over it. "Miss . . ."

"Miss Amy Corbett," Lord Bainbridge supplied.

"Ah, yes, of course, Miss Corbett. What a crush this ball is already. Would you like to stand or sit someplace less crowded?"

Amy, thrilled and surprised by his notice and courtesy, agreed immediately, and the three of them moved closer to the chaperon's area, a bank of seats already occupied by elderly ladies and matrons with turbans and plumes nodding as they put their heads together and gossiped. Amy saw Mrs. Bower and knew she ought to go over and speak to her — her plan to learn more about Lord Pierson and what chance he stood of gaining the duke's acquiescence in any courtship of Lady Rowena was still in her head — but she was dazzled by the viscount's courtly affability, and she could not have moved even if someone had shouted "Fire."

She noted Lord Bainbridge's quizzical look as it shifted back and forth between them, and then he bowed.

"Excuse me, Miss Corbett, Pierson, I see

some acquaintance with whom I must speak." He stalked away, joining a group of ladies.

Amy, flustered, knew she would not be able to speak first, so she was grateful when Lord Pierson began the conversation.

"Are you enjoying the Season, Miss Corbett?"

"It is not my position to enjoy the Season, my lord, but rather to . . . to make sure my charge enjoys the Season." Oh, how prim she sounded!

"Indeed. So, you are . . . Lady Rowena's chaperon?"

She heard the incredulous tone and looked up. His warm golden eyes were fixed on her and his brow furrowed. It was not the first time she had seen that expression, that puzzlement. Her first couple of balls had been awful experiences, since she had little more than the village assemblies she had been accustomed to, to go by. Many had looked down their long noses at her, and many more had ignored her. It had been close to disastrous.

Since then Amy had done what she could in the way of making herself look older and more serious; she wore sober colors and scraped her hair back in a staid bun. She had perfected a haughty stare, even though she generally forgot to use it. Short of donning a gray wig and using a lorgnette, she didn't know what else she could do, but it was vital that she not expose her employer to any criticism for his choice of a chaperon for his exquisite daughter, or it would all fall on her own head, she knew that. She had quickly assessed the duke, once he had shown his true colors, and realized that he would never *ever* admit that his own precipitate actions could be misguided or wrong, and would always find someone else to blame. In this case that someone would be herself.

At least since she had met Mrs. Bower and accepted that woman's tutelage, she felt much more at home in the ballrooms of the elite. Knowledge was power. "I *am* Lady Rowena's chaperon," she said, straightening her shoulders, happy for the reminder of her position. It would never do to be seen mooning over Lord Pierson. "His Grace hired me just after Christmas."

"You are so young," the viscount said, with wonder. "You look barely twenty yourself."

Stiffening, Amy replied, "I am almost twenty-five, my lord, and it is not my first such position. I am certainly old enough to guide Lady Rowena."

At the name of her charge, Lord Pierson's gaze slewed out to the ballroom floor again. He sighed, "She is lovely." His gaze swiveled back around to Amy. "Excuse me, ma'am, I know bloody . . . er, I know well that I should not be commenting on Lady Rowena's appearance; not the done thing. But difficult not to think of it, at least, when one sees her. She is magnificent."

Amy followed his gaze once more as Rowena whirled past them in the arms of her partner. "She is," she murmured. But instead of keeping her eye on Rowena, she watched the viscount, the shifting emotions on his handsome, hard-lined face, the flickering expression of his golden eyes, now clouded, now clear. She thought of all that Lady Rowena had told her of this man and wondered what it meant, in light of his attraction to the duke's daughter. As the girl's chaperon, should she be alarmed? He was dismissed as a rake and a reckless, dissolute wastrel. And yet, there was certainly no indication he was a despoiler of innocents, for he would not be allowed in this ballroom if that was the case.

Would he? Or did a title blot out many sins? Again, she was cursed by her lack of knowledge of tonnish ways. She would need to consult with Mrs. Bower.

Why, of all the young men in love with her, did Rowena have to choose to express interest in an acknowledged rake and scoundrel?

For it was all too true that Rowena had a multitude of admirers. Amy had been in company with scores of young gentlemen in the brief Season so far; earls, marquesses, viscounts, and sons of the same titles. There was even the foreign-born prince, Prince Verstadt, who was still enamored of Rowena, though he barely noticed Amy. She had had to remind him repeatedly that he must *ask* her if he wished to take the young lady for a drive. Rowena had seemed to like him well enough, so Amy had let the brief courtship proceed, only to have the prince's proposal rejected when he made it.

Was this just another flirtation for the duke's daughter, this fascination with Lord Pierson? As Rowena disappeared from sight again, Lord Pierson turned back to her.

"Have you done this sort of thing before, Miss Corbett?"

Amy sighed, having already told him she had. "I was last in Ireland, but not exactly as chaperon. I was a governess."

"Ireland! That is quite the journey, from being a governess in Ireland to a chaperon of a duke's daughter in London during the Season! How did that come about?"

Fearing she had already said too much, for her dignity as a chaperon lay partially in the belief others must have that she knew her profession, and yet realizing how small a circle the *ton* was, and that she would not deceive anyone who chose to ask the right questions, Amy paused. Did he ask the question to find fault? Should she beware?

"Pardon my prying, ma'am." His golden eyes changed, the gleam softer. "But you do seem so different from what one thinks of as a chaperon. It cannot help but make one curious about your story. Shall we speak, instead, of your family?"

If it were anyone else, Amy would have suspected that he was trying to find out just how unsuitable she was for the post she held, but the viscount's expression was so open and amiable. "I have no family to speak of. I was born and raised not that far from London, really," she said, and named her home village in Kent. "I still have an aunt living there, and I hope to return there soon."

The viscount's expression clouded. "That is only a hundred miles from my own estate, if my memory serves me," he said.

"Really?" His downcast expression made her pause, but then she said, "It is a very pretty part of England. We were quite near the sea, and I think I miss most the salt mist rolling in over the meadows."

"Yes. The mist."

"Lord Pierson?"

Pierson, his name catching his attention, shook himself. "Yes, Miss Corbett?"

She was silent, and he stared into her gray-blue eyes for a long moment. He still couldn't fathom how such a delicate, youthful looking creature had become a chaperon. In his limited experience — limited because he was not one much for attending tonnish balls — chaperons were elderly dragons with more hair on their chins than the young men they intimidated could grow in a month. But Miss Corbett, slim and girlish, with golden hair, a pointed chin and inquisitive, bright eyes, was a slight young lady even dwarfed by the potted palm, which they stood near.

"We were speaking of our home county," she said. "Do you miss your home when you are in London?"

He took in a long breath and regarded the pointed toe of his shoe. He amended his opinion of her to include the fact that when she caught hold of a subject, she worried at it like a terrier. Perhaps she made a better chaperon than he would have thought, for inquisitiveness was surely a valuable attribute for that breed of lady. "Miss my home? Well, I haven't . . . uh . . . spent much time there, really."

"You haven't?"

Her tone was startled and he could hardly blame her. "No, I mean, I went to school young and spent holidays with friends. My mother died when I was just a baby." He suppressed a bitter exclamation, for he had always suspected his mother died of a broken heart; his father's treatment of her was legendary in its cruelty. "So, I spent little time at home, in short."

"But when the Season is over, do you not go home?"

Her bright eyes, the blue-gray color of the sky over the channel, he thought, absently staring into their depths, were almost challenging. How to explain himself?

"It's a very large house and lonely. I have little incentive when there are so many other places to see, so many other things to do." He had forced a very merry inflection into his words, wishing to convince her of his claim, that he had too many friends and activities to spend much time at his country estate. "And I am always invited here and there during the hunting season and the Christmas season. Wouldn't do to disappoint friends, would it?"

And it appeared that he had been successful in appearing carefree, but the effect was to disappoint her. "I see."

He could see in her worried frown that she was thinking of all of the work there must be to run a large estate. Somehow he knew how she thought, and he felt a spurt of anger that she would judge him and find him lacking. "I have a very competent estate manager and he assures me that everything is run smoothly in my absence." Why he lied, he was not sure, but if it would wipe away those worried lines between her eyes he would do it again.

She looked startled at his addition. "I am sure you do, my lord, have a competent manager."

Too late he wondered if this exchange would hurt his reputation with her, and therefore with Lady Rowena. He had only been considering Miss Corbett's disapproval, when he should have been thinking of his fair divinity, and how her chaperon would view his suit when he made it. For the duke hired her; he must trust her judgment, even if she did appear as young and naïve as her charge. He wished he had taken pains to appear steady and sober instead of frivolous and pleasure-seeking. It was important, as the lady closest to Lady Rowena, and the one with the most influence on her, that she had a favorable impression of him.

That same moment the music ended and his companion scoured the crowd for her charge, who was now returning to her on the arm of her first partner. His curiosity piqued, Pierson watched Miss Corbett rather than Lady Rowena. What was the duke thinking about to put such a sweet-faced young lady in such a position? It could not be easy for her, when all the other chaperons were aged dragons or society matrons. It was a pity a girl of such grace and simple beauty should be required to work for her living at all, instead of being happily married to some gentleman and raising a troupe of sweet-faced tow-headed children.

And what was the matter with his head that he was even concerning himself with such matters? Wouldn't his wastrel friends laugh to hear such maudlin musings from a rake of his renown! He should not be paying attention to the companion anyway, for the duke's daughter was his object, and he must focus all his efforts on gaining her heart.

Amy watched Rowena, smiling up at her dance partner and gaily laughing at some witticism as they strolled back to her. She then glanced over at Lord Pierson to see his gaze fixed, of course, on Lady Rowena, too. She thought back to her and the viscount's conversation. There had been something in his tone when he spoke of his estate, some . . . What was it? If she knew him better she could say for sure, but it had certainly sounded like desperation, or anxiety. It had concerned her, for his joviality had seemed forced. He would have her believe he was carefree, but there was something that worried him deeply. Or was she just reading something into his expression, when she did not know him well enough to do so?

One thing that was on his face for the world to see was his attraction to Lady Rowena. Sadly, she realized that it was quite likely Lord Pierson was just the sort of man her charge would fall in love with, for not only was he more handsome than any of her other suitors had been so far this Season, he added to his appearance a depth of feeling in his golden eyes and a regal bearing that even Prince Verstadt had not had, in Amy's estimation. And his reputation, far from hurting his chances, only seemed to enhance his prestige in Rowena's eyes.

"How pleasant to see you again, my lord," Rowena said, as her guide bowed and disappeared back into the crowd.

"How could I go anywhere but here, my lady, knowing you would again return?"

Amy stifled a sigh as she realized her duty lay in promoting this match, if she felt it would offer a chance at happiness. She resolved to do the best for herself, which meant just that; if Lady Rowena appeared to favor Lord Pierson — and it certainly seemed so far that she did — then Amy must do everything in her power to assist the couple, and then to convince the duke that the viscount would make a good match for his daughter. The duke was so angry and displeased with his daughter, he would likely hand her off to Lucifer himself just to be rid of her from his house. They never saw one another without quarreling, and the duke was unlikely to place any barriers in his daughter's path when she finally decided to marry. That was

Amy's conjecture, anyway, but she would need Mrs. Bower's opinion to bolster her own before she would feel in any measure secure.

Lady Rowena and Pierson had been chatting amiably. It seemed Rowena's dance partner for that half hour had been called away unexpectedly, and she had the time free. The Marquess of Bainbridge approached them again, his gaze darting from one to the other of the trio.

"How goes the ball, Pierson?" he asked.

"I'm enjoying myself quite well."

Bainbridge glanced at Amy, who was feeling rather *de trop* at the moment, with the lady and her ardent admirer so engrossed in conversation.

"Miss Corbett, would you like to dance?"

Amy, startled, immediately said, "Oh, no, I couldn't. I am a companion and chaperon, my lord, not here for my own entertainment!"

But Rowena, with a significant expression, said, "Don't be ridiculous, Amy. You will not insult Lord Bainbridge by refusing his kind offer. Lord Pierson and I are quite able to remain unchaperoned in this crowded ballroom for everyone to see. Go. *Have fun.*"

It was virtually a command, and Amy, mindful of her eventual aim, which was that Rowena and Lord Pierson make a match of it, thought it might be wisest after all to leave them a half hour of free conversation. "All right," she said, reluctantly.

"I am flattered by your enthusiasm," the marquess said, dryly, as he took her arm and led her into the figures of the dance.

Nine

"My lord, I hope you do not think my reluctance made any reflection on you, for . . ."

"No, no, I understand," Lord Bainbridge said, guiding her to a line of couples.

But he couldn't possibly, Amy thought, glancing back through the crowd at Rowena and Lord Pierson. Determined, she turned her gaze away from them and looked up at her dance partner. "It was very kind of you to ask me to dance, my lord."

"Not kind at all, Miss Corbett. You looked as though you could use a break from your duties and I was unengaged, that is all."

Separated by the figures for a moment, Amy glanced around the elegant ballroom. The Parkinson home was large by London standards, and their gathering August. Mrs. Bower was chaperoning a pretty little chit in her first Season, a Miss Naunce, daughter of an admiral who had been knighted for his courageous service to the crown. Amy wanted desperately to speak

144

with her friend, for she still had some questions to ask about the likelihood of the duke approving Lord Pierson as a suitor for his daughter's hand. Despite her own certainty, she wished the added assurance of the experienced older woman.

She touched the hand of the last lady in the line and was rejoined by Lord Bainbridge, who then promenaded her around in a grand, sweeping circle.

"My lord, I believe we were at your home for a literary tea just recently."

"And I believe you're right," he said, with a wicked grin. "I must say that my sister remembers your visit very clearly."

Rowena's disastrous flirtation with Lady Harriet's beau came back to Amy and she fell silent.

"Miss Corbett, if I do not mistake your silence, you are concerned about my sister and her beau, Lord Newton-Shrewsbury. Please set your mind at ease. My sister was not, I think, seriously interested in Shrewsbury, and I say thank God, for I don't like the milksop. And I acquit Lady Rowena of any culpability in the affair even if others do not, for a lady so beautiful must attract men, whether she attempt so or not."

Amy sighed in relief, but could no more

speak than she could breathe right that moment. That she could not acquit her charge of guilt was reason enough to say nothing. And too, what had the marquess meant by adding *"even if others do not"*? Was there someone who saw Rowena's game and remarked on it?

"Pardon my curiosity," the marquess said. "But how did one as . . . well, as young as you come to be a chaperon? Most of your ilk are rather more . . . uh, seasoned veterans of the London set."

Amy sighed at the repeated question and told him an abbreviated version of the truth, leaving out that she had no choice but to take the position due to her impecunious state, and making it instead an honor that she gladly accepted. She was getting quite good at the tale by now.

"So this is your first Season. And your first charge is the daughter of a duke."

"I'm very fortunate, am I not?" Amy asked, with as much verve as she could summon, smiling up at the marquess.

"Yes. Very fortunate. All of London is puzzled by one thing, you know," he said. "How is it that a young lady of her beauty and stature has remained unwed? And why does she continue to refuse suitors? Does she not wish to marry?"

Amy's mouth went dry. She had been faced with that same question in many guises in the last few weeks, but no one had been quite so blunt. She thought for a moment and then said, "Lady Rowena is as . . . as romantic as she is lovely. She has determined to wait for a man she feels she can love. I know that is unusual, given her status, but her father is very indulgent and wishes only what his daughter wants."

"Indulgent, the Duke of Sylverton? Is that so? I had thought the answer would be somewhat different."

"What did you think, my lord?"

"No, let my musings remain my own, for we are all free in our own minds to think unflattering thoughts, you know, and not say them. It is what preserves a pleasant society."

Amy, unsettled, glanced up at him, but they were separated again by the figures of the dance. She passed by Lady Rowena and Lord Pierson, who were so deep in conversation that they did not even see her. That was a good thing, she said to herself with great firmness.

The marquess was silent through most of the dance, but finally, as the last notes sounded, she worked up the courage to say, "My lord, your friend . . . he has a certain reputation in London. I am surprised he is even allowed into this ballroom, with what I have heard. What say you in his defense?"

Lord Bainbridge took her arm and looked down at her, feigning alarm. "Ah, now the chaperon begins to show her teeth! So now I must defend my friend. Oh dear. Pierson has indeed managed to acquire quite the reputation over the last few years. But I may say with complete honesty two things; he has never ever, even in rumor, been cavalier with a lady's reputation or safety. And I truly believe that for reasons of his own he has decided he must mend his ways and begin life anew. He wishes to make amends for his past faults."

"Good. That's comforting, since he appears quite taken with Rowena."

"Yes. He's gotten it into his mind that she is everything he approves in a lady, that is, she is mild and meek of temperament, gentle and loving with pets and children, as sweet of nature as she is fair of face."

Amy felt a quiver of apprehension at the marquess' list. A more inappropriate description of Rowena she had never heard, save the "fair of face." "My lord, if you would be so kind, would you guide me over to yon bank of chairs by the wall where my friend, Mrs. Bower sits, and if you would bring Lady Rowena to me as well?"

"Are you feeling quite well, Miss Corbett? You look excessively pale."

Amy, leaning heavily on his arm, could say nothing to refute that assertion. Once near Mrs. Bower, though, she straightened and said, "Thank you, my lord. I think it was just the unaccustomed heat of dancing that made me feel faint for a minute. If you would bring Lady Rowena to me I would be eternally grateful."

With one backward look of concern, Lord Bainbridge disappeared into the crowd and Amy sank into a chair at her friend's side. Miss Naunce, Mrs. Bower's charge, a pretty, fluttery girl, was just taking the arm of a young gentleman and heading for the dance floor for the next dance. Amy waited until she was gone and then said, "Mrs. Bower, I am sorely in need of your advice."

"What is it, my dear?" The elderly lady shifted closer and her stays creaked alarmingly.

Amy related her current concern. Since Mrs. Bower was already the trusted recipient of her worries up to that point, she only needed to add her new concerns about Lord Pierson, his intentions, Rowena's feelings in the matter, and the viscount's viability as a candidate for her hand, especially given the duke's fractious and unpredictable nature.

"I could encourage both in their friendship, Rowena and Lord Pierson, only to have the duke fly into a rage at the mere thought of his daughter with a gentleman of such a reputation. And then where would we be? It's going to be difficult enough to get Rowena wed, but if the only man she has appeared to be truly interested in so far this Season is ineligible for her hand, I don't know what I shall do."

"Why does every girl love a rake?" Mrs. Bower queried, fretfully. She frowned and clicked her teeth. "I would say this, my dear; if Lady Rowena appears truly taken with Lord Pierson, then I think you ought to encourage him. There is a much greater chance that the duke will approve his suit just to rid himself of his daughter than that he will reject him."

"What do you know of Lord Pierson's situation?"

The lady twisted her mouth and chewed her cheek. "Lord Pierson, eighth Viscount Pierson; old name, but not so honorable in the last few generations. I will say this for the present viscount; unlike his father before him, there truly seems to be nothing vicious about this lad, he is just a little wild. His father, now, he was a different sort; he was a tyrant and a bully, from all reports. This one merely seems to drink too much wine — and where, I may ask, will you find a gentleman who does not? — and likes ladies of loose morals, and there again, what gentleman does not? I think he has been damned by his name, for some part, and then . . . there *have* been incidents."

"Incidents?"

"Incidents. Ahem . . . your charge is coming this way."

"Quickly then," Amy said, leaning toward her friend. "Tell me at least some."

"He is said," Mrs. Bower whispered, "to have ridden his horse through a Venetian breakfast and directly to the fountain in the garden of a certain Lady Decker, a social climber of the most odious sort." She chuckled. "I would have given much to see that. But anyway, he has been said to take part in debauched revels at some of the less stately residences, and there was one incidence of public nudity." The older woman cleared her throat and tried to look censorious, but she ruined it by chuckling.

"What a scoundrel! There were various other revelries, but on a more serious note he is said to play deep at the card table, money he can ill afford."

"Is he poor?" Amy was alarmed, for the duke was notoriously clutch-fisted, and if he thought his daughter could be a claim on his purse even after marriage, it might prove to be an impediment.

"Not poor," Mrs. Bower said, frowning. "I have heard of no claims against his estate, such as it stands. But he will have much to do, I think, to bring his country estate back to its proper beauty. Mind, I do not know this for certain. He could be into moneylenders for all I know. *Or* he could be making great strides in turning his fortunes around."

Amy sighed staring down at her gloved hands. "You don't think he is a fortune hunter, do you?" She looked up at her friend. "I will *not* countenance that, even if he should be Rowena's choice. I will not let her be unhappy for the rest of her life just so I may be free of worry."

"I've seen no sign of that, nor heard a word, dear. And surely, if he had been on the look-out for a fortune I would have heard from someone in my circle," said Mrs. Bower, with a sympathetic expression. "Chaperons are very careful about that kind of man, and we tell each other what we know and hear. It is the same with gentlemen of a violent bent; we are very careful of them. I would not subject one of my girls to that anguish. But as to Lord Pierson's financial situation, I will ask around . . ."

"Oh, no, Mrs. Bower, I would not have him embarrassed by inquiries . . ."

"My dear, please!" Mrs. Bower said, putting one hand on Amy's arm. "Credit me with subtlety, at the very least. I'll make my inquiries discreetly. I will say, that he has been admitted to the Parkinson house speaks well of him, for they are very high sticklers." She looked thoughtful, her gaze settling on Amy's face. "And what of his friend, Lord Bainbridge?"

"He is a very pleasant man, certainly."

"And he danced with you?" Mrs. Bower said with an arch look.

"Out of kindness, ma'am, I assure you," Amy said, shocked at the implication behind the woman's words.

"Kindness is not a quality the young gentlemen are noted for. He seemed most gallant. I would not turn him away, if I were you, for he may see in you just the sort of young lady . . ."

"Mrs. Bower!" Genuinely shocked, Amy stared at her friend. "I cannot believe you would think a marquess would look upon me with matrimony in mind, and there is not another end I would countenance for myself. But my background, my connections are not such . . . not that I have aught to be ashamed of, for I haven't — my father was a gentleman and my mother the granddaughter of an earl — but my origins are humble compared to Lord Bainbridge . . ." She faltered to a stop as Rowena approached on the arm of the man himself, trailed closely by Lord Pierson.

"I have delivered the young lady, Miss Corbett; now as my reward may I ask to sit with you and this charming lady," he said, bowing to Mrs. Bower, "while Lady Rowena goes off with her next partner?"

As Mrs. Bower snickered and elbowed Amy, Amy saw Rowena's extreme pique, and was grateful when Lord Newton-Shrewsbury, her next partner, appeared promptly to claim her. Lord Pierson glowered darkly at the other man, who scuttled off with his prize on his arm.

As Lord Bainbridge took a seat by her, a fact that was noted and was providing fresh gossip among the other chaperons, Amy watched Lord Pierson, studying his expression. What had he and Rowena spoken of? Was he happy with the outcome, and did he still feel the same attraction to her that had been evident from the beginning of their acquaintance?

She turned to Lord Bainbridge. "Thank you, my lord, for fetching Lady Rowena. I hope you did not have to interrupt a conversation between her and Lord Pierson?"

He shrugged and lounged back in an unforgivably lax attitude for a public ballroom. When Mrs. Bower gave him a stern look he straightened. "Uh, I believe it was mostly maidenly blushes on Lady Rowena's part and manly silence on my friend's."

Lord Pierson joined them at that point and said, "Bainbridge, shall we hie ourselves off to the card room until my dance with Lady Rowena?"

"I'm in the middle of a conversation, pudding head," Bainbridge said, irritably.

"I am sorry," Pierson said with a contrite expression, bowing to Amy. "My apologies, miss. It's so unusual to see my friend making an attempt to be pleasant to any member of the female sex, that I was taken by surprise."

"What he is trying to say is *he* is so seldom in the company of proper ladies,"

Bainbridge returned, acidly, "that he has not seen me speaking to any lady at all."

Pierson gave him a look of disdain. "Miss Corbett, please ignore my friend's attempts to blacken my reputation. He is clumsily trying to make himself look better at my expense."

"I would never do that. Why would I," Bainbridge said, airily, "when you are so adept at making yourself the goose?" His gaze caught on something in the distance. "Excuse me for a moment, Miss Corbett, Pierson. I believe my sister is summoning me from across the room and I must obey."

Amy watched him go, his stride long and loping. She desperately hoped his sister's urgency was not occasioned by Rowena's dancing with the lady's former suitor. In spite of all Lord Bainbridge had said to acquit Rowena of any wrongdoing, it was clear that someone had interpreted her behavior far too accurately and had openly said so.

"Lady Harriet wished to tell Bainbridge she is leaving, I believe," Pierson said, crouching down at her side to speak to her more easily. "I think she is promised to another ball this evening, as well as this one."

Relieved, Amy turned to the viscount,

and was startled to find his face so close to her, his warm breath mingling with her own. "D-do you know Lady Harriet well? I must say she is my idea of the perfect lady."

"If you like being challenged on every word you utter, I suppose," Pierson said, doubtfully.

Amy thought, wryly, that he had not experienced being challenged until he had seen Rowena throw down the gauntlet. "An opinionated lady is not to every gentleman's taste."

"Opinions I do not mind, I suppose, but ridicule is another thing. And Lady Harriet is just a little too swift to make a fellow feel as though he has just misspoke."

"Are you so unsure of your opinions, then?"

Lord Pierson smiled and Amy felt her heart thump.

"Not at all, but a fellow does say the occasional thing he would rather not have to defend. I sometimes talk nonsense. Do you not do so?"

"I? Yes, on occasion, I suppose."

"Well, Lady Harriet has never said or done a foolish thing in her life and it is unnerving." He stood, pulled a chair close to her and took a seat. "She will require a paragon before she will marry, I say."

"I think most ladies would not mind a man who spoke foolishness to her once in a while if he truly cared for her. That makes up for much."

"Do you think so?"

Lord Pierson was gazing at her steadily, and Amy felt herself flush. "I do. No person, man or woman, is without folly. There are more important attributes than great wisdom."

"Yes, like wealth."

Amy watched his face, his golden eyes and brooding expression. "Some may think wealth vital, but I don't think, beyond a competence — I'm not so foolish as to think one can do without money at all — it is so very important." Her tone gentler, she added, "You cannot eat jewels, nor drink gold."

His gaze caught on hers and held. He was so close his warmth radiated through her thin gown and petticoats. Surely, she thought, someone could not seem so sincere and good-natured and be the rogue he was reputed to be?

"Do you truly believe that, Miss Corbett?"

"I beg pardon?" She had lost her train of thought, but swiftly recalled their conversation. "Oh, yes . . . I do. As one who has never been wealthy, I don't think happiness is dependent upon such ephemeral things. I have seen a flower girl happy, just in the warmth of the sun and a fresh breeze. And I have seen a lord, with all his wealth and glory, wretched." She plucked at the folds of her dress and thought of the duke, who never truly seemed happy. And she thought of the Donegalses' tumultuous, riotous home, where happiness permeated even the rafters, though they were not rich by any measure.

Pierson was silent, his eyes searching hers. "I don't think I ever believed that until this moment, that one could be truly happy without wealth. But you have a way, Miss Corbett, of convincing me."

Ten

Whether she was trying to tell him, subtly, that his suit would not be dismissed if Lady Rowena should favor him Pierson did not know, but he felt unaccountably jubilant, of a sudden, sitting with Miss Corbett and talking to her. Money didn't matter. Life could be joyful without it.

Or could it? It was all very well in theory, but what of the destitute unpaid serving staff of his estate and the tenant farmers? What would they do with no money to feed themselves and their families? It was a new sensation, this feeling of responsibility, and it was unnerving.

No, worse than that . . . it was deeply distressing.

The music played and the dancers danced, and he gazed through it, seeing nothing. Instead he saw imploring faces, outstretched hands, barren land. What was going on at Delacorte? Would they ever track down Mr. Lincoln and the stolen money?

Lord but he needed a *drink!*

And yet he would not have one. He stiffened his spine and felt a hand on his arm. He glanced over to find Miss Corbett's face a mask of concern.

"Are you quite well, Lord Pierson?"

Her gentle voice was soothing, her blue-gray eyes clouded with worry, and he found himself wanting to reassure her. "I am, Miss Corbett. Say," he said, suddenly caught by something she had said a few minutes before. "You said you met Lady Harriet. That would have been at Lady Bainbridge's literary tea the other day."

"Why, yes."

He felt an urge to laugh out loud, hysterically. It had only just occurred to him that while he had been in an artist's garret looking over the poor likeness of his fair angel, she had been sitting in the drawing room of his best friend. If Bainbridge had obeyed his mother's wish and attended the literary tea, and if Pierson had stayed with him, he would have seen her there.

Of course he *knew* that she had been there, but somehow he hadn't yet realized that at the exact minute he was trying to describe her for that artist fellow, she was sitting in Bainbridge's drawing room.

"What is it, my lord?"

He shook his head. "Nothing. Nothing

at all. Do you believe in fate, Miss Corbett?"

She knit her brows. "If by fate you mean providence or divine intervention, I suppose I do."

"Well, so do I, now. Now I am more sure than ever that the road I have set myself upon is the right one, guided, as you say, by divine intervention."

"However," she added, eyeing him with a thoughtful expression on her pale face, "I think it is often man's mistake to attribute to God whatever we please, and to call it divine intervention or providence when it is only chance and our own will."

He shook his head. She had no idea what he meant. How could she, when she didn't even know about his first sighting of Lady Rowena, and the way his heart had taken flight, and now this proof that he was meant to meet her, if not by one chance, then by another. She was meant to be his savior, his inspiration, and to give him the strength and incentive to work and bring his estate back to where it should be. She would be the lady of Delacorte, and all of his staff and tenants would someday thank him for courting her and bringing her home.

Miss Corbett could have no idea that his

life's path was now stretched out before him, a shining ribbon of hope winding through the green acres of Delacorte. He must cling to that hope and add to it determination.

Bainbridge watched from a distance as Pierson and the pretty chaperon bent their heads together, talking. He could see in her animated expression and the way her eyes followed his movements, that she was fascinated by Pierson. She seemed a mild and intelligent young woman. Lady Rowena, too, *seemed* so. And yet it still struck him as odd that a young woman of such impeccable breeding, beauty, wit, and wealth as Lady Rowena should be single. Was it truly her choice, as Miss Corbett had stated? Or was there more?

The lady in question was being walked, at the end of the dance, back to her chaperon. From a distance he could see the action like a pantomime. Pierson looked up at her approach and his gaze never left her again while she remained with them. Miss Corbett faded back and watched the couple, now engaged in conversation. Lady Rowena was perfectly demure, yet seemed to accept Pierson's devotion as her due, and that sat ill with Bainbridge. What he expected he did not know, but such absolute graceful recognition of Pierson's ardor as her just deserts made him edgy.

If she was attracted to him, should she not be more unsettled, more agitated? Did the calmness of her demeanor, as habitual as it seemed, bespeak an unfeeling heart? He had heard nothing ill of her, and yet his mind wasn't satisfied. But for now he would just watch and wait. Pierson was in the first stage of infatuation, and there was little danger yet he would become officially engaged to her without a suitable period of courtship. His attentions might appear particular still for a while with no poor reflection on Lady Rowena's reputation.

So he would just watch and wait.

Amy didn't need to see her charge herself to know Lady Rowena was on her way toward them. Lord Pierson's attention shifted suddenly and was riveted on the approaching couple, and, though Amy was speaking to him still, he didn't appear to hear her. This should be an encouraging sign, for hadn't a very wry novelist of recent years commented that rudeness was the first sign of an advanced state of love?

And yet she couldn't help but be offended. It didn't seem fair that Lady

Rowena, spoiled, rich, and with every other advantage of face and fortune, should also have the ability to smite an otherwise sensible man dumb with love. And even a man of Lord Pierson's seeming intelligence and good sense. It just was not fair.

Yet it did no good to rail against the way of the world. And in this one instance she should be grateful, not resentful, that men were men, attracted by a fair face.

Lord Newton-Shrewsbury approached with Lady Rowena on his arm, returning her to her chaperon. The two men nodded a stark greeting, their antagonism toward each other like a scent on the air, and Pierson stood, bowed to Rowena and said, "This is my dance I believe, my lady."

"It is, my lord," she answered, curtseying gracefully. The pair made their way to the dance floor.

"What would she want with that bounder?" Lord Newton-Shrewsbury said out loud.

"I beg your pardon, my lord?" Amy said, piqued at being treated as invisible. It was the outside of enough.

The gentleman whirled and bowed, his face coloring until even the tips of his ears were red. "Pardon, miss, just speaking to m'self, you know."

"I know," Amy said pointedly, folding her hands on her lap and trying not to pull at a thread in her gloves in her agitation.

"H'lo Norman," Lord Bainbridge said, sauntering toward them. "Didn't go on to the Duchess of Twylle's ball with my sister, I see."

"Uh, no, Bainbridge, I uh, had commitments here."

"Yes, I noted your commitment to Lady Rowena. Hear you met her at m'mother's literary afternoon. With my sister."

Lord Newton-Shrewsbury reddened even deeper and bowed. With a murmured excuse he backed away and fled.

"Ninny. I don't know what my mother was thinking of to imagine him half good enough for Harriet."

"What a devoted brother you are!" Amy commented.

Bainbridge glanced down at her and chuckled. "How my mother would stare to hear me praised so. I do not do half of what she would like me to, on my sister's behalf."

"Yet I imagine you do twice what many other brothers do," Amy countered.

"I like you, Miss Corbett. You are good for my battered feelings of self-esteem."

Amy giggled and then hid her mouth behind her hand, glancing around at the other chaperons with alarm. It would not do to sound like a giddy girl. Mrs. Bower caught her eye and gave a significant look at the handsome marquess standing by her side. Amy shook her head and had no trouble assuming a more sober demeanor. She would certainly not mistake his kindness as anything more. And in truth, she had no wish for anything more than his kindness. She did not think she could ever return his regard if he felt for her anything warmer than friendship.

He indicated a chair with a quizzical look.

"Of course, my lord. Please sit."

He did not make the mistake of lounging again, but sat correctly, both black leather-shod feet firmly on the marble parquet floor. "Lady Rowena is somewhat of a puzzle to me, Miss Corbett."

"Oh?"

"Yes. She has every advantage of face and fortune, and yet she has not married. You say it is because she is romantic and will only marry for true love, but for all the men dying of love for her these past two Seasons, you say there is not one for whom she felt any emotion at all? I am no idiot; I know there is a fashion among the young men to be expiring of unrequited love for every fair diamond of the Season. It's this ridiculous culture of Byron's poetry that is to blame, I say. But still . . . not one of those young men appealed to her?"

"You cannot expect me to comment on past years and Lady Rowena's love or lack thereof when I was not here?"

He cast her a sharp side look. "No, I suppose not," he replied, reluctance in his tone. "That is the perfect evasive answer."

"Why would I be evading anything, my lord? I have nothing to hide."

"Ah, is that so? Then tell me; is Lady Rowena as perfectly demure and sweet-natured as she appears at every ball?"

"Are any of us exactly what we appear to others? Are we to have no private foibles at all, then? Are you, my lord, always perfectly correct in dress, manner and, ahem, *posture* as you appear now?"

"You answer a question with a question."

"And you answer a question with a comment."

"Routed. Very neatly routed. But my curiosity is not sated, and so I'll observe, still, the beauteous Lady Rowena and her future behavior. You see, my friend, Pierson, is

168

smitten, but not just any lady will do for him. He is far more romantic of nature than I, and he idealizes the ladies. It is a dangerous characteristic."

"He's a man, my lord, and not a boy. Do you think him foolish?"

"No. Not at all. Pierson is very intelligent or I would not be his friend, for I can't abide a fool. Hence my distaste for Shrewsbury."

"Then you cannot mean to interfere in his life and decisions."

"Interfere in *his* life? No, of course not. Not at all."

What did he mean by that emphasis, she wondered, throwing a swift glance his way and catching a secretive smile on his lips. How strange it was, she thought, that with all of the attention he paid her and the conversation they shared and even the dance, it was still not *his* face and voice that moved her, but Lord Pierson's. How incalculable were women, she sadly pondered, that self-interest could not inspire love. Mrs. Bower had been urging her, subtly, to make the most of her time with Lord Bainbridge, for stranger things had happened in the world than a lord falling in love with a chaperon. Amy knew that, but she could not be so self-serving.

If, by some miracle, Lord Bainbridge decided he was desperately in love with the meek Miss Corbett and offered her his hand in marriage, what would she say? She suppressed a smile at the notion, for his behavior toward her, in her estimation, had been more like a friend than a lover. But if he did, what would she say? She supposed she would have to say yes. What kind of idiot would not, even if she did not care for him as a wife ought to care for her husband?

The music played on. Lady Rowena and Lord Pierson whirled by, their eyes locked together.

But no, her self-interest would best be served by promoting a match between her obstreperous charge and the handsomest gentleman in the ballroom that night, in her own estimation. And she would be stern with herself and do it. Lord Pierson could do worse than Rowena. She was spoiled and tempestuous and could on occasion be rude and thoughtless, but there was no real evil in her. And given how little time husbands and wives spent in each other's company in the usual marriage, as far as Amy could glean from her brief time in the world of the *ton,* they should do just fine together.

That was *if* Lord Pierson truly fell in love with her, and *if* Lady Rowena felt the same, and *if* the girl could come to see that marriage was in her own best interest.

Amy sighed. It was only the beginning of the Season. She could hope for a miracle or two, but she didn't know if they came by the gross.

"Your chaperon is so very young," Pierson said, as the last strains of the music sounded and the dance came to an end. "She looks so . . . so out of place sitting with the other ladies, all of them so much older and dressed in black. She looks like a flower against a field of ravens."

"How very fanciful, my lord," Lady Rowena said, gracefully taking his arm as they strolled the perimeter of the ballroom back toward the bank of chairs set up for the chaperons and mothers of the closely guarded young ladies.

"I suppose it is. But just look at her! She is so very pretty. Bainbridge seems taken with her, if you notice. They are deep in conversation. I wonder what about?" Lady Rowena's fingers tightened on his arm and he glanced at her in concern, but no emotion marred the perfectly smooth forehead, silvery hair drawn back, and clusters of curls drooping near her shell-pink ears.

"I cannot imagine what they are speaking of," she said. "But I suppose it is I."

Pierson, not sure how to respond to that, remained silent as they approached the chatting pair. Lady Rowena's next partner was already waiting and whisked her away, though she gazed back a couple of times, Pierson noted with satisfaction. Perhaps he was making some headway after all, though it was impossible to tell with so well-bred a young lady as she.

He turned his attention to his friend and Miss Corbett. It was true that she did not have the spectacular beauty of Lady Rowena, say, but Miss Corbett was a very pretty young woman, gowned in pearl gray and lace, her golden-brown hair drawn back in a too-tight style that emphasized the perfect shape of her fine-boned oval face and how large her blue-gray eyes were.

Was Bain truly taken with her? He had asked her to dance, and that was an outrageous thing to do, given her status.

"Miss Corbett, your protégé does you credit. Lady Rowena has delightful manners."

The young woman looked up at him, her expression unreadable. "I can hardly take credit, my lord, for anything about Lady Rowena, since I have been her chaperon only these last three months, and both her manners and her character were taught long before that."

Pierson sat down in a chair near the lady as his friend watched, with an amused twist to his lips. "Do you believe that character is taught, then, ma'am? I had thought our character was set in the cradle."

"By taught, I suppose I mean that life teaches us who we are and how we must be. Our position, our family, our experience; it all melds together to make us who we are."

"Are we then past learning, past improvement, once we reach the age of maturity?" It was a subject he had thought seriously on in the past days, and he was interested in her opinion.

"Never, my lord. I think we are capable of change well into life, though folks seldom do once they become men and women."

"I would not have thought you so cynical, for some reason," Pierson said, catching a glint of sadness in her eyes that disturbed him.

"Cynical? I don't think myself cynical. I said *'seldom,'* not *'never,'* after all."

"Lady Rowena seems very intent on young Mardisham, doesn't she?" Bainbridge airily observed, dangling his quizzing glass on its black ribbon and swinging it.

Pierson looked up and saw the young lady in question float by, her expression unchanged since he last saw her. "She looks just the same, Bain. Whatever are you talking about?"

"My mistake. Thought you might be interested, that is all." He smirked.

"I say, Bain, whatever is wrong with you?"

"Nothing at all," he said, and stood, stretching his long legs. "Think I shall go and cause trouble elsewhere and let you and Miss Corbett discuss life and the ills of the world."

He sauntered away. Pierson watched him go and said, "He is really acting in the most peculiar manner. What did you two talk about during your dance?"

"Uh, well, we spoke of Lady Rowena and how I came to be her chaperon, and we . . . we spoke of you, my lord." She colored and turned her gaze away.

"Did he say anything unflattering? He

has an odd sense of humor, so if he did, you must disregard him."

"Unflattering? No, I believe he said you were becoming more serious in your life and were quite taken with Lady Rowena. Was he not correct?"

Her steady gaze directly into his eyes was unsettling. He did not feel at all ready to confess his emotions, and especially not to the girl's chaperon. Damn Bain! Why did he have to become so loquacious?

"I think Lady Rowena is a beautiful young lady with exquisite manners, and I am intrigued by her gentle character and mild temperament. More than that I do not think it necessary to say." Damn, he sounded so stiff, like a methodistic prig.

She chewed her lip.

He took a deep breath, and said, "I *would* ask if I might take her for a drive tomorrow afternoon, if that's permissible."

Her uncertain expression pokered up into a formal rigidity. "I don't have my engagement calendar with me, my lord, but I'll send a note by post or footman first thing in the morning."

"All right." He frowned down at his leather shoes, noting a fray in the tying ribbon as he pondered how to get Miss Corbett back to her formerly relaxed and chatty self. She was glancing around uneasily, as if noting for the first time that many of the other chaperons were looking askance at them. He wondered how his uncertain reputation would affect the young chaperon. Would she be a cast out for allowing him so much time? Should he have thought of that already and gone away? He leaped to his feet.

"I . . . I shall await your answer tomorrow, Miss Corbett, concerning the carriage drive. Until then, your servant." He bowed very formally, and sauntered away to find Bain.

Amy sat perfectly still, wondering at her own state, her nerves on edge, her stomach in knots. She hadn't felt that way when Lord Bainbridge spoke to her, and yet just fifteen minutes in Lord Pierson's company left her anxious and miserable. What was wrong with her?

Mrs. Bower moved over one chair and whispered, "That young man is making efforts I have never seen him make with anyone. He must be terribly in love with Lady Rowena already to be mending his ways so thoroughly."

"Do you think so?" Amy asked.

"I do. It is the talk among all the ladies. Some don't approve, but I've done my best to help his reputation, reminding them that many a young gentleman sows his wild oats before settling down, marrying, and begetting an heir."

"He wishes to take her for a drive to-morrow."

"What did you say?"

"That I would send him a message to-morrow morning."

"Good. Don't let him be too sure of himself."

"It's not that, Mrs. Bower. I can never be sure what mood Rowena will be in when she awakes. She sometimes takes it into her head not to do things at the last moment, and then blames me or her father. And then I can't lay the blame where it belongs when she does that or I risk painting a very unflattering picture of her nature."

"Hmph. A very *truthful* picture, you mean."

"A truthful picture of her nature will not catch her a husband. I must protect my own interests. Better I should appear capricious and unmannerly than that she should."

"Good, I'm happy to hear you speaking so sensibly." Mrs. Bower nodded her purple plumed head, the feathers dancing, little bits of the fragile plumes breaking away and floating to the marble floor. "You've wisdom in that head of yours far beyond your delicate years, and I have no doubt that if you stay the course you'll prevail."

"Oh, I haven't given up the fight, Mrs. Bower." Amy took in a deep breath and stiffened her spine and her resolve. "It is a risky affair and may all come to naught, but I may as well do the best I can and hope it works out. If Rowena does marry, and His Grace does honor our agreement . . . well, I won't have to work for a while. I shall have my cottage and my sewing and life will be easy for a time for both myself and my poor Aunt Marabelle. I have never seen Lady Rowena so intrigued with anyone as she is with Lord Pierson. And he *is* handsome and amiable, or so he seems anyway." She chewed her lip. "Tell me, you don't think there is anything vicious about him, do you? He would not hurt her?"

"Of course he would."

Shocked, Amy blurted out, "What?" Heads turned their way and she lowered her voice below the music and whispered, "What do you mean?"

"Oh, I don't mean he would beat her, though a good beating might teach her a thing or two . . ."

"Mrs. Bower!"

"All right, child, I know I speak m'mind too coarsely. Don't mind me. Anyway, all men are capable of hurting a lady. Men have interests and needs we can't even begin to understand. Stands to reason. Got that thing between their legs doing all their thinking for them."

"Mrs. Bower!" Amy felt red flood her face and her cheeks burned. Sometimes the other woman's country coarseness slipped when they spoke intimately, though she would never say such a thing in public.

The older woman chuckled. "Keep forgetting you're an unmarried gel. The other old bats like me would have a good chuckle over that. In my day we spoke our mind, with none of this false delicacy. Anyway, to frame it differently, the gentlemen will do things that injure our poor, frail hearts, but the dears don't mean to. It's just their way." She shrugged and heaved a philosophical sigh. "They drink and they wench and they gamble. As long as they come home at the end of the night, it's best if a wife doesn't know too much more than that."

"That is painting a very bleak picture of married life, Mrs. Bower," Amy said.

She grimaced. "I buried two husbands of my own, an' each of 'em was worse 'n the other. I was glad it was just other women, for if it had been gambling or drinking it would have been the worse for me. Another woman kept 'em happy and docile, like. But it's not all bad, you know. A woman can always take a lover or two of her own, once the begetting is out of the way."

Amy did not reply. Surely a gentleman of Lord Pierson's nature would not take a mistress? But his reputation spoke ill of such a forlorn hope. Even if he was trying to mend his ways now, would he keep to his resolutions? And who even said he was trying to mend his ways? If she managed to marry Rowena off to him, would she be condemning the girl to a lifetime of unhappiness with a rake and a scoundrel?

She must think seriously on the topic, and in the meantime not allow him to advance his cause too much. She wished to observe him more, speak with him more, gauge his character for herself before allowing even such a termagant as Rowena to fall in love with him. The girl was her responsibility and she would not hand her off to a rogue just to receive her reward.

With that resolution made, she felt a fraction better. For the rest of the evening, though Lord Pierson remained at the ball, he did not approach them again, choosing instead to speak to the host and hostess at length. Lady Rowena danced every dance, and Amy sat with Mrs. Bower, wondering how her life had become so far removed from the humble circles in which she had grown up.

Eleven

"Look, Amy, that is the very spot where James splashed that drunken sot last week! I wish I could see that again."

The ride home had been silent up to this point, but Rowena, apparently forgetting her anger with her chaperon, was in a merry mood. She knelt on the seat and pointed out the window toward the curb, the spot lit by gaslight.

"I would rather not remember that, Rowena." That image had haunted Amy since that night, and she wasn't sure why. Perhaps it was just that the fellow had seemed so abjectly miserable, and she disliked seeing anyone in such a sorry state. "I hope the poor gentleman got home that night and I pray he didn't catch pneumonia."

"He was likely not going home," Lady Rowena said, sitting back down on her seat and twisting her face into a grimace. "And he very likely deserves it if he did catch something nasty, though I doubt it would be pneumonia."

"Rowena, don't . . ." Amy shrugged and decided against any attempt at correction. Rowena was who she was. That she concealed her true nature in public proved that she knew it was unpleasant, and that she could curb her tongue when she so desired. So what made her so sharp and shrewish?

"Don't what?" Rowena's lovely, pale face glowed in the faint light from the coach lanterns.

"Never mind," Amy said.

"No, go on. Say it. What am I doing wrong now, in your estimation?"

Her tone was acid and Amy had had enough. She folded her hands in her lap, squeezing them together, and turned to Rowena. "Don't speak to me like that again. I will *not* stand for it. I'm not in your employ, but in your father's. If you wish to address me, do so with civility from now on."

Rowena's eyes widened in shock and Amy waited for the outburst of vitriol that was sure to follow such a dressing-down. Then the young woman's lip quivered. She bit down on it, but finally emotions burst forth.

Lady Rowena laughed, throwing back her head and guffawing in a most unlady-

183

like way. When she recovered, she said, "I can't say I like you any the worse for your impudence. I had thought you incapable of speaking your mind, but the last few days have shown me to be wrong."

Amy was taken aback and unsure how to respond. The girl continually surprised her. Slowly, she said, "I will not stand for ill-treatment anymore Rowena; I mean that most sincerely."

"I understand. Whether I choose to honor your declaration or not, you shall see. You may demand all you like, and I'll choose to go along with you . . . or I may not."

Amy watched her. "Why do you take such great pains in public to appear to be demure and ladylike, when in private you behave however you wish?"

The girl's eyes were calculating in their assessment of Amy. She finally said, "Gentlemen do not like an ill-mannered lady, is that not so?"

"Yes," Amy agreed.

"And I find it amusing to be the most sought after lady of the Season."

"You mean you enjoy gentlemen falling in love with you, only to reject them ultimately."

"Don't mistake my laughter of a moment ago for a license to be impertinent, Amy," Rowena said, a hard glint in her eye and a pugnacious lift to her chin.

"And don't mistake my statement for empty posturing. I meant what I said. I will not allow you to speak to me in a way I find discourteous or uncivil." Amy swallowed back her fear at speaking out in such a bold, harsh manner. She must do this or be miserable.

"And what will you do to stop me?"

It was a moment of truth, Amy realized. She had bluffed and was being called on it. Now what could she do? Rowena held all the power, in truth. The carriage creaked and swayed in the utter silence between the two ladies. It was time for a gamble, Amy finally decided. "I will quit and go home," she said, sure that Rowena did not know all the details of her life, and her inability to do that.

"And how will that affect me?" Lady Rowena watched Amy's eyes, her expression blank and calm.

"You cannot go out without a chaperon and maintain the fiction that you are a demure young lady. Your father will have to hire someone else, and it may be someone you will not like half so well as me. You detested your chaperon last year; I have heard all about it from the servants. Despite your efforts to appear in harmony with her, the woman, often the worse for her fondness for gin, spoke openly of your irascibility and her dislike of you. It damaged your reputation ever so slightly. Another such Season will erode your reputation even more."

The two women stared at each other for a long moment.

"All right," Rowena finally said. "I accept your terms." She leaned over and stuck out her gloved hand. "I cry peace between us."

"Peace, then," Amy said, taking her hand and shaking, even though she was under no illusion that this was in any way a final resolution.

"But you *will* call me Lady Rowena," the duke's daughter said, a haughty lift to her head.

"Then you *will* call me Miss Corbett."

They stared at each other for a long moment in silence, the monotonous rattling of the carriage the only sound.

"What did Lord Pierson speak of to you for so long?" Lady Rowena asked, finally.

"Various things. He asked if he could take you for a carriage ride tomorrow afternoon."

"What did you say?"

"That I would answer tomorrow morning."

"I think I shall go."

"You will if I say you may," Amy said.

Rowena narrowed her pale eyes, her blonde brows squinting to a pinched "V." "Don't imagine our agreement extends to you truly deciding on all of my social engagements."

"I will agree to consult you on every engagement if you promise to at least honor the ones you say you will and don't change your mind at the last minute. It is incredibly rude."

The young woman stared at Amy for a long minute. "All right."

"That said, there are still some that one must not shun. You do see that don't you, Lady Rowena?"

"I suppose," the young woman agreed, reluctantly, twisting a corner of her fringed shawl into a knot. "Why are they always the most boring ones?"

"I don't know. But they are generally the ones that reflect most on one's social standing. As the daughter of a duke, you will always have social duties that you cannot neglect."

"That is quite enough of a lecture, Amy.

I don't need to be told my duty; I have lived as the daughter of a duke my whole life, you know. I will allow that I do have some engagements I must attend, even though I would rather not. I just wish . . ."

"Wish what?"

Lady Rowena turned her face away to the window. "I just wish my father would give me my due, and acknowledge that I am a grown woman now. He treats me as a child still."

"Have you considered," Amy said, "that you very much act like a child in his presence?"

"That's absurd!"

"No it isn't," Amy returned, as gently as her agitation would allow. Their new footing was being tested, and she must go carefully. "You view every word from him as a challenge. You become petulant and have even, on occasion, stamped your foot. That is the action of a child."

"But he is just as bad! He rages and shouts and stomps off to the library as if he . . ."

"His behavior is no excuse for yours," Amy interrupted. "He is a man and a duke, and as such, will determine his own behavior. Besides, we aren't speaking of him but of you. Adults are in control of their emotions and will not let others irk them into poor behavior. A lady even more so, for a calm demeanor is to be wished for in all cases, even, or more pointedly *especially* in front of the servants. They do talk."

Rowena was silent after that, and Amy thought it best to let her be. She longed to ask the young woman what she thought of Lord Pierson, whether on further acquaintance she thought she might like him, but it was best, after such a breakthrough as they had had, to let her think on it.

And besides, she had her own thoughts to mull, and her own emotions to ponder.

The letter, received at Pierson's townhouse very early in the morning from a liveried footman with the Sylverton emblem, merely said that Lady Rowena would be free for a drive in the park between four and five that afternoon, and that she would be pleased to see Lord Pierson. But it was all he needed to know. Miss Corbett was as good as her word.

"How do I look, Rupert?" Pierson said, standing before his glass and preening for his valet.

"Very presentable, my lord," Rupert murmured, brushing lint from his employer's best black hat.

"Presentable! Someday I shall wrench a compliment out of you, you dour curmudgeon."

"When that day comes we may both expire from astonishment, my lord."

"No doubt. I am off to court a young lady, Rupert." He turned and took the hat from his valet.

"Very good, my lord."

"Things may change drastically, Rupert, if I am successful."

"And if you are not?"

Pierson, for the first time, glanced at his valet's face. It was very lined for a fellow so young, was his first thought. He knew for a fact that his valet was several years younger than himself, but life and worry had scarred his visage. "I say, Rupert, have you found a replacement for Dorcaster yet?"

"I did not know if I should. Is there . . ." His voice trailed off, though his gaze never left his employer's face.

"What is it, Rupert?" Pierson stopped fussing and waited, but Rupert was silent. "Is there *what?* Spit it out, my good man."

"Pardon me, my lord, but is there money to hire a new butler?"

Pierson sighed and sat down heavily on the chair by his dressing table. He ran his hand over his carefully coiffed curls, but the valet did not even flinch. "You seem to know very much about my private affairs, for a valet. S'pose that's the way of a good servant. Is there money for a new butler? Strictly speaking, no. Can we do without one?"

"Yes," Rupert said, straightening. "We can certainly do without one. I shall put it about that since Mr. Dorcaster left you do not see the necessity of hiring a new one for what is left of the Season. That should stop any rumors."

Pierson nodded. "What a good fellow you are, Rupert. I don't know why you have stayed with me, when I have at times been a sore trial."

"But there are better times coming, my lord," Rupert said, handing him his walking stick with a weary smile.

Pierson stood and nodded. "There are, old man. There are better times coming. I have a purpose now. I have seen a vision, and if I can only snatch that fair vision from heaven, I shall be a changed man."

Rupert's smile died just a little. "Yes, my lord. I wish you luck, then."

On his way out Pierson startled a maid by whistling, and tipped his hat to her with a smile. His groom was waiting with his carriage, seldom used in the tight confines of London streets. He frowned to see that it looked shabby in the brilliant light of a sunny spring afternoon. He should have it refitted, but couldn't afford to. Would Lady Rowena notice? He hoped not.

He pulled up to the ducal manse and his cheery self-confidence took another blow. Lord, but it was a splendid house! Tall and regal, made of spotless pale gray granite, with marble steps that shone in the sun, it was fronted by a black wrought-iron fence and gate. Urns of flowers adorned the steps up to the house, where a gleaming brass knocker as big as a turnip glinted.

Pierson jumped down from his carriage as his groom raced lightly up the steps to employ the knocker for him. A tall, sturdy butler, dressed immaculately in dark green livery, bowed and offered to show Lord Pierson in. Lady Rowena would be down in just a moment.

He was ushered into the great hall, an echoing high-ceilinged chamber lined with marble statuary and more Grecian urns. The duke's coat of arms worked in marble mosaic was the central motif on the floor, and the theme was repeated in paint over the doorways and in the banners that lined the upper gallery.

It was a very grand house, designed to impress and intimidate. The design was working.

What in God's name did he have to offer a lady from this house? His worthless name, dragged through the mud of at least three successive generations of degenerates? An estate stripped of every item of worth except a few tired paintings and dirty, antiquated gems? His own useless self, steeped in alcohol, with no skills other than at cards?

Lady Rowena Revington, youngest and no doubt most cherished child of the eminent Duke of Sylverton, could have any man, even up to and including one of the royal dukes. Why would she ever deign to marry a lowly viscount with not a groat to his name?

His sigh echoed off the high ceiling and whispered in the gallery. A door closed somewhere and a maid scuttled above from one door to another. A footman carried a massive silver epergne through the great hall.

If he could have, he would have slunk away, but just as he was feeling at his lowest, from above came the sound of soft shoes on the marble floor and the object of his feverish affections appeared at the top of the stairs, trailed by her chaperon.

Lady Rowena Revington, fairest flower of the London Season, was adorned in a pale pink gown with a moss green pelisse over it; she appeared as a tender rosebud would, still clothed in a mantle of spring green. From the top of her head, her lovely silver hair topped by a saucy bonnet and pink plumes, to the tips of her toes, shod in pink leather slippers embroidered in silver accents, she was a vision.

And he was breathless and speechless.

Finally he found his voice as she stood, blushing and with downcast eyes, before him. "Lady Rowena, you do me so much honor I am . . . I am breathless with wonder."

"Shall we go, my lord?" came another voice.

It was Miss Corbett, whom he had not noticed was standing there as well, and she gazed at him steadily.

"Are . . . are you to join us, Miss Corbett?" he asked, eyeing her bonnet and plain gray spencer.

"I am, Lord Pierson. I thought that was understood?"

He sighed. Ah well; slowly. He must be prepared to woo slowly such an infinitely valuable treasure as Lady Rowena Revington. If he was to be so fortunate as to make her his bride, he must know it would be a great effort.

"Then my pleasure in the ride is doubled," he gallantly said, and bowed, sweeping one hand toward the door. "Shall we go? It is a lovely day, and the park awaits."

Twelve

The first part of the ride was accomplished in silence, if a ride through the London streets at the height of the Season and in lovely weather could ever be called silent.

The wheels of the open carriage clacked as the hooves of the horses clopped. Drivers swore at each other over close calls on the narrow streets, disputing whose fault it was. Children screeched, hawkers yelled, and horses whinnied and neighed. There was no end to the noise and dust of the street, and it was a relief, Amy thought, when they finally reached the park. It was crowded, but at least the pace was slow. She breathed deeply and more freely, having green space around her just beyond the fringe of the crowded walkways and lanes of Hyde Park at the perfect hour for promenading.

She had been reliving, on their silent journey, the humiliation of knowing how little she was wanted as a companion, judging by Lord Pierson's evident disappointment when he found she was to accompany them.

And yet, what did he expect? He had a reputation he was only recently, it appeared, trying to mend. She would not even allow him near Lady Rowena if it were not for the fact that the young lady seemed to fancy him, and any acceptable beau was to be welcomed, even one with a shady reputation. But Amy was not going to abdicate responsibility so easily, for she would not just hand Rowena over to the man if she decided he was in any way vicious or unprincipled.

He and Rowena were chatting over the side of the carriage with a mutual acquaintance in another carriage for the nonce. Amy examined Lord Pierson. He looked familiar somehow, still. Or perhaps it was just that if she were to design the perfect gentleman to her own taste, it would be he.

She had seen many men in her weeks immersed in the London Season so far. Handsome and plain, tall and short, thin and fat, and in between. And so, though the physical was only one small part of a man, she knew, it amused her, during the boredom of a chaperon's role at the balls, to design her own ideal gentleman.

Short herself, she did not want a gentleman to tower over her, so a man of medium height would be fine. And she rather found the men of a darker cast to be attractive. Black or brown hair and darker of complexion. Lord Pierson embodied those characteristics. His hair was a dark chocolate brown and curled on its own, it seemed, and his skin was rich-toned, as if there was a gypsy ancestor somewhere in his background.

He was smiling and describing something to Rowena that was making her and the lady in the other carriage smile, and he used his hands a lot as he spoke. That was another thing she found attractive, she mused. He had an eagerness of spirit that bespoke a warm heart. She had seen so many gentlemen — and ladies too, for it was a fashionable attribute — with such a lassitude of personality that it was difficult, sometimes, to tell if they were even truly awake. There were many more who were like Lord Bainbridge, cynical and cool of temperament, amused onlookers rather than participants in the grand spectacle of life.

But Lord Pierson . . . he was a different sort altogether, and instinctively she knew he was warm of heart and impetuous of spirit, engaged in life even when it let him down. It could be accounted a fault if it led him into trouble, but it could also be con-

sidered a valuable attribute to someone —
someone like her — who had lived such a
careful and tedious life. What would she
give to be loved by someone who would
make her smile, who would take her hand
and lead her down joyful paths?

At that very moment he was describing
some grand prank he had only recently
been involved in. Vivid and eager, his
golden brown eyes sparkled with joy as the
two ladies laughed.

Rowena actually *laughed*.

Amy's gaze turned to her charge and she
watched the duke's beautiful daughter, her
expression lively and her laughter ringing
out in the clear spring air. Pierson was
staring at her, his mouth open and longing
on his face.

How could they not fall in love with each
other, Amy thought, with so much happy
infatuation on his side, and such self-
absorbed determination on hers to capture
him? It made her sad, for some reason,
though she knew she should be dancing
with happiness. Rowena appeared to be
genuinely taken with Lord Pierson, and he
was clearly enamored of her. Amy had long
known that the girl had a determined,
stubborn cast of character. She knew that
once Rowena decided to marry, it would

not be a matter of "if" but "when" the marriage would take place, no matter how unsuitable some might consider her beau.

Amy reminded herself that such an outcome was to be considered the best of all possible endings for herself. Once Lady Rowena and Lord Pierson had plighted their troth and published their intentions, she, Amy Corbett, would be in possession of a fortune, or what passed for a fortune in her mind. And then she could go back to her village, buy her tiny cottage near her Aunt Marabelle and live quietly, taking in sewing when the money began to dwindle. They would all have what would make them happy.

So why did that future seem so bleak now?

"I tell you," Pierson said, much later in the day, "she is exactly what she appears, Bain, a lovely, unassuming, well-bred lady, mild of temperament, gentle . . . everything."

Bainbridge examined his enthusiastic friend, noting the flush on his cheeks and the hectic glitter in his eyes. "Have you been drinking, Pierson?"

They sat in a quiet room at their club, where Bainbridge hoped to catch a friend of his before that fellow went on to his evening's pursuits.

"Don't be ridiculous. I had some wine with dinner, that's all." Pierson's tone was indignant. "Everybody drinks wine; what would you have me drink, water? That's hardly healthful."

Abandoning his censorious tone, Bainbridge commented, "It seems you must have had a delightful afternoon, then, eh? With the two ladies?"

"Two . . . oh, yes, Miss Corbett accompanied us."

"She seems a very good sort of young lady, if a little young and delicate for the role of chaperon, wouldn't you say?"

"I suppose." Pierson squinted through the gloom to the doorway. "Hello, there is old Carver. Remember him from school? Haven't seen him in an age. I'm just going to say hello for a moment, Bain; I'll be right back."

Bainbridge watched him lope across the room and greet their mutual acquaintance, a fellow now portly from too much good wine and food. Watching the two together talking, the portly Carver and slim, eager Pierson, Bainbridge considered his friend, and what he knew of him both from fact and by instinct.

Dante Delacorte Pierson had been raised the way they all had been raised, all the expectant sons of wealth and privilege, educated at the right schools, intimate with the right set of other young men. In fact they had both been Oxford men, brought together in friendship by the various miseries of poor food, lack of desire for learning, and inadequate quarterly allowances.

But when Pierson was just eighteen his father had died in embarrassing circumstances, the habitué of an opium den, and Pierson inherited the title. He had left school and embarked on a series of adventures envied by his former classmates, quickly becoming legendary for his exploits. Of course, once the rest of them had graduated and joined his London set, it had all quickly become too familiar and Pierson, at first their guide in the usual depravities of young London men, was just another wastrel with no goals and little real motivation to do anything at all other than drink, gamble, and trade expensive mistresses with other like-minded young men.

But there was more to Pierson, and it was that "more" that had made Bainbridge his firm friend. For all his troubles — and Bainbridge well knew his financial worries and had remonstrated with him too many times about mending his fortunes — Pierson had an optimistic, romantic view of life that was attractive to a cynic such as himself. Just being in the other man's company made Bainbridge long for things he knew he would never have with his own tired fatalism. He had often wondered what it would be like to be his mercurial friend, but they were so different he could not even imagine and gave up the futile exercise every time.

Pierson would do anything for those he loved, and so Bainbridge had, for the last couple of years, suspected that falling in love with the right kind of young lady would be the making of the viscount. He was one of those who needed an object, a purpose in life before he could settle down to the toil of recovering his estate. Perhaps it was not admirable; perhaps he should have, with his intelligence and abilities, been willing to immure himself at Delacorte and settle down to the business of building his holdings back up with no incentive other than family honor, but if Bainbridge had learned anything in his life it was that humans were all different. He had always believed that his friend would eventually do the right thing. With his loving heart, though, he needed an object, some lady who would inspire him to do right.

But was Rowena Revington, spoiled daughter of privilege, the right one? Bainbridge doubted it and further, suspected she was about as much the wrong lady as there could be on the face of the earth. The woman who married Pierson would have to have the internal fortitude to make do with little in the way of material comforts for a while, for with his estate depleted, Pierson would want to right that wrong first if he married and had to think of future children, and an heir.

True, Lady Rowena had money, but Bainbridge knew Pierson too well to think that he would ever take his wife's money to improve his inherited estate. Other men could do that, and surely there was nothing wrong with it, for it was for the betterment of their children's inheritance, but the viscount was of a chivalrous cast and would protect his wife's money, before even paying for improvements to their home. He would be ashamed to take money from her dowry, ashamed of looking like a fortune hunter.

No, Bainbridge knew that Pierson, as lax and irresolute about his estate as he had been for too many years, would never do that.

And so though it would seem an heiress of Lady Rowena's status would be a great boon to Pierson, the opposite was likely true; he must marry a lady who would not care about material discomfort for a few years, one who was frugal by nature and who did not need expensive trinkets, trips or costly friends to make her happy and content.

Was the duke's lovely daughter that kind? Was love enough for her, and could she give up her status, her London Seasons, her expensive yearly wardrobe, for the love of a warm-hearted man?

Bainbridge was dreadfully afraid she was not, but equally as afraid that it was already too late; with his warmth of heart and impetuous nature, Pierson had already fallen in love and would never be happy without the object of his desires.

And in the meantime he would completely fail to see that the perfect young lady, modest, pretty, mild of temperament but firm of character, was right in front of him eating her heart out for him.

For Bainbridge had seen all the signs. Miss Amy Corbett, a truly odd choice for companion and chaperon to Lady Rowena

Revington, for she seemed gentle, retiring, sweet-tempered, and good natured, was fascinated by and attracted to Pierson. She became flustered and distracted in his presence, and there was a longing in her eyes she could not possibly know was so very stark and visible. She was the one more like Pierson's described ideal of a lady, pretty and mild, sweet-natured. And no doubt Lady Rowena had her completely wrapped around her little finger, unable to exert any control over the headstrong duke's daughter.

Or was he misreading the beauteous Lady Rowena? He had made some assumptions based on his own observations, but perhaps . . . Bainbridge stopped his restless tap-tap-tapping of the table leg, arrested by a plan that had crept into his brain.

He wanted to know Lady Rowena's true nature and felt it would be beneficial for Pierson to see it too, if it had a negative side that was being concealed. He caught sight of his friend, who was clapping Carver on the shoulder and turning to stride back to their chairs. It would satisfy his own curiosity, too, and ease his worry that his friend might be walking into a serious commitment to a lady who was exactly wrong for him.

And it could be fun.

Should he do it? Why not? Pierson would thank him someday. Indeed, he might be able to set his plan in motion that very night, if things went the way he had planned.

Marcus Fallstone, an old friend of his and the lover of a very wealthy, well-titled lady of great respectability, entered the room and followed Pierson to Bainbridge.

"Hello, fellows. Good news. My little buttercup says of course you are both invited to her ball, and if that stuffy old butler of hers says nay, then you are to tell him that the mistress especially desires your company, or some such rubbish. She'll make it right, though, before the evening."

Bainbridge stood and took his hand, wringing it with gratitude. "What a good friend you are, Fallstone! Your lady friend and my mother are great enemies, and as a result even I have been banned from her invitation list."

"Well, *poof,* you are back on it," Fallstone said, waving his hand in a magic gesture.

"Thank you, old man," Pierson said and stuck his hand out. "I shall be forever in your debt."

"Oh, likely not. My little buttercup will not want her bumblebee forever," Fallstone said, with a wry twist to his lips. "And when she decides she don't want me anymore, I shall have to make shift like the rest of you, or at least the rest that ain't as rich as old Bainbridge, here. Then I shall very much need the kindness of my friends."

"And so speaks the pet of a very wealthy woman," Bainbridge laughed.

"It is only a matter of time, Bain, truly," Fallstone said mournfully, then pulled a funny face. "I ain't got brains like you have, and I ain't charming, nor near as good-looking as Pierson here, so she is sure to move on to greener pastures to graze. But for the nonce I amuse her with my youthful frame and *joie de vivre,* so I shall make merry while the sun shines and think of darker days another time," he said, with a cheery wave, as he moved away from them. "Hey there, you," he said, loudly to a waiter. "Brandy, man, and make it quick. I am perishing for a drink."

Bainbridge turned to Pierson. "So, we are invited to the Earl of Larkhurst's ball tonight, where Lady Rowena, accompanied by her chaperon, shall be awaiting your attendance."

"Excellent," Pierson said. "I suppose I should go home and give Rupert enough time to make me over into something worthy of the lady."

Bainbridge watched him exit the club and pondered his plan. Should he go through with it? Was there any danger? He didn't think so. If Lady Rowena was the sweet natured, good-tempered, amiable young lady she appeared then there could not possibly be any harm done to anyone.

And if not . . . well, it was much better for Pierson to find that out before he was irrevocably committed.

Thirteen

Yet another ball to attend that evening, this one at the home of the Earl of Larkhurst. Amy was tired to death of balls and all the attendant fuss and bother of getting ready for them. It was relentless, the pressure to be there, to be perfectly coiffed, dressed and comported. And yet Lady Rowena did it effortlessly. But then she was born to it, and thrived in the hothouse atmosphere like an orchid.

Amy was more of a marigold, a meadow flower transported to the dirty, noisy city. She had to say there were some aspects she enjoyed; she loved the opera and the music recitals, and she had made a good friend in Mrs. Bower. Even the balls had their moments of interest for an observer of humankind. But the truth was there were those for whom the city was their natural milieu, and those for whom it was not. She would place herself firmly among those for whom it was at best a treat to be taken in small doses.

The one good thing about the Season

and its accompanying necessity to be dressed properly was that the duke, recognizing that she did not have a wardrobe vast enough for the depth of their social calendar, had allowed her a dress allowance in addition to her wage. Amy had furnished herself with gowns that would be, at a later date, convertible into wearable dresses that would last for years.

Rowena took all the hustle and bustle in stride and Amy envied her her placidity about this one thing. She was very good at standing still for her maid and hairdresser for hours, if need be. They were presently in her room as her hairdresser coiled her platinum hair into an elaborate style incorporating a gorgeous strand of pearls that had a pinkish hue.

"It was a very enjoyable afternoon, riding in the park with Lord Pierson."

"Yes," Rowena said.

Amy paced behind the chair, watching the hairdresser, a graying woman with stooped shoulders, working. "Lord Pierson is very amusing."

"Yes."

Amy gritted her teeth. She wanted to establish how Rowena felt about the viscount, but one syllable answers were not going to help. "Mrs. Bower said that he will not possibly be able to get an invitation to the Larkhurst ball this evening, because the countess is a stickler, and very prim and proper. Lord Pierson's reputation is too awful for her to allow him in her ballroom."

"Really?" Rowena said. Her tone was still placid, but her eyes glittered in the candlelight, reflected in the mirror.

"Yes," Amy said, carefully, watching the reflected image of her charge's lovely face. "What you told me of his notoriety appears to be true. He is not accepted in much of polite society, though there are those who say his foibles are in the past and he should be given a chance to prove himself."

Rowena's expression was unreadable, but she was certainly pondering something. Amy wished she understood the labyrinthine maze of Rowena's mind, but she feared much of what the girl thought and felt would remain an enigma. And yet it seemed to Amy that one thing was clear; Rowena was attracted to Lord Pierson because of his terrible reputation, not in spite of it. Was that any healthy basis for a marriage?

Or . . . was Rowena just toying with Pierson hoping it would get back to her father and enrage him? Their complex relationship was a puzzle to Amy, for so much of their antagonism was buried in past interactions and long-established patterns of mutual disregard.

Amy sat on a nearby chair to bring herself eye to eye with the younger woman. She must try to be forthright with her charge, honest and open. Maybe someday the girl would trust her. "Rowena, you have not repeated in the last week your usual diatribe against marriage. Does that mean you have softened your stance? Have you begun to think about marriage in a different light?"

"No, of course not. Whatever gave you that idea?" she said, batting the hairdresser's hands away finally and doing the last touch herself. She stood from her dressing table and the hairdresser exited while Jeanette, her lady's maid, came forward and with her habitual dour expression brushed her mistress' gown thoroughly.

Amy sighed and stood. "I don't know. Nothing. It was just a question."

"Well, it was impertinent."

"It was not impertinent coming from your chaperon. It is my duty to ask such questions, and to pry unforgivably. To do less would be to abdicate responsibility." Amy glanced at Rowena and caught the faintest hint of a smile. "And you know that, so stop roasting me, Rowena."

"Shall we go?" Lady Rowena said, as her maid brought her her shawl.

"I suppose," Amy said, grudgingly. "Another night, another endless ball."

Pierson followed Bainbridge into the Larkhurst house and up to the ballroom, really a series of three rooms thrown into one. "Will Fallstone be here?" he asked his friend.

"You must be joking! He and the countess are carrying on an illicit affair; she would hardly invite him to a ball with her husband there. Besides, Fallstone is not on most invitation lists."

"Hmm," Pierson mused, glancing around himself and noting the elaborate decor, the urns of flowers, the verdant topiaries. How vastly expensive were such entertainments to host! "Has he done the unthinkable, like me?"

"No, not at all, but he is untitled and has few connections. He just isn't on the list."

"You say 'the list' as if there is an actual list somewhere that some aristocratic dragon keeps and updates to aid in the exclusion of outcasts and social pariah."

"I have no doubt such a list exists somewhere," Bainbridge said, "for ladies like my mother to consult. I'm sure it has two sides; on one, those who are welcome into the inner circle, and on the other, those who have misbehaved. And on the reverse is listed every infraction you, my friend, have ever committed." He jabbed his friend in the arm.

"I feel, suddenly, like Sisyphus, doomed for eternity to perform an impossible task." They strolled to the edge of the ballroom floor near a group of chattering ladies, some of whom eyed them hopefully. One young lady's mother or chaperon dragged her away and whispered to her fiercely, and Pierson could not help but imagine that the young lady was being warned against him. "Will the damned stone ever stay up where I pushed it, Bain? Or will it keep rolling back down the hill, crushing me every time?"

"Don't be gloomy, Pierson. You have only just begun to make your way, after all; you're here, aren't you? Continue to mend your ways and soon you will not need the intervention of Fallstone or anyone else. Sisyphus didn't have *my* help."

They continued strolling until they

neared the door into the card room; two gentlemen were exiting. Pierson bumped into one accidentally, and the other fellow drew back as if he had been insulted.

"Pierson," he said, with a snarl. "How did you get in?"

Pierson gazed steadily at the fellow, a gentleman of about his own age, and tried to place him.

"Sanson, what is wrong with you?" Bainbridge said.

"I cannot believe that you are with this worm, Bainbridge."

"He's my friend."

"He's unworthy of that honor."

"What on earth did I ever do to you . . . Sanson, is it?" Pierson stared at the other fellow and tried to place him, but could not for the life of him imagine they had ever met before, much less that he had offered the man some kind of insult.

"I don't suppose you even remember, you horse's ass," Sanson grunted. "Probably too drunk. I was lining up the services of La Belle Delice . . ."

"La Belle . . . that dancer? Good God, I haven't seen her in five years! She disappeared off to the continent with some foreign count."

"Nevertheless," Sanson said. "She was

to be mine and you cut me out! Can't believe you would show your face in polite society."

Bainbridge interrupted, stepping in front of Pierson. "Really Sanson, that was five years ago. Can you not let bygones be bygones?"

"What do you know? You were not even in London at the time."

Pierson, tamping down his spurt of anger at the intransigence of the silly fellow, pushed Bainbridge aside and said, "Sanson, if I did you wrong, I apologize. I didn't know you had an interest in La Belle Delice, or I wouldn't have cut you out in that unmannerly way. Again, I apologize."

His friend murmured something to him and Sanson reluctantly nodded. "I guess I must accept your apology."

The two men moved off, but Sanson continued to throw dark looks his way.

Pierson leaned against the wall and said, "I suppose there are likely to be more of those encounters in my future. I've likely a list of old offenses to apologize for."

"That did not strike me as the kind of thing the old society matrons are concerned about," Bainbridge commented, wryly.

217

"No, I suppose not. But what else have I done that people *will* hold against me?"

"You worry too much, old man. I tell you, behave from now on and folks will either forget your transgressions or think they were vastly exaggerated."

"Easy for you to say, Bain. You have never blotted your copybook."

"Say," Bainbridge interrupted. "Have you heard anything yet about that wretched thief, Lincoln?"

"Anything to change the subject, eh?" Pierson frowned down at the floor. "All right, then. My solicitor says that there seems to be some mystery in the case. Lincoln was last seen in a tavern. He had been to the bank and collected the quarterly wages for dispersal to the staff, but after leaving that night he was never seen again. His purse was found several miles away near the sea. It has been suggested that he was robbed, but some just think he had finally had enough of Delacorte and absconded to the continent. I think I'll have to take a trip down there myself to straighten this out."

Bainbridge was silent and when Pierson looked up it was to find his friend staring at him.

"Now I am sure you have been transformed," Bainbridge said. "Travel all the way to Kent to straighten out a matter pertaining to your estate?"

Stung, Pierson straightened and said, "See here, Bain, there is no cause to become sarcastic. I just . . . well, I cannot stop thinking about the staff at Delacorte, and how they are doing. What if they cannot get credit at the butcher anymore with Mr. Lincoln gone? He was the one who paid all of the accounts. And the grocer and coal merchant . . . old Mrs. McCracken has been cook at Delacorte this age. She must be near sixty by now. It's not fair that she should have this kind of worry."

"I'm not being sarcastic, Pierson, I was just surprised into a hasty statement, that is all."

But it was more than that, and Pierson knew it. He put one hand on his friend's sleeve to stop him just as he was about to resume their stroll about the ballroom. "Look, Bain, I know I have not been the most assiduous of landlords, nor the most responsible of landowners. I mean to make it up to Delacorte someday, when . . . if . . ." *When* did he mean to make it up to them all, all the people of Delacorte and the village beyond? He shook his head. He would think of that another day, another —

A stirring near the door drew his attention and he drew in a sharp breath. Lady Rowena and her chaperon had arrived, but they were not alone. With them was the Duke of Sylverton, Lady Rowena's esteemed and lofty papa, and in their midst was Lord Newton-Shrewsbury, looking as smug as a cat at the dairymaid's skirt.

How it had all come about, Amy did not know. The duke had announced just as the carriage was being summoned that he had a mind to go to the Larkhurst ball. As if she did not have enough trouble, now Rowena was going to be forced to be in company with her papa, whom she appeared to despise most of the time, and the duke would be looking down his beaky nose at Amy and judging her performance as *chaperon extraordinaire!*

What a muddle! But as if that was not bad enough, just as they entered the Larkhurst ballroom, Lord Newton-Shrewsbury had spoken to the duke. It appeared that the young man had, before ascending to his title through the death of his late father, been an aide of some sort of His Grace during the war. This was a fine pickle indeed, Amy worried, as they entered the already over-heated ballroom, pausing only to murmur a greeting to the earl and countess, who looked overwhelmed with the honor of the duke's visit. The duke was entirely capable, once he heard of Lord Newton-Shrewsbury's affection for his daughter, to demand that she, Amy, somehow make his daughter decide on him as her future hus-band. The duke was wont to mishandle his daughter completely, thereby ensuring more scenes, more acrimony, and more trouble for herself.

Perhaps she was worrying for naught, but she had a dread feeling in her gut that her fears would come to pass. She put one hand over her stomach, feeling the quiv-ering there already. She caught sight of Lord Bainbridge and Lord Pierson, and far from giving her pleasure, as she had ex-pected, she had a dread of the two making their way over and speaking to Rowena. Just to irk her father, the lady was capable of ignoring Lord Newton-Shrewsbury en-tirely in favor of the viscount.

"Too soon, too soon," Amy muttered to herself. She had hoped the duke would not meet Pierson for a few weeks, until he and her daughter were practically, in the public eye, betrothed.

"I shall claim the honor of the first dance and the supper dance, my lady," Newton-Shrewsbury said, bowing low and grabbing her card, suspended by a pale blue ribbon from her wrist.

Rowena snatched it away. "You may have the first, but you will not have the supper waltz, sir, as it is already spoken for."

"By whom?"

Haughtily, she said, "That is not your concern, my lord."

Pierson and Bainbridge were fighting through the crowd, and Amy felt perspiration already on her upper lip.

"You rude child," the duke thundered. His dark eyes were fixed on his daughter. "You will give the Earl of Newton-Shrewsbury exactly the dances he has requested."

"I will not," Rowena said, her gaze darting around until she found Lord Pierson. "Why, here comes the gentleman to whom I promised that supper dance!"

The duke's expression looked thunderous for a moment, but then relaxed into a smile. "Why did you not say so, Rowena? Of course, I approve. Shrewsbury, you will have to select another for your second dance, for the Marquess of Bainbridge has reserved the supper dance with my lovely daughter!"

Fourteen

"Lord Bainbridge? But Papa, that's not . . ."

Amy stepped up to greet the two gentlemen, who were looking mildly confused, as was Lord Newton-Shrewsbury. "Just go along with this, my lords," she muttered, shielded by a couple who were squeezing past them from the door, "and we shall all have a better time of it." In a louder tone she said, "Yes, Lord Bainbridge is the very man who was promised the supper dance, is that not so gentlemen?"

Bainbridge stepped forward toward the duke and his daughter. "Correct. My lady?" He held out his hand for Rowena's card and she, with poor grace, handed it to him. He signed for the supper waltz and a later dance.

Amy could see that he was hard put to keep from smiling, and if the situation were anything but desperate she would have smiled herself.

The duke, rather taken with the idea whispered to him by Lord Newton-Shrewsbury that he was doing the ballroom a great honor by being there, thankfully decided he owed it to the good earl and countess to personally greet each person present and stepped away to commence his charitable endeavor. Since there were over a hundred already and more pouring in every minute, Amy thought it might take a while, but at least he was not near his daughter.

Rowena, grasping Amy's arm in a grip as tight as death, pulled her to one side. "What do you mean by making me dance with Lord Bainbridge for the supper dance? I was meant to dance that one with Lord Pierson. I promised him!"

"I did not think it wise to bring your father's attention to Lord Pierson yet. If he should hear of his reputation . . ."

"He might have one of his temper fits," Rowena said, her expression smug. "Don't you think I'm aware of that?"

"Rowena, do you mean the only reason you wish to dance with Lord Pierson is to irk your father?"

"No, of course not!" Her eyes wide, Rowena said, "I would never be so contemptible. It is not the only reason, it would just be a . . . well, an unexpected benefit."

Amy's stomach clutched as if in the

grasp of a fist. She examined her charge with distaste. "Do you have any feeling for Lord Pierson at all?" With her mind's eye she could see the naked longing in the viscount's golden eyes and she could imagine how those eyes would become clouded if he was rejected by the love of his life. Why it hurt her so to consider his pain she didn't to want to examine.

Rowena shrugged as she glanced around the ballroom. Pierson and Bainbridge were standing a little distance away engaged in what looked like a fierce argument.

"I . . . I don't know," she answered. She gazed at the two men. "I have only just met him after all, Amy. One cannot form an opinion after such a brief acquaintance."

Amy had to allow that was a sensible rejoinder. Trying to calm her nerves, she replied, "So I would advise that until you know how you feel, you not deliberately antagonize your father into despising Lord Pierson. Anyway, you will likely not have to dance the supper dance with Lord Bainbridge, for I can't imagine your father will spend more than an hour or so here. He is not one for balls and will become bored, I warrant, very shortly."

But her assumption proved to be false.

The duke's elevated title meant he always received a high degree of reverence and obsequious attention, but his arrival at the Larkhurst ball had inspired an unprecedented wave of flattery and fuss. After all, though he was fifty-five and a widower for many years, it was not unknown for a gentleman of his age to take a second wife, and many of the chaperons and matrons saw his attendance as a sign he was in the market for that commodity. As a result of the adulation, he stayed. And stayed.

And *stayed!*

"It is eleven," Amy said, taking a seat by Mrs. Bower. "And he still has not left. What am I to do? What if Rowena refuses to dance the supper waltz with Lord Bainbridge?" She fidgeted restlessly, moving to the edge of her seat.

"Then she will look like a miserable little chit, not you, dearie. I know, I know; that is cold comfort when you are trying to marry the girl off. But don't concern yourself. If ever a girl knew how to behave to fool others into thinking she is a well-behaved young lady it is Lady Rowena."

"I wish I could be sure." Amy sought out her charge in the crowd. She was dancing a second dance with Lord Newton-Shrewsbury and smiling up at him with a brilliance that had the young man looking dazzled. As her gaze traveled the perimeter of the ballroom, Amy saw more than one male gaze directed her way, including, she found, Lord Pierson's, who stood off to one side and glared at the couple.

A second later there was a gasp around the ballroom, and dancing in one area stopped completely. Some commotion was taking place.

Lord Pierson was already in action and Amy bolted to her feet, wondering if anyone needed help. She started forward and the crowd, now completely stopped dancing, cleared just enough for her to see the center of the disturbance. Lady Rowena and Lord Newton-Shrewsbury were in a tangled heap on the floor. Amy, without conscious thought, started toward her, watching the panoply as it unfolded.

The gentleman scrambled to his feet first, his face red all the way up to his ears. Some of the ladies who had been dancing just moments before were trying their best to look concerned, but in truth, for all her vaunted perfection, not many of them liked Rowena, so there was more than one hastily concealed smirk. The gentlemen around them looked truly troubled, and a couple were reaching out to her to attempt to disentangle her from her skirts when Pierson struggled through the crowd and reached her.

With an aplomb that Newton-Shrewsbury was unfortunately lacking, Pierson reached down and pulled her gently to her feet and took her arm, escorting her off the floor, toward Amy.

"Are you all right?" Amy asked, as the pair approached.

"I'm fine," Rowena muttered.

Oh dear, Amy thought. She recognized the signs, the two hot scarlet patches high on Rowena's alabaster cheeks and the grim set to her mouth. Her charge was in a towering rage, and any minute would let loose in a stream of verbiage that would come as close to swearing as a lady ever could. Just then, Lord Bainbridge approached.

"What has happened?"

"Lady Rowena fell," Pierson said.

"I didn't fall, some dund . . ." Rowena stopped before she let loose a tirade, though, and clamped her mouth shut.

Amy, holding her breath, watched Rowena's face as she took in a deep breath. The young lady then attempted a trembling smile as she sank into a chair.

"I don't quite know what happened," she said, weakly, still clutching Lord Pierson's hand. "One moment Lord Newton-Shrewsbury and I were dancing, and the next we were on the floor. It almost felt as though he had been blundered into by someone else."

"Clumsy ox," Bainbridge said. "Imagine anyone ungainly enough to stagger into someone on the ballroom floor."

Amy let out her breath as she glanced up and caught the faintest trace of a smile on the marquess' lips. But he returned her gaze with an innocent expression.

"It's a good thing you weren't hurt," Pierson said, kneeling by Rowena, and patting her hand. "You weren't, were you?"

At that moment the duke strode toward them. "What is going on here? What is this unseemly fuss? Rowena, you misbehaving?"

Amy rolled her eyes and knew she must say or do something to stem the tide of the duke's disapproval, or he would undo all of the good work already accomplished. "She just had a nasty spill, Your Grace, but is better now."

"Well, it is the supper dance now. She can recover with young Bainbridge here," the duke said, pulling his daughter to her feet as if she were so much baggage and thrusting her into the marquess' arms.

Disastrous. Completely and utterly disastrous, Amy fumed, at the duke's high-handed behavior. But how did one chastise a duke who was also one's employer? One didn't, one gritted one's teeth and . . . Bainbridge dropped her a wink and whispered something to Rowena, whose bottom lip was beginning to jut alarmingly. Sulkily the girl nodded, and Bainbridge then whispered something to Pierson.

The viscount turned to Amy and bowed low. "Miss Corbett, would you do me the honor of allowing me this dance?"

"I . . . I . . ." Amy caught the marquess' raised eyebrows and nod, and she muttered, "Certainly, my lord." Anything to leave the duke's company.

As the music started, the two couples joined a set just forming. As they stood waiting, Pierson murmured, "Bain pointed out to me that if we all dance the supper dance, we may go together into the supper room, or walk on the terrace after."

"Yes, I thought that might be his intent," Amy said, gazing up at her escort. She supposed she should be grateful that the viscount seemed to have formed an attachment to Rowena in a remarkably short time. He had seen her that day on the steps of the dressmaker's shop and appeared to have fallen head over ears in love, as ludicrous as that seemed to her. What did he know of her, after all? That she was pretty and well-dressed; that was it. But then, to be fair, what did she, herself, know of *him,* and yet right this moment, gazing up at him, his golden eyes glowing and his dark hair carelessly swept back, she felt her own heart sorely in danger.

Was that all there was to the game, then? Was it no more than animal attraction, male and female seeking mates? There had to be more to it than that.

Didn't there?

And then they were waltzing and Amy lost the ability to reason for a while, for it is well acknowledged that the grand sweeping movements of that dance are in direct opposition to the human animal's ability to think and reason.

That is why so many fall in love waltzing, Amy thought, when conscious thought would again be heard.

Pierson's hand was at her waist, and she could feel the warmth seep through. His strong, straight jaw was just above her, and she could feel the flex and movement of every sinewy muscle of his shoulder as he effortlessly directed her over the floor.

What a lucky girl Rowena was, that such a man as this wanted her so badly!

Rowena! She had even completely forgotten to keep her eye on her charge. What a terrible thing for a chaperon to admit. But then most chaperons did not have to try to keep their mind on their charge while they themselves were being expertly guided over the dance floor in the waltz by the handsomest man present.

"My lord," Amy said, realizing they had not spoken one word to each other since beginning. "Have you thought more, since our last conversation, about your estate in Kent?"

He gazed down at her. "I seem to be often thinking of my estate in Kent lately."

His tone was mournful, almost.

"I hope all is well with it?"

He shrugged and said, "Who can speak of estate business on the dance floor, Miss Corbett? Do you not enjoy the dance? Is it not intoxicating to you? I thought that was so with every young lady."

"But it is my responsibility to not let myself be so carried away, my lord, that I forget my duty." Amy caught sight of Rowena and Lord Bainbridge just then, nearby. They did not appear to be speaking at all, but that was not strange. What would two such different characters, thrust together by necessity, have to speak of?

Pierson had not answered her and when she looked up, it was to find him regarding her with a serious expression.

"Did I . . . did I misspeak, my lord, or step on your toes?"

"You seem so very intent on duty, Miss Corbett, and yet you are a young and pretty lady yourself. Have you never had time to just enjoy yourself? Have you never let duty go for just a time?"

Her mouth was dry and Amy swallowed hard, trying to find her voice. It was difficult with his intent gaze and his focus solely on herself like that. "I — I have been on my own for a long time, my lord. I have found that when I forget about duty, that is the very moment when I will forget that my duty is also to myself. What good will it do me to forget about my obligations when that is the only thing that keeps me employed and able to fend for myself another day?"

"So serious," he murmured. "You need a lesson in enjoyment."

With that he whirled her and his steps became lighter, his movements more sweeping. Amy, lightheaded, lost sight of everything but Lord Pierson, every other person on the dance floor disappearing into a blur of color and movement.

Pierson had never in his life wanted to make another forget their troubles, but Miss Corbett's sad little speech about duty, and duty to herself, had made him realize that while he had spent his youth seeking pleasure for himself, she had likely never had a single day devoted to mindless joy and her own fulfillment. He swept her up in the grand movements of the dance and she was as light as a feather, her expression changing in a second from serious and concentrated to giddy and smiling.

Rapidly he swept her through the crowd, finding in his own almost forgotten skill as a dancer a dizzy enjoyment. It was like racing down the long sweeping hill to Delacorte when he was a very young child. There had been a broad expanse of grass down a long slope to the stone and marble edifice that was his home. When he was very young, he and his playmate, the land steward's son, had raced down the slope, breathless, tumbling, falling, and rolling and finally coming to a stop on the lush green grass.

It had been such fun he and his friend would make the long climb to the top, just to do it again.

He steered his partner through the crowd, aware that people were watching them but he didn't care. This was too much fun and Miss Corbett was laughing out loud now at the rapid movement, her head thrown back, her giddy giggles intoxicating to the ear.

But then, inevitably, the music stopped.

It was only then that he realized that his reckless enjoyment would have a price, and not one that he would have to pay this time.

Fifteen

Her heart throbbing wildly, Amy finally felt her dizziness start to subside, and she glanced around to find that every eye in the crowd was on her and Lord Pierson where they had come to a stop by the chaperons' chairs. As was the duke's leaden gaze.

She dropped her hand from where it rested on Lord Pierson's shoulder and stepped away from him, appalled at being the center of attention. She caught Mrs. Bower's eye, but that lady just shrugged and sighed. Lord Bainbridge, at that very moment escorting Rowena, returned to the chaperon chairs and seemed to see what the problem was.

With a quick word to Pierson he turned and bowed to Amy and said, "Miss Corbett, my friend and I would be delighted to escort you ladies to the supper room."

That broke the spell and the others around them returned to their whispered conversations. The duke grimly said, "Miss Corbett, we shall have a word when we get home."

"Yes, Your Grace," she said, trembling. She took Lord Pierson's arm and walked swiftly away.

The supper room, a long chamber with tables at one end laden with meats and breads and sweets, was overly warm, or so it felt to Amy. She sat at a small table with Rowena while the gentlemen went to fill their plates, her mind a-buzz with fear and worry.

Rowena glared relentlessly in another direction, and Amy had a feeling that even her charge was furious with her for making a spectacle of herself, and more especially with the gentleman she had singled out as her current beau.

But that concern could not hold her attention when she thought about the duke's thunderous expression and ominous pronouncement. Was this it, then? Would her few moments of absolute enjoyment in Lord Pierson's arms be the end of all her hopes for the Season?

Would the duke, as impetuous as his daughter and imperious in his own right, let her go?

With a sick conviction in the pit of her stomach, she knew that he would. She would be released from her employment with no recommendation and nowhere to go, for no one would dare hire the Duke of Sylverton's cast off. If the duke chose to give her the wages owed her so far, it would not keep her beyond a few weeks at the most and then what? The workhouse? Her home parish and the poor list?

Poor Aunt Marabelle?

What had possessed Lord Pierson to suddenly whirl her like that in a wild dance the like of which those gathered had never seen?

Too many questions and no answers. Too much heat, too much noise. Amy felt the sickness well up in her and for a moment she thought she would compound the hideousness of the evening by vomiting and fainting. All her careful plans for naught, only to become the cynosure of all eyes, the one thing a chaperon should never be.

She would need to make a plan for the future, but for the moment, all she could think of was —

Hadn't it been grand for those few moments at least to be in Lord Pierson's arms and to be recklessly joyous?

"What were you thinking of?" Bainbridge whispered fiercely to Pierson while they filled plates for the two ladies.

"I don't know, I don't know, I don't *know!*" Pierson muttered as he wielded a pair of tongs to lift lobster patties onto a plate. He paused and thought back to the moment and the madness that had overtaken him. "I just know that we had been speaking, and I looked down into her eyes — very pretty eyes, really, if a little crossed — and I realized that the girl had probably never had a moment's pure fun in her life without worrying. It's damnable. She is rather lovely, and really very young yet. Younger than you and I, anyway. And so I thought, on an impulse . . . and she laughed, Bain." Stricken, he looked up into his friend's face. "She laughed aloud and I was right, I don't think she ever had that before, just to let go and enjoy."

"Yes, well, now, judging from the old duke's look, she will certainly be 'let go.' He looked like thunder. You have to have known, Pierson, that it just isn't the done thing. I mean, dancing is one thing; that, indeed was stretching it, for not many of the chaperons dance. But in that wild manner, careening around the dance floor like the veriest hoyden . . ."

"I know," Pierson said, wearily, dropping the lobster patty onto the plate. "Leave off, Bain." He glanced toward the table where

Lady Rowena and Miss Corbett sat. "My impetuosity has had a heavy toll this time. Do you really think the duke will let her go?"

Bainbridge regarded them through the maze of tables. "I think there is every possibility, but if the young woman relies on her . . . that is, if Lady Rowena should intercede, it may be all right. We don't know what the duke is like but I have heard that he is a hard old piece of flint. And precipitate."

They began back toward the table with the plates. Anger flooded Pierson's heart as he caught sight of the two young ladies, and saw the distress evident in Miss Corbett's very posture, her shoulders slumped and her hands clenched in her lap. "I swear, Bain, if that ass, the duke, should toss Miss Corbett out, we must do something for her. *I* must do something for her. But damned if I know what. I haven't an acquaintance in the world but the immoral type, not a one that could help the girl out with a position. But p'raps you, or your mother . . ."

"I can imagine explaining that to my mother," Bain said, grimly. "But I could try, I suppose. Harriet might help. She's a calm one in a crisis."

They reached the table and both men made a move to lay their plate in front of Lady Rowena.

"Pierson, you dolt," Bainbridge muttered. "Yours is for Miss Corbett, your partner on the dance floor."

"Oh, yes," Pierson stammered. "I beg pardon, Miss Corbett."

Her cheeks were pink and she would not meet his eyes. He regretted terribly making her the focus of censure and wished he could say so, but couldn't think of a way to without embarrassing her further. And yet he must find a way to tell her that if she suffered for his actions, he would move heaven and earth to make it right for her. Then he glanced at Lady Rowena and all further thought was lost from his head.

What a princess she looked, daintily picking through the delicacies on her plate. Poor dear, too, just recovering from that spill on the floor with that lout, Newton-Shrewsbury. At least the idiot had disappeared after his clumsiness, likely too embarrassed to be seen by Lady Rowena. She glanced up at him and smiled, her tiny rosebud lips curving upward sweetly. She took up her glass of wine-colored ratafia and raised it to her lips, her every movement a seductive ballet.

And poured the whole glass down the front of her chin and dress.

"Damnation!" she shrieked, leaping to her feet, dark wine dribbling down her chin and the bodice of her lovely gown. "Who jogged my arm? How did . . ."

Miss Corbett was at her side in a second and took her by the arm, murmuring soothing words. Bainbridge, concern on his handsome face, was on her other side.

"My lady, how terrible — your lovely gown!" He took the empty glass from her hand and set it on the table.

Lady Rowena, that brief outcry her only concession to the shock of the event, was taking deep and shuddering breaths, her cheeks mottled by two high red patches on her cheekbones. Miss Corbett was dabbing ineffectually at her chin and then her stained dress. Around them many at other tables were chuckling or laughing outright at the duke's daughter's continuing misfortune.

"I think it is best if we just go," the chaperon said. "It has been a trying night and perhaps . . ."

"I don't wish to go," Rowena said, in her most stubborn and queenly accents.

Pierson gazed at her in admiration. She looked truly lovely with her bosom heaving and those two rosy patches on her cheeks.

"But my lady," Miss Corbett said, glancing around in alarm. "Your gown is in such a condition that a trip to the repair room will not suffice, I fear."

"I wish to walk on the terrace."

"May I volunteer my services as your escort?" Pierson said, hastily, as Bainbridge cleared his throat.

Lady Rowena dimpled as her cheeks lost some of their violent red. "That would be delightful."

He took her arm.

The night air was cool so early in the season. It was only March and Pierson began immediately to regret acquiescing to the lady's request. After all, her gown was saturated with wine and there was a breeze outside. He guided her to a protected area where there was yet light from the supper room, and eyed the sky uneasily as a low rumble vibrated through the night air.

This was his chance, his opportunity to show her how much she meant to him, how absolutely enchanting he found her to be. In fact, she seemed to be waiting for just such an overture.

"My lady," he said, holding her arm close to his body and trying to impart some of his warmth. "You are radiant tonight. I have never seen such a . . . such absolute divinity."

"Thank you, my lord." Slyly she gazed up at him through her lush lashes. "Tell me, my lord, do my looks compare with the attractions of the ladies I have heard tell of, ladies who frequent certain establishments of low repute?"

Shocked and speechless, Pierson gazed at her in confusion. What exactly was she asking him? And how could he possibly answer? "I don't think it would do you justice to make such an inadequate comparison."

"But do I? I have heard it whispered that there is one girl whom they call Mademoiselle Divine. Is she beautiful?"

Pierson took in a deep and shaking breath. Mademoiselle Divine was an opera dancer of spectacular beauty and no morals at all. She was running through the younger portion of the peerage register at such a rate that she would soon need to expand her net to those of more years or lower title. However, as indiscriminate as she was in imparting her favors, she had her methods for benefiting and gave away nothing without a gift in exchange. He knew that well, for he had given her a spectacular sapphire ring he could ill afford. But that was before, in the last Season, before his life had changed in one glance at a passing carriage.

His mind worried at the problem, though: How had a young lady heard of Mademoiselle Divine, and what could he answer? He was repulsed even to speak of such a thing to Lady Rowena and was afraid his distaste showed on his face.

"My lady, may we not speak of another subject?"

"Why, my lord?" she replied, her tone arch. "Is my beauty not a fit subject?"

Pierson gazed down at her. "Of course it is, but that of the woman in question is not. Your beauty stands apart from one such as she, as you must know. You are radiant and lovely and innocent, the picture of health and comeliness. Girls of her ilk . . ."

"Are very attractive to gentlemen such as yourself, are they not? Are you not a rake, then? I have heard stories that you are? Will you not confess?"

Pierson felt as if he were in some bizarre dream, but no, when he had dreamed of Lady Rowena she was refined, ladylike, and not chattering of unfit subjects. "My lady, let's speak of something else. How are you enjoying the Season so far?"

The lady stared at him and shrugged, elegantly. "You will not answer," she pouted.

With an enormous sigh and dainty yawn, she made plain her displeasure. "The Season is just as usual, I suppose. Until I met you, my lord. You have not generally been in the way of coming to the balls. What has changed for you?"

Pierson hesitated, but then said, "You, my lady. I was stunned by your beauty and could not stay away if I wanted to."

She looked pleased, her eyes sparkling in the light from the supper room. "Really? How gallant!"

"It is not mere gallantry," he said, gazing at her. "Sometimes a gentleman will be touched by beauty, and all he can do is follow and hope that that beauty radiates from the inside as well; it is evident to anyone with eyes that you are as lovely clear down to your soul as your external shell would seem to promise." He reached out and caressed one silvery ringlet, the glow from it like moonlight. "You are pure and sweet and as gentle as a lamb."

A smile still turned her lips up, but it appeared to have frozen in place. Had he said something wrong?

"I rather thought," she said, slowly, "that a gentleman such as you would be attracted to a different kind of lady."

Puzzled, he said, "What do you mean?"

"I mean, why is it that . . ."

Just then the sky, which had been clouding over, the moon disappearing finally, opened up and a deluge of icy rain sluiced down as if the rain gutters had burst. Pierson hurried to shepherd Lady Rowena toward the doors into the supper room, and at the door they were met by Bainbridge and Miss Corbett, who carried a shawl for Lady Rowena.

Damnable timing, Pierson thought, cursing the rain. He watched the chaperon tuck her charge in, pulling the shawl around the young lady's damp shoulders as he pushed the sodden hair out of his eyes. Just at that moment he met Miss Corbett's eyes and the most extraordinary thing happened. She stared at him, really stared; her blue-gray eyes widened, and her mouth dropped open.

"My lord, you are soaked through," she gasped. "You are . . . your hair is . . ." She fell silent and her cheeks bleached of all color. "Lady Rowena and I must depart. Her gown is stained beyond help and she is soaked through. We must go."

Bainbridge, who had followed her, said, "I agree Miss Corbett, that you must get your charge home. She has had a very . . . wet evening."

Pierson glanced at Bain with suspicion. It had never been clear who had jogged Lady Rowena's elbow, though there had been several people squeezing past their table just then. And yet it was unlikely that Bainbridge should be so clumsy. "I will escort you to your carriage," Pierson said, guiding the ladies through the second set of double doors from the supper room into the great hall.

"That won't be necessary," Miss Corbett said hastily, still staring at Pierson, her eyes large and luminous. "I have ordered the carriage and His Grace is awaiting us. Good evening gentlemen. Thank you for a memorable evening."

Lady Rowena, her skin dewy from the rain, curtseyed and gave Pierson a melting look. He stuttered into speech.

"My lady, Miss Corbett, would you consider a carriage ride tomorrow, or . . ."

"Pierson," Bainbridge said. "I was thinking that the ladies might like to engage in a spot of sport, perhaps an afternoon of archery. I have a friend with an archery court set up. Could we interest you?"

Miss Corbett, her expression grim, said, "I think, sirs, that I must engage us for nothing at the moment. I . . . well, you heard the duke earlier. He wishes to see me, and I'm afraid I cannot be sanguine about the future of my tenure as Lady Rowena's chaperon."

He had forgotten all about her position, Pierson realized, stricken. How could he have been so cavalier? He frowned down at his shoes and said, "Miss Corbett, I feel responsible . . ."

"Please don't," she said, softly, putting out one delicate hand and touching his sleeve. "I would not take back that dance, not even for my position."

Lady Rowena's gaze shifted back and forth between them and her eyes were narrowed.

Pierson examined Miss Corbett's face and she was smiling, though it was tremulous and there was trepidation there too. It was a gallant lie, he thought, and well done. She would not suffer for his sake, he vowed, no matter what he had to do.

"Good evening then, ladies," he said and bowed.

Arm in arm they left, gliding through the great hall and to the steps down toward the front door.

Sixteen

The drive home was accomplished in silence. Rowena was brooding about something and the duke was in one of his resentful silences. Amy should have been trying to ameliorate his mood and stave off his certain dismissal of her, but the quiet was blissful, and gave her a few moments to examine her emotions.

For she had made a discovery, and she was not sure how it changed or affected her experiences of the evening.

When Lord Pierson had come into the supper room from being drenched by the sudden downpour, Amy had known suddenly why he had seemed familiar to her from the very first moment of meeting him. He was soaked and his dark curls hung in his eyes, even as he tried ineffectually to push them away. In that moment she had realized with a bone deep certainty that he was the man their carriage had splashed as he knelt in the gutter. He was the poor fellow she had been worrying about for a week.

Was it coincidence only that he now frequented every venue where Lady Rowena was to be found? Was the meeting on the steps of the dressmaker a coincidence? Or had he seen her that night and in the most romantic of fairy tales, fallen in love at first sight and sought a meeting?

She would need to ask him. As Rowena's chaperon, she supposed it was her duty.

If she still was Rowena's chaperon come morning, that was.

When they arrived at the ducal mansion, the duke summarily dismissed his daughter preparatory, Amy was sure, to giving her a complete dressing-down and a dismissal from the ducal manse, but Rowena did not leave them alone without one last parting word.

"Father," she said, her voice echoing in the ghostly silence as she mounted the great curved staircase that spiraled up to the gallery overhead. "Despite her poor judgment in waltzing with Lord Pierson, I will not have you disrupt my Season by letting Amy go. Just think of all the fuss and bother of finding another chaperon at this late date. And remember last year's chaperon, the one who drank. And the one before that, who was caught in bed with the first footman, that lanky fellow you had to dismiss as well. It is fatiguing to find good help."

Amy bit her lip, chagrined, and yet, despite the gravity of the moment, entertained by such a unique bit of arm twisting. Who would have expected her fractious charge to be her "white knight"? Rowena went upstairs to bed and in the end, though the duke gave her a lecture on the impropriety of a chaperon waltzing at a ball, he harumphed a great deal and let it go with what he termed "a stiff warning," after extracting from her a promise never to do such a thing again.

And so all her worry and anxiety had come to naught. And that night, instead of worrying about her position for the time being, she could dream that she was again on the dance floor in Lord Pierson's arms. Though in the dream his hair was in his eyes and he had the unfortunate whiff of the gutter on him.

Pierson spent a troubled night, not able to sleep for worry that he had done irreparable damage to the young chaperon's position. As morning light poked fingers of brightness through a gap in the draperies and into his gloomy bedchamber, he sat on the edge of his bed and contemplated possible solutions, but he could come to no conclusion. He could not go to the duke and plead her case, for he would certainly only make matters worse. If he had learned anything, it was that he must rein in his impulsive whims or risk hurting others besides himself. It was a salutary lesson and came not a moment too soon.

But he was troubled by the notion that he was helpless to ameliorate her calamity; his hands were tied.

Why he suddenly felt so solicitous toward Miss Corbett he could not fathom. He only knew that the new start he had made in his life did not include getting harmless young women in trouble for things they had no control over. He had been swept up in the mood of the moment when he waltzed so wildly with her, and though he was delighted by the look of surprised rapture on her face — in fact it had affected him deeply to be able to transport her with such a simple action — he wished he had been more circumspect. Bainbridge would never have made that error in judgment. And therein lay the reason he was perpetually offending society with his wild antics while his friend always knew the absolute correct moment to pull back from the brink of disaster.

His valet entered the room and started to find his master already awake.

"Don't look so appalled, Rupert," he said, wearily. "You aren't late; I'm up early."

Rupert put his tray down beside Pierson and moved to draw the curtains open. "It is a beautiful day, sir, just right for archery."

"I'm not so sure of that, old man. Whether we do that or not depends largely on a certain chaperon and her continuing employment with Lady Rowena."

"Yes, well, Lord Bainbridge sent you a note, so perhaps it will clear up the mystery, my lord." The valet indicated a note on the tray.

Pierson grabbed it. Bain's note read,

The invaluable Staynes has it from a fellow gentleman's gentleman in the duke's employ that Miss Corbett has retained her position. This, apparently, is a relief to the duke's staff in general, though my valet's source will not elaborate on why that is so.

"Thank God," Pierson sighed, refolding the note. With a more cheery outlook he glanced up at Rupert, who was pulling out linens from the wardrobe. "You already knew what it said, you fraud. Reading my mail! I should sack you on the spot."

"It is my duty to know these things, my lord. And I needed no letter, for Staynes told me."

Pierson chuckled. "You say it is good weather, Rupert? Then dress me appropriately, for I go a-wooing with a bow and arrow, appropriately enough!"

"Are you out of your mind, Bain? Bringing that froggy-faced wet cloth with us?" Pierson's mount shied at his master's unwonted emotional outburst.

They were on a quiet road to a private estate on the outskirts of London, the whole party headed for an afternoon of archery in the brilliant sun of an early spring day.

"Wasn't my fault. I merely invited my sister," Bainbridge said with a shrug, indicating Lady Harriet, "and said she might bring a guest. Thought it would add variety to the party. How was I to know she would bring along Newton-Shrewsbury?"

"What was she thinking about? She said herself he is nothing to her." Pierson gloomily watched his competitor for Lady Rowena's hand as that fellow rode alongside the ladies' carriage, bending over and monopolizing the most beautiful occupant's time.

"You can't possibly be worried," Bainbridge asked. He pulled his black gelding into step with his friend's bay. "Newton-Shrewsbury has nothing on you; not for looks or dash. Said yourself the fellow's a wet blanket. Look how he disappeared after that disaster on the ballroom floor last night! You would never do that."

"Thank you for your confidence. No, I'm not worried about his charm. But the fellow does have a tendency to be there always. And he is certainly a more acceptable beau for a young lady like Lady Rowena than myself. He is damnably steady and responsible. You saw how her father favored him at the ball last night."

"I have a feeling that Lady Rowena is a strong-minded enough maiden that she will make her own choice of a future husband."

"I hope so."

"Relief that the little chaperon was not sacked, eh?"

"Yes," Pierson said, letting out a gusty sigh. "I cannot tell you how that worried me all night. I did not sleep for thinking of it."

"Never seen you take any responsibility so to heart," Bainbridge said, with an interested look. "Why so concerned, besides the obvious inconvenience to Lady Rowena?"

Pierson grimaced at him. "Thank you for pointing out how lax I have always been." He brooded for a moment, trying to answer his friend's question. "I don't know. It was yet another example of how my precipitate actions led to misfortune for someone else. I don't mind when I'm the one who suffers for my own idiocy, but for that young lady to, when she has done nothing but be kind to me . . . it was beyond bearing. I would have done anything for her rather than see that happen."

"Yes, I rather think you would have," Bainbridge said.

Amy glanced back at the gentlemen on horseback following their open carriage. It was an invigorating spring day, and now that they were out of London proper the sky seemed bluer, the breeze fresher, and the birdsong clear and trilling.

How magnificent Lord Pierson and Lord Bainbridge looked side by side, quite the handsomest men in London in her estimation, and she had had the opportunity lately to view those who were considered the best looking beaux in the *ton*.

She resettled herself, aware that it would not do to be thought craning her neck for a look at the men. Examining her companions in the carriage, she wondered why she felt a hint of tension between Lady Harriet and Rowena. Was it just that Lady Rowena insisted on flirting with Lord Newton-Shrewsbury? But surely if the older lady was interested in him, knowing who would be with her that day she would not have invited the viscount. No, the tension seemed to have another source, one Amy could not put her finger on.

She was about to introduce some subject of talk — any subject! — when Lord Bainbridge shouted out, "Here we are!"

From there the afternoon proceeded with the sport at hand. The estate was a pretty Tudor manse with an extensive system of gardens: herb, vegetable, rose, and the obligatory Elizabethan "knot" garden. It was too early in the year for much show of color beyond tulips and primrose, but the delight Amy most felt was in the long sward of green grass that swept down to a stream. For the first time in a while she felt that she could breathe away from the limitations of the duke's stiff presence and the confines of London.

As she was not partaking in the sport herself, she was free to wander and indulged herself for a time, before remembering her duties and rejoining the party on the archery green.

They had made it into a competition, and it seemed that either Lord Pierson was not very good at archery or his mind was not on it, because he was the first to lose and be ejected from the match. Amy joined him where he stood and watched the others.

"Lady Rowena is a fierce competitor," Amy said to Pierson.

The lady in question was crowing about her victory over Lord Newton-Shrewsbury, and that gentleman was taking it in very good stride. Against all Amy's intuitive beliefs, it appeared that he was a very good loser.

"She does seem to succeed at whatever she tries," he replied. He turned his gaze from the competition to his companion. "May I say, Miss Corbett, how happy I am that you have retained your position. I was in horrors all night that my precipitate actions may have cost you your employment."

She was touched by his concern and laid

her hand on his arm, squeezing briefly before letting go. But she would be honest with him. "And so it might have, had not Lady Rowena made it clear to her father that I was not to be let go."

He gazed back at the lady and sighed. "A steadfast friend. I admire that."

It was to his credit that he saw her in such a positive light, so Amy did not correct him. She felt herself that Rowena was just unwilling to have her Season disrupted by the inevitable search for a new chaperon. Since she *was* still Rowena's chaperon, though, she needed the answers to many questions and was trying to decide how to ask them when he suggested that since the competition looked to go on for some time, a walk down by the stream would be a pleasant way to spend a half hour. She acquiesced readily and he took her arm in his.

With just the touch of his arm, she was flooded with memories of the waltz they had shared the night before and the heat rose in her cheeks. She must get over this foolish preference she felt for him if he was to become Rowena's suitor, and she rather feared that was a conclusion that must be expected.

"Miss Corbett," he started, as they

strolled down the soft green slope toward a budding willow at the water's edge. "I would be honest with you always, and I would ask the same from you in return."

She nodded in reply.

"I would like to be considered a suitor for Lady Rowena's hand."

There it was, and Amy didn't know what she had expected, but her heart jolted at the bald statement. So it was to be thus; he wished to court Rowena. It would be her job now to promote the match if she thought it one that would bring both parties happiness.

"I'm not surprised, my lord."

"I'm sure that there are many more worthy suitors. Lady Rowena could not fail to be courted by men with better rank, and certainly better prospects. Perhaps if I told you how I feel and what she means to me, you'll see that I'm best suited, as I have her best interests at heart."

With her new knowledge of where she had first seen him, she wondered if he would tell her about that night. She had reasoned through the night that he must have recognized Rowena or even, perhaps, sought her out, and that must have been the genesis of his infatuation . . . or preference, she supposed she must call it. Infatuation implied a heady but brief rush of emotion.

Certainly if he had any intelligence he would not tell her of that night, his drunken state and his first view of Lady Rowena. And did it really matter? All she was truly concerned about just then was the sincerity of his feelings for Lady Rowena. "I honor your intentions, my lord," Amy said, referring to his last statement and the sincerity she heard in his tone.

They stood on the banks of the stream and watched it slip by in silvery shimmers of light, reflecting the blue sky above and the white puffs of cloud, looking for all the world as if they drifted on the surface of the water. The willow stretched fingers down to the water and lazily trailed them in the burbling brook.

"I'm not, by most standards, a wealthy man, Miss Corbett. If that is a primary consideration for Lady Rowena's hand, you will soon find my superior. But . . ." He paused and kicked at a bit of turf. "But my life has completely changed. I have a very pretty estate in Kent — I've spoken of it to you before — that has suffered badly at the hands of my father and grandfather, and, truth be told, myself. I haven't lived as I should since attaining the title I now hold."

Amy let out a breath she didn't know she had been holding. "My lord, don't tell me anything you will regret later."

He gave her a swift, sideways smile, and she was utterly charmed. There was so much self deprecation in that look, so much humility, that her heart went out to him.

"Somehow I feel my confidences will be safe with you."

"Should you not be telling this to Lady Rowena?" Amy stuttered, feeling suffocated by a longing to be close to him, to soothe the two lines of worry that slashed between his dark brows. The breeze lifted his dark curls and tousled them, and she almost reached out to smooth them, but restrained the urge.

"As much as I . . . care for Lady Rowena," he said, "she is sometimes difficult to speak with on serious topics. Perhaps it's to be expected that one so lovely and young and one who has never faced trouble should not wish to drone on about such things, especially in the ballroom! But I was speaking of my estate. I'm going to try, now — I'm still young enough to make this attempt, I think — to undo the damage of many decades of neglect. I should have started ten years ago, but I can't regret what I cannot undo."

"Very true, my lord, and a very wise way of looking at it."

"My estate has been depleted through bad management and neglect on my part, and lately the problems have reached a crisis."

He told her a tale of his land manager, Mr. Lincoln, and how the man was missing; no one was sure whether he had absconded or whether there was an even darker reason for his disappearance. "I should even now be there, and in a couple of days I need to make the trip to set some things straight. I haven't lived as I ought, this past decade, and my reputation is . . ." he took a deep breath. "It's damaged, Miss Corbett. I won't try to hide the truth. Indeed, it would do me no good to make the attempt, for a discreet question here or there would reveal all. But even now I am working to mend it. Indeed, I think I've made some strides in the right direction already." He turned toward Amy and took her gloved hands in his own bare ones.

She gazed up into his eyes. They were honest golden brown and shone with determination that melted her heart.

"But I believe that to do this great task," he continued, "I need the inspiration afforded me by Lady Rowena. If I could just believe she might care for me . . . if such a perfect, tender, delicate, unspoiled dove could say she might someday be mine . . . I would toil until my skin cracked in the sun. I would spend every day in my own fields. I would in short, do anything to be worthy!"

How could Lady Rowena resist such a man, if he made his case to her? Amy felt sure that even her charge, as difficult and contrary as she sometimes could be, would be melted by such a frank and passionate speech. If it had been directed to *her* . . . but it hadn't and never would be. Amy turned away from the secret longing of her own heart and thought about Rowena. And she considered her own best self-interest. If she gave him permission to woo Rowena and he should be successful, the duke could likely be made to see that marriage to a viscount was an honorable fate for his difficult daughter.

But was it right? Would it serve for both of them? She squeezed his hands and pulled hers away.

"My lord," she said, softly, quieting the clamor of self-interest and the warring desires of her own heart. "Would it not be best, if you have so much work that you must accomplish on your estate, to return there and commence? It sounds as if you should be there even now and indeed, I sense an underlying impatience with London and your stay here. I think if you search your heart you will find that you truly would prefer to be in Kent right now setting things to rights on your estate."

Pierson considered her words. He had expressed himself to Miss Corbett in way he never had with another soul, not even Bainbridge, and felt unburdened in a way. She listened and believed him. So many would have scoffed at him, and many more would never believe him until he succeeded, but she took his aims seriously and it warmed him.

But perhaps she didn't understand. "I think, Miss Corbett, that I've failed to explain myself. I can't leave London yet, for I believe that Lady Rowena is my destined helpmeet, my future. I would do all of this for her, but I must feel sure of her affection before I can depart London and set myself to my task."

"I think, my lord, that you must do this for yourself and for your name. Perhaps if you do . . ."

A scream from above interrupted their earnest discussion, and Pierson felt it pierce him like an arrow. Lady Rowena! That was her own voice; she must be hurt. With a hasty word for Miss Corbett, he turned and ran up the slope to the archery field. What would he see? What would greet his eyes? Nothing less than his lady love laid out on the green grass with an arrow in her shoulder could account for such a heartrending shriek.

He galloped up, his breath coming in gasps. A strange tableau greeted his eyes.

Lady Harriet and Lord Newton-Shrewsbury stood to one side of the green and Bainbridge was in the center. Lady Rowena, her hand clutching something, stood at the other end of the green and she screeched again and stamped her feet.

Approaching her he gasped, "What is it? Lady Rowena, dear one, what is wrong? Are you hurt? Are you . . ."

Panting with some strong emotion she held out one hand, her tan kid glove stained a dark hue. "Someone . . . somehow . . . There was a blot of dark ink on the arrow in my quiver!" she uttered. "And these are my favorite gloves! Ruined! Stained beyond repair! Who did this? I will know!"

Seventeen

"My lady," Lord Newton-Shrewsbury remonstrated, pacing toward her. " 'Twas surely an accident. Could've happened a hundred ways."

"How? You tell me how!" Lady Rowena, her face pinched into a grimace and with two hot red spots high on her cheeks, held out her gloved hand and waved it in the man's face. "It was deliberate! And I resent that you would say such a thing. What am I, some raving idiot then? Is that what you're calling me?"

Lord Newton-Shrewsbury, his face pasty, stumbled in his backward perambulation across the turf and away from the lady. Pierson glanced around to find Lady Harriet looking truly concerned and Bainbridge with a frown on his face. Miss Corbett had arrived at the scene that moment and took her charge in hand, stripping off the offending glove and saying, "Rowena, it's just a glove, after all."

"But it's my favorite," she said, her expression clouded and pinched. "I shall never have another pair I like as well, I know it."

"Nonsense. You have a dozen just like these."

Pierson frowned and watched the exchange. Bainbridge strolled over to him and said, "Such a fuss over a glove! One would think it was the end of the world the way she shrieked."

"I thought she had been hurt," Pierson admitted. "I heard her scream and ran here, picturing her on the ground with an arrow through her!"

"No, just caterwauling over her glove. She reached into her quiver to draw out an arrow, and that is when her glove became stained."

"It is odd, you must admit," Pierson mused.

"What is?"

"This string of bad luck she has been having. Her fall on the dance floor last night, and the wine spilled on her dress."

Bainbridge shrugged.

"And how did the ink, or whatever the stain is from, come to be in her quiver when it was not there earlier?" Pierson said. "Poor girl; she's merely high strung. That is a testament to her breeding."

Bainbridge snorted, but Pierson hadn't

time to ask him what he meant by such a noise, as Miss Corbett approached them just then. "Lady Rowena's maid is fetching another pair of gloves for her," she said. She glanced back at her charge, who was speaking to Lady Harriet and pointedly ignoring Lord Newton-Shrewsbury. "I don't understand how these things keep happening."

"We were just discussing that," Bainbridge said. "I find it highly suspect that Lord Newton-Shrewsbury just happens to be near whenever these things occur."

Pierson glanced in surprise at his friend, as did Miss Corbett.

"You cannot think that Lord Newton-Shrewsbury would do anything like this?" she said.

"Why not?" Bainbridge said with a shrug. "He does seem always to be near. I think I saw him last night just as the wine was spilled; he was among those who were squeezing by our table."

"I didn't see him. I thought he left after their fall on the dance floor." She frowned and fell silent for a moment. "What would be his motive?" she continued. She shook her head. "No, I can't believe that it has anything to do with him. Just a string of coincidences."

"Perhaps you're right," Bainbridge said. "Just unfortunate coincidences."

Archery was abandoned in favor of a late luncheon. After lunch the party broke up to some extent and Pierson, with Miss Corbett's tacit approval, led Lady Rowena on a walk. They were silent as they strolled at first and he glanced at her often, admiring the curve of her cheek, the silvery blonde of her exquisite hair and the rose pink of her lips. No portrait artist in the world could ever capture the happy unity of her features and coloring, he thought.

His heart full to bursting, he felt a need to speak to her of some of the things he was thinking and feeling. With the memory fresh of Miss Corbett's advice, he wondered if he was rushing things too much. If he had some encouragement from her —

"My lady," he said, taking her arm as they strolled down the grassy slope. "How I wish you could see Delacorte, my country estate. It is on a prominence much like this place but it's wilder, and I confess that appeals to me more than this ruthless subjugation of nature. I'm going back there soon to take care of some estate business."

She was silent.

"I'm worried for my estate staff," he continued, "for my land manager seems to have disappeared, and . . ."

"Lord Pierson, do you think me spoiled?"

Stuttering to a halt, Pierson did not know how to answer, except, "Well, of course not, my lady. Who would say . . ."

"Lord Bainbridge, while we were competing, said I had been spoiled so badly that I was a poor loser. He beat me handily and then said I was moaning when I remonstrated with him about his shocking joy over having bested me!"

"I'm appalled he would be so ungentlemanly!" Pierson said.

"But is he right?"

"Of course not! You are completely unspoiled and the image of perfection."

"And so I told him," she said, with a nod and in a better humor.

They strolled on, but no matter how much Pierson tried to raise the subject of his hopes and dreams, his estate, all the work that remained to be done, he found himself talking into a void. It was only when he spoke of her stained glove that he elicited any emotion from her that afternoon.

And then his only reward was to listen to her rail against the unseen forces that were conspiring against her enjoyment.

★ ★ ★

The sky was golden with slanting rays as they left the estate and began their two hour journey back to London. The roads were dusty, so about halfway there Bainbridge suggested they stop at an inn for a cup of restorative tea for the ladies, and though there was sulking and much exhaustion, his notion was greeted with some relief.

Amy had found, over the course of the afternoon, that she had her suspicions about the true state of Lady Harriet's feelings, as tight as that young woman's expression often was. It seemed to her that the marquess' sister nursed a *tendre* for Pierson, one which she had no hope of seeing come to fruition, but a preference nonetheless.

It made Amy's mood melancholy, for it reminded her of her own tender feelings toward him, and she wondered why one man, Lord Bainbridge, with everything to recommend him including looks, wealth, and intelligence, should have no one expiring for love of him and the other, Lord Pierson, with such a reckless past and uncertain future, should have three ladies in their company languishing for love of him.

Granted she was too sensible herself to

be languishing, or expiring or any other such nonsensical feeling. But if she let herself —

Oh, if she let herself. She sighed again over the light in his beautiful eyes as he spoke of his home estate. He seemed to be, after neglecting it for years, discovering an awakening passion for his home. She only hoped he heeded it and stayed the course, giving back to his title and people what was owed after so many years of neglect. Every advice she could give him would be in that direction, even if it should countermand her own best interest, which lay in a hasty wooing and wedding of Lady Rowena.

Self-interest urged that path, and she felt that all things being equal, they would have as good a chance at being happy as the next couple. But how did she balance what was best for him, for Rowena and for his people, estate and title, together? In truth, it was not up to her. He was a grown man and would ultimately make his own choice.

At that moment the inn was in sight and the gentlemen guided the carriage driver to the front to allow the ladies to step down.

It was an ancient Tudor inn, low roofed and half-timbered, and the gentlemen needed to stoop as they entered the public rooms. The innkeeper bustled forth and, seeing their quality, immediately offered them his best private room for refreshments.

The company, weary after a day of outdoor sport, was quiet, with Lord Newton-Shrewsbury pointedly ignoring Lady Rowena in favor of Lady Harriet, and Bainbridge — just returned from conferring with his groom — sitting alone and staring into the fire that was welcome against the spring chill that had begun with a fresh breeze on their journey home.

Lord Pierson and Rowena sat together, with Amy just a little way away. She could overhear their conversation. Pierson tried to speak of his estate but Rowena pouted prettily until the subject once more came around to her, and how lovely she was in the firelight. He again tried to speak of his home and how he felt a mistress would give the old place life and cheer again.

Rowena was silent for a long minute, but then answered that she thought London much more cheerful than the country. Then she sighed and said what she truly longed to do was travel. She wished to see Italy and Greece and sail the Mediterranean. That was her dream.

Amy had heard her speak of such things

before, but had never realized how serious she was about traveling. Poor Lord Pierson's expression was glum, and Amy thought she could trace the hopelessness he must feel, knowing that his own finances would not run to foreign travel for many years to come, and perhaps never.

When the landlord personally brought in refreshments, the company gathered around the trestle table in the center of the snug room. Somehow, Lord Newton-Shrewsbury ended up beside Rowena at the table, and the frost between them was painfully funny to Amy, considering the assiduousness that young man had shown to the duke's daughter earlier that afternoon. She supposed she should not see the humor in the stiff little scene, but she could not help it and caught Lord Bainbridge eyeing the situation with a lift to the corners of his mouth.

She watched the marquess for a moment and considered his odd behavior to Lady Rowena. He watched her often, and in any other gentleman she would have thought his behavior an indication he was a fair way to being in love with her himself, but he seemed to watch her to criticize. He often made cutting remarks and was wont to point out her faults of behavior.

Granted, he did not do it in front of anyone else — she had only overheard him a couple of times herself by accident and because it was her duty to be near her charge — but Amy was fascinated by Rowena's response. She appeared to be doing everything in her power to impress him. And yet he would not be impressed, remaining stolid in the face of her most enchanting flirtatious behavior.

A serving girl brought in a plate of cream cakes, a pitcher of buttermilk, and a flask of port for the gentlemen. Tea was also provided, and an apple tart glazed to an exquisite sheen. Amy thought she had never tasted such fine country cookery and said so to the sweet-faced maid, by her looks the landlord's daughter.

The company fell silent as they indulged in the treats arrayed before them. It was an informal party, so the gentlemen helped the ladies to some of the food, and Lord Bainbridge poured tea with a twitch to his mouth and a joking comment that he was "playing mother."

All was well for a time until Rowena, taking a large mouthful of a cream cake, choked and her face turned a brilliant scarlet. She stiffened, but then spat out the food in her mouth in the most unladylike way and let out a string of vulgarities that turned Amy scarlet too, just to hear them. The young woman stopped only to take a long swallow of buttermilk, and it dribbled down her chin as she gulped deeply.

"What is wrong with you, Rowena?" Amy said, leaping up from her chair and approaching her charge.

"What is wrong is that this food, th-this cream cake has p-pepper in it! I got a mouthful of pepper!"

Lord Pierson had leaped up to aid her as well, but unfortunately his precipitate movement somehow unsettled the pitcher of buttermilk and it rocked and then tipped, spilling down onto Lady Rowena's fine spring cloak.

That was the end of any hope of peace as Lady Rowena leaped to her feet and pulled off her cloak, screaming like the banshees the Donegals used to tease their children about at Amy's last position. Amy called Lady Rowena's maid, who had been in the kitchen having tea, and sent the two out of the room to deal with the results of her string of misfortunes. Lord Pierson followed briefly to ensure that the landlord was informed of their need for hot water and cloths.

Lord Newton-Shrewsbury appeared almost smug, and Amy recalled Lord Bainbridge's conjecture that he, somehow, was responsible. But surely he was nowhere near Rowena just then, or was he? He had been seated beside her at first, but then had changed seats to sit beside Lady Harriet. Then she caught Lord Bainbridge's eye. That gentleman was doing his best to conceal a smile and Amy felt her instincts twitch unhappily. Lord Bainbridge? But why would he be intent on torturing poor Rowena?

She sat back down as the maid came in and cleaned up the spilled buttermilk and smeared cream cake. Lord Bainbridge winked at the girl and slipped her a crown surreptitiously, and Amy wondered if that was some sort of bribe or just an apology for the fuss and bother they had caused her. Should she accuse him outright, or was it ludicrous to even suspect he had anything to do with the recent spate of accidents?

He *had* been absent from the room for a while, supposedly out speaking to his groom. He could have tampered with the cream cakes . . . but that was ridiculous to even contemplate! Worried and puzzled, Amy paced outside into the fresh air to think for a moment, and felt rather than saw someone follow her. She turned to find it was Lord Pierson.

"Are you all right, Miss Corbett? This has not upset you, has it?"

"No, not at all. I'm puzzled by this continuing string of misfortune, but not upset."

"Lady Rowena is in a fair taking," he said, gloomily. "I apologized as best I could for upsetting the pitcher of buttermilk, but she would not listen to me."

"She will once she has calmed. She's just agitated right now."

They paced to the terrace overlooking a hedgerow and the gently sloping valley beyond. It was the end of a lovely spring day, Amy thought, and she should be as happy as the proverbial lark, since Lord Pierson appeared to be completely intent on wooing Rowena, and contrary to her long-stated objection to marriage, she seemed amenable to being wooed. If he just did it the right way, though. The duke's daughter was not a girl to be charmed by talk of an estate that needed work and years of toil ahead.

So how would she deal with the reality of such a life? Lord Pierson, for all he had the reputation of a rake and rogue, seemed a most sober young man now, intent on reformation. Amy felt an unwilling spurt of respect added to her attraction toward him, but didn't think his new steadiness would inspire such a feeling in Rowena, who would have preferred that he act as impulsively and erratically as he was reputed to do. Should she advise him on how best to court the fractious girl, or would putting such things into words be indelicate or even unproductive? It did seem, unfortunately, that Lord Pierson's feelings for Rowena were based on her appearance of dove-like mildness and sweetness of temper.

She glanced up at him, the strong line of his jaw just darkening from the bristle of beard coming in. His arms were folded over his chest and she thought that he looked the very image of a well-dressed Vulcan, dark and handsome but brooding, too.

"My lord, Lady Rowena is volatile, I know, but good at heart. Don't concern yourself with her outburst, please."

"What? Oh, no, Miss Corbett, I was not brooding on that, I assure you." He smiled at her. "Shall we walk?" he continued, indicating a winding path that followed the hedgerow. "It will take a while, I think, for her maid to dry Lady Rowena off. We must go soon, for it is beginning to get dark, but we still have an hour or more of daylight."

Amy acquiesced and the viscount gave her his arm.

They were silent for a few minutes, but then Lord Pierson cleared his throat. "You know," he said. "I've spoken more to you of my plans than to any living person, even Bainbridge, and he is my best friend in the world."

"I'm honored, my lord."

"You just seem to inspire me to talk. I feel like I am boiling up with things I'm thinking of and longing for and needing to do. But Lady Rowena is . . . Well, she's so lighthearted and spirited. I can't blame her for not wanting to speak of dry subjects like my recovery of Delacorte."

But if she loved you, anything you said would be fascinating. The thought came unbidden to Amy, and she tamped it down furiously, angry at herself for letting such a traitorous thought have a voice, even if it whispered only in her mind. She rushed into speech, reluctant to think too long on her own feelings and how they had become entangled in Lord Pierson's life and desires. "Is there so very much to do at Delacorte, then?" Twilight's golden hue colored the hedgerow and lush valley grass a brilliant green, and it took all of Amy's considerable willpower to keep her mind on any topic at all when she was so very content just walking on Lord Pierson's arm.

"There is. It's not irrecoverable at this point, I hope, but I will need to make plans, plans that will encompass decades, not just years. And I've never applied myself, so I haven't any idea of where to start. I'm taking advice from Bainbridge's man, who has been very helpful so far. Frankly . . ." He paused and glanced down at her. "I shouldn't be so very candid with Lady Rowena's chaperon, should I? However, you inspire confidence, Miss Corbett and I seem to forget, when I'm with you, that you will be the one with influence over Lady Rowena and her future."

He was silent for a long minute. "I really don't know what I'm doing. I've made a start by hiring a new land manager through Bainbridge, whose man was able to recommend someone. But I'll have to go to Kent soon and make some plans, and that, inevitably, will involve confessing to this new fellow my absolute ignorance. He'll despise me."

"Not at all," she said, softly. "He will respect you for your willingness to learn and your determination to do better than your father and grandfather."

"And I will do better. Miss Corbett, I've been wild, impetuous . . . My title has been dragged through the muck by three generations and stands at very low tide. I'm not saying anything to you now that hasn't likely been said by others. But I'm determined that I will be different. I'm willing to work long and hard at it. I just wish I had awoken to this ambition earlier in my life instead of frittering my time away in London."

"I cannot tell you how much I honor you for your determination and your brilliant plans," Amy said, squeezing the viscount's arm to her side in a reassuring manner.

"My first step, I have decided, is to attach and marry a young lady of worth, of morality and goodness. She will be my shining beacon, my moral compass!" Pierson's voice trembled, full of emotion. "I have vowed to be guided by her gentle hand and submit myself wholly to the joys of marriage. She will direct me away from vice and folly and toward respectability."

Doubt overwhelmed Amy. There was so much to fret upon in his words, not the least of which was the absolute lack of similarity between the young lady he described and Lady Rowena, his supposed object. But she must not contradict him there, and in fact her concern went much deeper, to the very heart of the problem. "My lord," she said, "I think . . . are you not approaching things from the wrong direction? In fact . . ." She took a deep breath. "I must say this, my lord; that is rubbish! Out of line totally!"

"What? What do you mean?"

Amy hesitated, but then plunged ahead. "You cannot make another person your moral compass. Really, my lord, it is every person's responsibility in life to come to his own understanding about correct behavior."

"But I have done wretchedly until now."

"Admit it, though; in your own heart you knew you were doing wrong . . . or at least omitting to do right. I think you *always* knew. And if you want to change, it is entirely up to you. No one else will be able to make you over, and certainly, with all the power in this world residing in male hands, no wife is going to be able to do that chore. And if she could, it would mean you could be intolerably hen-led, and I would never believe that of you."

He stood and stared at her for a moment, her hand still held in his. With his free hand he had just plucked a new leaf from the budding hedgerow and he twirled it in his fingers. "What should I do then? What would you advise . . . I mean, if you were going to give advice, which you are clearly loath to do."

She chuckled, gazing up at him, the golden light of twilight blazing in his warm golden eyes. He was so very different from his reputation, she mused, that she would never again judge anyone by what others said. And yet he clearly had a wild side, one she regrettably found intriguing. It exposed an impetuous and impulsive heart, and in her own controlled, quiet existence a little spontaneity would have been a welcome thing. With his infatuation for Lady Rowena, of course, he would never look at someone like her, but she could dream and she could be his friend.

But if he wanted advice —

"You cannot marry goodness and expect it to rub off on you, my lord," she said, her tone gentle. "I think you already know this deep inside but I will say it anyway; you have to start within yourself. I think you might be surprised at how true your own compass will be if you let it guide you. Change will not be easy, for you have a lifetime of habit to battle, but if you're sincere and really want to make a difference to Delacorte, the people who work for you, and for yourself, you can do it."

Slowly, he nodded. "You've given me much to think of, Miss Corbett. And now I think we should return to the inn, for it is past time that we should be on our way."

They walked back slowly, silently. Once back at the inn the carriage was waiting, and Amy was sure Rowena would question her closely about where she had been with Lord Pierson, but the girl was silent and stiff, sitting looking straight ahead. Even Lord Bainbridge appeared rigid with anger, and Amy wondered if she had missed some set-to.

But she had given up for the time being her usual role of mediator and smoother of ruffled emotions. She would let everyone be in a foul mood if that was their preference. For herself, she was going to go back to London and remember the golden light in Lord Pierson's warm eyes, and how it had bathed her for a brief time in delight.

Eighteen

The day had been a long one and they were committed to a card party that evening. Later, when they arrived back home from it — it had been exceedingly dull — and Rowena was in her room having her hair braided for sleep, Amy entered.

Lady Rowena had been unusually quiet all evening. The day's events had been upsetting, Amy surmised, and she was exhausted and agitated, an unusual state for the duke's daughter. Her own suspicions about the origin of the string of accidents was upsetting to herself, but unanswered. She could not imagine a reason in the world why Lord Bainbridge would plan such a nasty attack against Lady Rowena, and yet who else could she accuse? In truth, there were far too many incidences to dismiss it as chance.

She waited until the maid finished and Lady Rowena, with a tired wave of her hand, dismissed the dour woman, who took her mistress' clothes into the connecting dressing room to hang for repair and cleaning. Rowena met Amy's eyes and frowned. She opened her mouth to speak but then closed it again.

Answering some plea that went wordless, Amy knelt by her side and took the girl's hands. "Rowena, are you all right? You didn't get a chill today, did you?"

"No."

"Come, let me tuck you in," Amy said and pulled the young woman to her feet.

Rowena was no child, nor even a girl, but she obediently crossed to her bed, climbed in, and allowed Amy to pull the covers up to her chin.

It seemed to Amy from what she had gathered over the months living in the duke's household that as the youngest child, Rowena had been spoiled and indulged by her much older sisters to such a shocking degree that how she had turned out was a foregone conclusion. Would someone as infatuated as Lord Pierson ever exert the demands on her that would force her to grow up into a woman, or would she need to scramble into that learning herself over the years, as she became a matron and mother?

Or should she just not marry until some of that maturation had taken place?

Amy sat on the edge of the bed and

gazed down at her. "Are you happy with your life, Rowena?" she asked, without quite knowing why. The girl had never shown a moment of introspection; why should she think her even capable of it?

Rowena blinked and stared up at the canopy of her ornate bed. "I have always thought so unless I was crossed, which didn't happen often. But . . . I'm not sure now. Amy, have . . . Have you ever been in love?"

"I don't think so."

"Oh."

"Why?"

"I was just wondering how one knows? All the girls say it is when you can't sleep and can't eat and you're floating on a cloud. They say your beau seems just perfect to you. But then, most of them have since married and it appears to me that they went rapidly from that stage to detesting their husband, or at the very least, disliking him. I only know one girl who married and still has a pleasant word to say about her husband."

"I think that wedded happiness and the kind of love you're talking about, the not-eating-not-sleeping kind, have little to do with each other," Amy said, mildly. "I think a marriage can likely be very successful even without love, if the two are committed to being kind to each other."

"Kindness." Rowena stretched and yawned, blinking sleepily. "Do you think that's important in a husband?"

Amy smiled, thinking about Lord Pierson and his gentle nature, despite the wild stories about him. "Yes, I do think kindness is important."

"Then I'm quite sure Lord Bainbridge will never marry, for he's very unkind. He said the most horrible things to me!" Her pretty face was twisted in a scowl and she plucked at her bedspread.

"Lord Bainbridge?" Amy said, surprised. "I can't believe that; he has always been the soul of kindness to me."

"Yes, well, he detests me, I'm sure of it." Rowena punched her pillow and turned onto her side. "He says the most awful things to me. He says I'm spoiled and unpleasant and childish."

Amy was silent. What could she say to counter what was, after all, only the truth?

But Rowena didn't need an answer; she continued, "So how does one truly know when one is in love?"

Amy considered her answer carefully. Self-interest warred with a desire to make sure Rowena and Lord Pierson were really destined to be together in happiness, not discord. She would see neither of them suffer just because she was worried for her own future, and so she would urge neither into love before they were ready.

"I think that when you love a gentleman, you want . . ." She consulted her own feelings, for despite what she had asserted to Rowena, she suspected she knew what it was to love, even though that love expected no return. Softly she said, "You want what is best for him. You want to be with him and it doesn't matter where you are, just as long as you're together. You're willing to compromise, to bend and grow together and not insist on your own way in everything."

"Oh." Rowena, her expression thoughtful, frowned. "I . . . I'm not sure, then. That sounds very much like not getting to do what one wants most of the time."

Amy sighed. Had she even now pushed herself into poverty? She laid her hand over Rowena's on the pale coverlet and stroked the girl's hand. "I think if you are truly in love, and you examine your heart without vanity or stubbornness, you'll know."

Pierson and Bainbridge had spent the evening together too, though not at the card party Amy and Rowena attended. They were at their club and it was very late. They had both been silent for some time.

"Pierson, we must talk," Bainbridge blurted out, finally.

The viscount gazed at his friend, assessing him anew. The marquess was agitated, restless, and that was unlike him, for Bainbridge was the calmest, coolest fellow Pierson had ever met. "You were very cruel to Lady Rowena today," Pierson said. "You called her spoiled. It upset her."

"It's true, though, can't you see that? She *is* spoiled, and if everyone just smiles and lets her go on that way she will make herself unhappy in the end."

"You're not her father," Pierson ground out.

"No. Her father is even worse, for he just storms at her and calls her rude but offers no guidance. If he cared enough for her . . . Oh, there's no talking to you," Bainbridge said, getting up and pacing back and forth. "You won't see reason where she is concerned. You see her as she has always appeared in public, but haven't the last few days shown you what she is like? She is a termagant, wild, spoiled . . ."

"Stop! You're talking about the girl I'm

going to marry." Pierson watched his friend's face change, the expression cooling, calming to his habitual tranquillity. Whatever was wrong with the marquess, he was letting it go. And it was a good thing, for if Bain said anything more about Lady Rowena, he was going to have to face his friend's fist.

They fell silent again and there was no raising any subject that they could speak of. Finally they abandoned all pretense and parted ways to go to their separate homes.

As the days passed the weather became more even, and the sometimes icy winds of March softened as the days lengthened into April.

The duke was being patient and Amy could only be grateful. She had consulted with Mrs. Bower, but that lady knew of no other position that Amy could retreat to if Rowena did not find a husband by the end of the Season. Positions were not to be had so easily, it seemed.

Oddly enough, though the viscount had seemed intent on his wooing of Rowena, progress, if there was any, seemed slow and uncertain. Amy could not account for that, but was unwilling to urge either forward.

But in the meantime the Season was progressing happily in some ways and for some young ladies and gentlemen. Romances proceeded, engagements were announced, weddings planned.

Balls went on, card parties, dinners, the opera, and the theater. Lord Bainbridge, his mother, and his sister were often present, and it seemed to Amy that the marquess purposely threw them all together. And she also noticed that while the marquess' family group was gathered, no more "incidents" happened to Lady Rowena.

It was not always a happy company, for the marquess' mother had never lost her initial distaste for Rowena and occasionally made quite cutting remarks. Amy would have expected the duke's daughter to slyly find a way to return those jabs, but she remained silent, generally.

But it was Lord Pierson, of course, whose company Amy most enjoyed. He talked to her often, even as he sat and stared at Rowena. It should have made her miserable, she supposed, but she was resigned. If she could help it she would not make herself unhappy over the viscount, who was as out of her reach as Prinny himself.

It was another evening and another ball, a come-out ball in honor of the daughter of the house, a lovely young girl named Lady Penelope Harwicke.

Amy watched from the edge of the ballroom, near the large French doors that opened onto the terrace, as Rowena danced with Lord Bainbridge. The weather had turned truly divine, with spring flowers scenting the puffs of warm air from the garden outside. She had noted that recently, due solely to his good behavior, Lord Pierson had made enormous inroads on inverting his formerly soiled reputation. Some wise matrons were already pushing their daughters toward him — and it must be said that most of the girls were willing to be wooed, if only he had been so inclined — though if they had known the state of his finances as well as Amy did, perhaps they would still have been a little more circumspect.

Lord Pierson had traveled back to his estate for a couple of days on business that could not wait, but had said he would be back for this ball, so Amy kept her eye on the door, knowing she should not anticipate his presence so, but not able to keep her foolish heart from hoping, wishing, dreaming.

And there he was, strolling in alone, his splendid form expertly clad in black with immaculate white linen. But even if he had been clothed in poorly cut broadcloth, even if he had been as she first saw him, drenched and on his knees, she still would have considered him the only man there worth looking at, worth talking to. Why? Why him?

She had asked herself that many a night in the darkness of her elegant chamber, with Puss curled up purring in the crook of her arm. She could only think that her attraction to Lord Pierson lay in his kind heart, his earnest and deeply felt desire to strive for something better, and in the way he made her feel, that at least while they spoke together she was the only one of whom he was thinking. It was a heady sensation and one that, like strong wine, intoxicated her.

And one she would have to forget, for he seemed as intent as ever on wooing and winning the hand of Lady Rowena Revington, even if his pace had slowed and become uncertain.

He caught sight of her and made his way through the crowd of delicate belles and handsome beaux. "How good to see you, Miss Corbett," he said, reaching out and grasping her hands in his.

"My lord, how jaunty you look tonight. Has your business in Kent been resolved to your satisfaction?"

His expression clouded and he frowned. She castigated herself for raising an unpleasant subject when he had been looking so happy. But in a moment his expression cleared.

"I would speak to you of that alone, if I may, Miss Corbett. Would you walk with me on the terrace or in the garden?"

Amy glanced around and saw that the dance continued and Rowena was still in Lord Bainbridge's arms. If there was one man in the ballroom she would consider Rowena to be safe with, it would be the marquess; for all his cynicism and occasional temper, he was a steady and reliable young man.

She nodded. "Let us talk, my lord."

He took her arm and strolled with her out to the narrow terrace, guided her to the steps and they descended to the grassy lawn beneath. "Ah, this is much better."

They strolled down a path and Amy leaned on his arm, enjoying the closeness, inhaling his scent. Her slippers were silent on the verdant grass and if the breeze was still a little cool, she was wearing a merino gown and with Lord Pierson next to her would not have felt a hurricane.

"I have, as I told you before I left, been to Kent. Poor Delacorte; Miss Corbett, it's worse than I feared in some ways and better in others. The house needs so much work. The land is not in as bad a state as I feared, and . . . Well, Mr. Lincoln — that was my land manager — I'm afraid the news of him is not good. He truly has disappeared. He was on his way to Suffolk to his sister's a few weeks ago, but he disappeared on the way and I fear the worst. While all were suspecting him of malfeasance, I fear that something tragic, some accident has happened. I will not say I suspect Mr. Lincoln was running off with the money; it's not pleasant to think or speak ill of him when we know not what happened, so I will just surmise that he . . . forgot to leave the wages when he went, being upset at the report he had just received that his nephew was ill. It is a sad case. I . . ." He paused and thrust his free hand through his hair. "I didn't know that he was his sister's and nephew's sole support, so when I went to speak to her I gave her some money, what I could spare. Miss Corbett, there is so much I didn't know; I feel as though my eyes have been opened.

How could I have behaved with such care-lessness for so many years?"

She ached for him and the desolation she heard in his voice. "You mustn't blame yourself. That will help nobody. You're doing your best to rectify matters now. Isn't that for the best?"

"Yes, and that's the good news. Like I said, though the house needs repairs that can't be attempted yet, the land is in good condition and this year's crop is in the ground and flourishing. I met with some of the tenant farmers, and I even think I won some of them over. It'll take time, but some day it will be as it once was, a legacy to be proud of for my . . . for my son, if I should be so fortunate to ever have one."

"I'm so happy for you, my lord."

"Happy for *me?*" He paused as they stood in the dark shadows of a flowering crab apple on a carpet of pale petals, the sweet scent of the blossoms drifting over them. Light from the brilliant ballroom had faded there to a dusky purple gilded with moonlight.

She turned and examined his face in the dim light. "You've found work worth doing and you have a determination and commit-ment to do it. There is no nobler task for a man than what you've found."

"But . . . but would a lady feel the same?" He frowned down at their joined hands and played with her gloved fingers. "The house needs repair. It will be slow, though, since the land needs immediate attention. It's not in too bad shape, but will need some investment. The orchards have been neglected for too long and need replacing, and the greenhouses need repair." He shook his head. "And there I go again talking about it." He laughed at himself and squeezed her hands. "How would any lady find my conversation now anything but boring? Where did the charming wastrel of years gone by disappear to? I'm afraid if . . . If I marry, my bride and I will have to confine ourselves to a small portion of the house for a year or two until I can afford to repair the roof and see to the chimneys. And I won't be able to buy new furnishings for some time to come."

It was too easy for Amy to say what she felt truly in her heart, which was full to bursting with pride of him, pride for his reformation, and pride for his strength in the face of almost insurmountable difficulties. How much easier it would have been to just keep going on in the way he always had! "My lord," she said, her voice trembling with emotion, "anyone would be proud to have a husband who put the land and their future above trivialities like a grand house or new furnishings. You would do her honor by believing in her intelligence and ability to help in your endeavor."

He stared at her, his eyes shadowed in the darkness. What she expected him to do, she wasn't sure, but it was not what he did.

He put one finger under her chin, lifted her face and kissed her lips, gently, sweetly.

Nineteen

"You mustn't look so lovely, my lady," Bain-bridge said, staring down at Lady Rowena as the dance ended. "It isn't fair to all of the gentlemen who know they'll never have a chance with you."

The crowd swirled around them and the ballroom was hot and noisy, but when he looked down at her he may as well have been alone in a field of wildflowers. There was no denying it any longer, how he felt and what he wanted. What he would never have.

"What good is looking lovely, my lord," Rowena answered, tossing her head, "when all *you* do is look at me to criticize."

"I do that, don't I," he mused, taking her arm. "But it's only because I see so much in you. You are so . . . so perfect in your imperfection." He shook his head, de-spairing at his own ineptitude. "Lord, that sounds ridiculous but I'm neither a poet, nor a beau. I can't say the words you would want to hear. I know the ladies like a fellow like Pierson better. He has the romantic words that I don't."

Lady Rowena stared up at him. "Lord Pierson? All *he* ever wants to speak of is his gloomy estate and how much work there is to do there. It sounds a dead bore. I thought he would be entertaining. I thought a rake would be shocking and wild and lively, but he's not."

"My dear Lady Rowena, that is the difference between a rake and a reforming rake. Lord Pierson wishes to reform and he thinks to have you guide him to that reformation."

They drifted toward the open terrace doors near the band, at the opposite end of the ballroom from where they had left Miss Corbett at the beginning of the dance. But Bainbridge didn't want to release Lady Rowena just yet, not when he was hearing such interesting criticism of his old friend.

"I? I aid him to reform?" She snorted, an unladylike sound.

"He thinks you are mild and meek and sweet-tempered," Bainbridge said, heaping coal on what he hoped was a firestorm of disapproval as he guided her toward the open doors. Deliberately sarcastic, he said, "He thinks you will be his moral compass and tell him how to achieve religion and humility."

Lady Rowena stopped and stared up at him again, her brow furrowed. "A moral compass? Does he think me the Captain Cook of religion?"

Bainbridge threw back his head and laughed. It was what he most appreciated about the young lady, her unexpected sense of humor. She was much more intelligent and witty than she had ever let on in public, with an acerbic edge to her words that entertained him. But he immediately sobered. How had he come to this pass? How had he come to the point of falling in love with the real Lady Rowena while his friend still stubbornly insisted, beyond all reason, in loving the social face of the lady?

Could that even be called love, when one didn't know the real person? That was like falling in love with a portrait of someone. He hesitated, but then gave in to the powerful urgings of his heart.

"Will you walk with me, my lady?" He indicated the cool green shadows of the garden below the terrace.

"I . . ." Rowena glanced back into the ballroom, looking perhaps for Miss Corbett, and then down into the garden. "I shouldn't. I should find Amy. I should be dancing with . . . Oh, who was next? I . . ." She fumbled for her dance card, and then stopped as Bainbridge took her arm.

But she wouldn't meet his gaze. Even more interesting, for she had never failed to do so before. "Walk with me," he entreated. He stooped, grasped her shoulders and caught her eyes and held her, fiercely. "Defy society, Rowena. Let the poor idiot who is next suffer. I want to talk to you. I *need* to talk to you." He knew he was revealing his desperation, his turmoil, with every shake of her shoulders, but he didn't care anymore. There were more important things in the world than a calm façade and unruffled demeanor.

She looked up at him and her pale face glowed. "What about?" Her voice was a whisper, cracking with suppressed emotion.

"Something of great importance to both of us. You know what it is, Rowena; you feel it too. I know you do."

She hesitated, but then nodded. They descended the steps into the garden.

One night can change everything.

Pierson paced anxiously at his club. He was far too upset to talk to anyone, but he had left a message at the ball for Bainbridge, for he did need to talk to him, his best friend and most reliable guide to right and wrong.

What had he been thinking about, kissing Miss Corbett? He must have been out of his mind. And after, she had looked up at him, her wide gray-blue eyes stricken as if he had just struck her. He had fumbled to explain, had apologized . . . In fact he couldn't quite remember what he had said, except that out of shame he had mumbled some weak apology, guided her back inside and fled the ballroom, not even able to face Lady Rowena. He needed to talk to Bainbridge and get his mind straight, and then the next day he was going to propose to Lady Rowena.

He stopped pacing, arrested by the thought. That was it, that was what he must do. He had waited long enough. He was going to propose and then visit her father and ask for her hand in marriage. It was what he had set out to do, and he must hesitate no longer. Hesitation was what had gotten him into this mess.

What mess? No! He pushed away his tumultuous thoughts. There was no mess. He was going to wed the girl of his dreams, the vision of loveliness who had inspired him to change his life.

He spotted Bainbridge just entering and called out to him, earning filthy looks from some of the other men, the ones who came there for quiet. Motioning to Bainbridge to follow him, together they found a quiet niche away from other club members and sat down.

"What the devil do you mean, escaping the ball that way when you had just come back? I looked everywhere for you before that footman found me with your message." Bainbridge stared at him, a dark frown on his face.

Pierson took a deep breath. He had to calm himself. He was not the impetuous fool he used to be, he told himself. He had decided that Lady Rowena was the one and had wooed her for weeks now, steady and slow. It was all planned out in his mind, the proposal, the wedding, and Delacorte. She seemed to like him well enough, so now he would ask her to marry him and then ask her father. Then they would marry and he would take her back to Delacorte and they would live happily ever after.

Ah, but there was the rub. He couldn't see her at Delacorte. And yet, she was a strong young lady; she would adjust her life of luxury as the pampered daughter of a duke to the Spartan existence they would need to live for a while. Surely she would. It would test their love and they would triumph.

Bainbridge still stared at him. His tone gentler, he said, "What's wrong with you, Pierson? You look . . . quite awful. Ill."

"I'm not ill," he snapped. "I'm . . . I'm going to ask Lady Rowena for her hand tomorrow."

He expected some resistance. Bainbridge had been distinctly odd for a couple of weeks now, but he would hear of nothing against his ladylove. Bainbridge would just have to learn to love her as his friend's wife.

Bainbridge rose and paced for a moment, and then turned to stand in front of Pierson. "My friend, what I'm about to say will shock you. You may hate me, I don't know, but I have to say it. You don't love her, Pierson, and she doesn't love you. You only love who you think she is, some pure, sweet flower, and she's not that. She is gloriously wild and contrary."

"I knew you would try to talk me out of this," Pierson said, leaping to his feet and facing his friend. "I knew it! I was prepared for this. But you don't know her well enough, that's all."

"I know her better than you think," Bainbridge said, with an odd laugh. "I know her better than you. Do you know, Pierson, she remembers you from that mucky night when you were on the road and first saw her in her carriage."

Pierson gasped in alarm, his eyes wide.

"Oh, she doesn't know it was you and I didn't enlighten her. But she remembers you, kneeling in the filthy water, dripping wet, accompanied by two whores. She saw you from the safety and warmth of her carriage. She told me all about the incident, and Pierson," Bainbridge thrust his face closer to his friend. "Pierson, my friend, she *laughed*." He poked the viscount in the chest. "She laughed about you being soaking wet and inebriated with your two . . . friends. Miss Corbett wanted to go back and help you but Rowena would not allow it. She thought it was hysterically funny, and that you got what you deserved." He paced away, his fists balled.

"I don't believe you," Pierson said, his voice coming out in a hoarse croak. No, he would not allow Bainbridge to taint the memory of that moment of realization for him. He remembered with such great clarity Lady Rowena Revington's pale, lovely face in the carriage window, and how it struck him at that moment that he wanted that beauty in his life, that purity, that sweetness. He had transformed his life based on that one moment, and he would not allow Bainbridge to taint it, or to mock it. It was not a fraud. "I don't know what's wrong with you Bainbridge, but I will not smash you in the face as you deserve. I will hear nothing more against Lady Rowena, as she will be my wife. If we are to be friends no more . . ." He couldn't finish that sentence, for to lose Bainbridge's friendship was an awful consequence.

"I have nothing to say against Rowena, my friend." With a heavy sigh, Bainbridge paced over and put his hand on his friend's shoulder. "But you'll never marry her."

"I am ready to counter whatever the duke has to say against me. I know I'm not the richest man or have the best title. But I am willing to work. And I'll wait to marry, if he thinks . . ."

"No, Pierson, I mean you will not marry her because . . ." Bainbridge, his face white and his lips compressed in a tight line, swallowed. "I hate to do this to you my friend, but you don't understand her and you don't love her for who she really is."

"What are you saying?"

"I'm saying that you only love who you think she is; you love this simple, pure, sweet flower. But Rowena is willful and selfish and a little wild. You would hate each other within a se'nnight. You would

311

hate her because she couldn't forever be who you want her to be, and you would think she changed horribly after marriage. She would hate you for expecting things from her that she can't possibly live up to. No one is that perfect, Pierson. *No one.*"

"You're out of your mind."

"No, I'm not. And . . ." Bainbridge stared at Pierson. "Oh, God, this is so much harder than I even thought it would be." He took in a deep breath and let it out slowly. "You're going to hate me but I can't help it, I can't! If there was any other way . . . Pierson, she doesn't love you. She loves me. We're eloping this very night."

"Eloping?" Pierson felt a strange urge to laugh at his friend's words. Instead he blurted, "Are you out of your mind? You're lying, or you're imagining . . ."

"No, hear me out!" Bainbridge put out one hand to ward off Pierson's vituperation. "I had to do it this way. I knew that if I went to the duke he would accept my suit in a second and bring pressure to bear on Rowena. But I want her to want me. I believe she loves me, but I want her to choose me and to be willing to defy society, to do what she has never done and expose herself for the wild girl she is."

Pierson felt sick inside. Could this be

true? Surely not! He felt weak inside, as if his very entrails were collapsing. "But Bain, you . . . No, I won't believe it. You would never do such a mad, impetuous, wild thing! You are staid, respectable . . ."

"And sick to death of it!" Bain was shouting now, red faced and angry. "I will do this," he said, jabbing the air with one finger. "I will run away with her and cause a scandal, and then joyfully do my damnedest to live it down."

"How can you do this?" Pierson mumbled, his voice sounding hollow and sick even to himself. This was a bad dream only; it must be, for everything in the world was strange to him that moment, including his own feelings. He should be devastated. He should be angry. He wasn't, but neither did he know *how* he felt. But still he said the right words, the words that expressed how he *should* be feeling at that moment. "How can you do this knowing how I feel about her, knowing of my love, and how I have . . ."

"Leave off! You don't love her," Bainbridge said, savagely, pacing like a caged lion. "You love some chimera, some . . ." He stopped pacing and glared at his friend. "Think about it, Pierson. Who do you really love?"

Pierson dropped into a leather chair and covered his face with his hands. "Rowena, of course! Have I not told you so?"

"Time and time again, but I don't believe you." Bainbridge took a deep breath and his voice was calmer when he spoke again. "I hope you don't hate me, old man, but I must do this. If I did things through the proper channels I would never know if she married me for the right reasons, Rowena being who she is. If she does this, if she runs away with me, abandons all her rigid training, and all the effort she has put into forming her public face, then I will always know what a great sacrifice she has made for me. And I will spend the rest of my life making it up to her."

Pierson uncovered his face and gazed up at his friend. "But Bain, your mother, your sister . . ."

"Harriet will laugh. Mother will be furious, but she'll come around once the first baby comes."

"You're out of your mind!"

Bainbridge laughed. "You know, I think you're right! Isn't it wonderful?" He turned on his heel and strode to the doorway of the private room, but turned back just before leaving. "Wish me well, Pierson, and don't hate me. This will be best for you, you'll see. If you search your heart, I know you'll find the truth."

Cold fury clutched Pierson. This was the death of all his carefully laid plans, all his hopes for the future. How could Bainbridge think he would just accept this outcome? "I will despise you for the rest of my life, Bain, I swear it."

Amy awoke at dawn to the sounds of crying, a long keening wail that could only indicate something was terribly wrong. Puss had heard it too and was glaring at the door, her green eyes holding something like irritation. After a night of too little sleep, tossing and turning, Amy drew on her robe and wearily left her room, trying to find the source of the lament. She had not far to go, for it was from Lady Rowena's room.

She ran into the bedchamber, fearing sickness or injury, to find Jeanette standing by the bed holding a piece of paper in one hand and tearing at her hair with the other.

"Jeanette, what is it? What's wrong?"

"Milady, Milady Rowena . . . she is gone, zut, like that, *gone!* What have she done? Where have she gone?"

The maid's voice was rising to hysteria and ended on a shriek. She fell to the floor.

"Jeanette, slow down! What do you mean?" Amy trotted across the room, knelt by the woman and yanked the piece of paper out of her hand. She looked it over, could not understand it and read it again, more slowly.

Amy, I have gone to follow my heart. I know you won't understand this, any of you, but I have decided there are some things more important than my reputation, and being with the man I love is one of them. I know we should have waited, but I didn't want to. Good-bye. Tell Papa to treat you well, and I'll explain all when I come back.

Rowena

Amy plunked down on the smooth bedcover and laid the paper carefully down as the maid collapsed and wept softly on the carpeted floor. So, Rowena had run away with Lord Pierson after all, and after what happened last night! How could he do that?

How could he, after kissing her —

She pushed away all personal feeling. First, Amy thought, she must find a way of concealing this from the duke and recovering Rowena before word got out of her precipitate action. If the pair could be brought back to London and married quickly, or —

Amy could not get past that. Marriage, to Lord Pierson. She had known it was going to happen, but for it to be so sudden! And why had he done things this way, forsaking his new steadiness, his intent to recover the Pierson name from decades of infamy? An elopement would just undo all the good work he had done in the past month. It was a shocking conclusion to the Season for both Lord Pierson and Lady Rowena. Was it because of his embarrassment over kissing *her* that way in the garden the previous night? She covered her face with her hands. Oh, Lord, she hoped not, but he had seemed horrified by what he had done, even though she would never forget the moment of his lips touching hers and the way her heart had soared for that brief, precious instant.

She took a deep breath and stood. She had to act and quickly; she had to make sure no one —

The roar from down the hall was her first inkling that she would never have the chance to hide Rowena's elopement from the duke. It was already too late. Servants' gossip had no doubt been the rapid carrier of the awful truth.

It struck her in that second that of all the people in the whole affair it was likely *she* who would pay the highest price.

The day passed in a blur from there, from her initial encounter with the enraged duke, through the shocked murmurings of the serving staff — whom she finally had to gather and, with the help of the house-keeper warn not to spread gossip — and on through a mind-numbing hour of writing notes to cancel engagements with feeble excuses. Only one brief encounter stood out with great clarity.

She had a visitor in the early afternoon just before she was scheduled to meet with the duke, who had demanded a formal audience. Apprised of her waiting visitor, Amy wasn't sure who to expect, but entered the drawing room to find Lady Harriet waiting, ankles primly crossed and gloved hands folded.

"My lady," Amy said, with a curtsey. "I . . . I take it you have heard of our . . . our trouble." She couldn't imagine any other reason for the lady to visit.

"*Heard* of it? Well, of course." She laughed, but it was a mirthless sound. "But surely not *your* trouble only, Miss

Corbett," Lady Harriet said, compressing her lips in a tight line.

"What do you mean?"

"Your charge has beguiled my poor, infatuated brother into eloping with her. Surely that is as much to do with us as it is to do with your household?"

"Your . . . brother?" Amy sat down abruptly, that seeming her only reaction to things lately, she thought. Her knees were perpetually weak. "Lord *Bainbridge?*"

"Yes, who did you think . . ."

"Lord Pierson, surely! He was . . . I know for a fact he wished to . . ." Amy couldn't finish her words. Her mouth had gone suddenly dry.

Lady Harriet shook her head. "Another poor fool. What is it about that girl that has men acting like idiots? Shrewsbury, Pierson, and even my sensible brother." The lady rose. "Well, I just came here to find out if you knew where they would be heading; my mother, as you can imagine is distraught and beside herself. But clearly, if you did not even know it was Bain, then you wouldn't have any idea where they would be."

"Oh, poor Lord Pierson!" Amy said. "How crushed he will be."

"Yes, well, I heard from Bain's valet that

Pierson had an urgent message from home; something about his land manager being found, or something like that. Anyway, he has departed from London and no one expects him back after this humiliation. It was so very clear he was courting Lady Rowena; he will not want to face London society for some time, the object of a jilt like your precious Lady Rowena! If we do not learn something this day, we are leaving London, too. Neither my mother nor I wish to be here for any length of time. Good day, Miss Corbett. Next time you take on a charge, perhaps you should consider the efficacy of locks on bedroom doors." She departed without another word.

It was a lot to take in and Amy was stunned still when she had her confrontation with the duke.

He was wild with baffled fury. How could Miss Corbett betray his trust in her so contemptibly, allowing such shame to fall on his old and untarnished name?

Amy tried to defend herself, and asked how could she be considered to blame when she hadn't even known who Lady Rowena had eloped with. She informed the duke that it was Lord Bainbridge who was the culprit, not Lord Pierson as she had originally surmised.

But no. The duke was emphatic; it was clearly all her doing. Base, treacherous, despicable: His Grace used all of those words and more, and within two hours Amy found herself on the other side of the ducal door, with her shabby bag in one hand and Puss in the other and a few coins tucked into her reticule, the duke having deducted from her quarter's wage the cost of her dresses, despite what he had originally said, which was that they were part of her pay.

It was the great fear of her life; no position, no money, and nowhere to go. A hollow pain rumbled in her stomach, the twisting, coiling sensation of fear roiling in her gut. The staff had been aghast at the duke's actions, but not a one dared defend or aid her except the housekeeper, who pressed a couple of coins into her hand and a bundle of food.

Where would she go? Mrs. Bower was a dependent like her; she couldn't help. Amy's Aunt Marabelle down in Kent had no room, for she had taken a lodger in to her tiny cottage to make ends meet. Amy was alone in London, with only her own wits to guide her.

What was she going to do?

Twenty

The cramped boardinghouse where Amy found temporary recourse was a noisome place. The odors of cooking — mostly cabbage and fish — unwashed bodies, and other unsavory smells clogged her nose and fouled her clothing. The stairs were dark and cramped, her room shabby, and yet the landlady was kind, despite her appearance of tottering around in a gin-soaked haze most of the time.

Sleep came, as each night closed in, only after exhausting hours tossing and turning on the narrow, thinly padded bed and only because with Puss there, at least, to curl up and purr, Amy felt some small measure of comfort. She wasn't alone in her misery.

But for all her frugality in choosing the cheapest boarding house she could find, Amy's money would run out soon and she didn't know where to turn. She had to plan, had to find some work, *anything* to feed and house herself and precious Puss. She was frightened and her stomach always ached, but she refused to give in to fear.

"I don't know what we shall do, Puss," Amy said, as she walked along a dingy street carrying her carpet bag, in which Puss resided. Amy couldn't stand to leave her cat in the boarding house, not with the way other inmates of that place eyed the animal. In fact she couldn't stand to leave anything of hers there, and so she carried her meager belongings as she walked, trying to find a decent job, or *any* job.

It was the most frightening feeling, having no home, no family and no one to whom she could turn. Mrs. Bower had offered her what money she had and Amy wasn't proud; if she was destitute she would take it.

But it didn't solve her problem, and that was employment and a place to reside.

The backstreets of London, even on a lovely spring day with a blue sky overhead, were dull and grimy, a coating of filth over everything. Amy shrunk from the scurrying rats and slimy, malodorous heaps of offal and considered her limited choices. She had tried a couple of employment agencies, but had met with a blank stare when she tried to skirt around her lack of recommendations. Apparently the assurance that her last but one family, the Donegals of Ireland, had been very happy with her was not enough to make them enthusiastic about her chances at a respectable position. A commendation from an Irish family was almost as good as no recommendation at all.

And so she had tried seamstress shops to no avail. The proprietors looked her over, her soft hands, her ladylike demeanor, and apparently decided — Amy was not privy to their thoughts, but it was all she could conjecture — that she was unlikely to work hard enough, nor take the pitiful wage they were willing to pay to an untried worker.

It had been three days since that awful afternoon that she had been tossed out of the duke's home. Three days of little sleep and endless worry. Though her own survival had taken the uppermost place in her mind, she had spared some late night thoughts, as Puss curled up to her and purred, to wonder how Lord Pierson had taken the news that his intended bride and his best friend had run away together. He must have been so sad, she thought, aching to reach out to him and knowing she never could.

She should be happy, she supposed, that he had retreated from London to his country home, but it made her feel just so much more lonely.

What was Lord Bainbridge thinking? He had seemed such a level-headed gentleman, and Amy had had no idea that he and Rowena had even come to like each other, much less love each other. It was unaccountable. It had occurred to her though, that perhaps she had been a little too taken up with talking to Lord Pierson to notice her charge's emotional changes.

For when she looked back, she could remember subtle changes in Rowena's demeanor. She had been more thoughtful, and her pettish outbursts had almost disappeared in the last few weeks. Often she had asked odd questions of Amy, like that one about how to tell if one was in love. Had she even then been falling in love with Lord Bainbridge? Amy had been so sure that Lord Pierson was her object that she had failed to notice anything else. How blind she had been. And yet, what good would it have done to know ahead of time? Would she have been able to change how things came about?

And why on earth had Rowena and the eminently respectable, eligible Lord Bainbridge eloped? It was a puzzle with no answer.

She trudged down the alley, taking what she hoped was a shortcut to another employment agency and sidestepping yet another pile of refuse, where skittering movements indicated the presence of creatures best left to her vivid imagination. Puss growled in his hideaway and she muttered, "Yes, I know you would like your chance to rid the alley of such creatures, but I will not risk your precious life in the pursuit of such diseased vermin."

As she was scampering past an open door, Amy heard shouting and a woman's scream and stopped, undecided as to whether someone needed her help. Just then a female form, slovenly and staggering, reeled out the door.

"And don't come back again, you drunken sot!" That was a man, his face red with anger.

The woman stumbled to a halt and screamed back at him, an unintelligible string of words that Amy could not make out the meaning of.

"Ya had yer chance," the man returned, apparently understanding her quite well. "Ya wouldn't find a better gent to work fer than Mr. Lessington, but ya abused yer place, and now yer gone. Yer never could sew a straight line h'anyway!"

The woman reeled off, cursing and mut-
tering. The man was about to close the
door after an incurious glance at Amy, but
fear and desperation made her bolder than
she would have believed possible.

"Pardon, sir, but did I hear you correctly? Was that woman a seamstress, and
has she been let go?" Amy clutched her
bag to her, hoping Puss did not let out a
yowl just then.

"Yep, she were. What's it to you?" He
looked her over, his words more unfriendly
than his look.

"Just that . . . I happen to be a seamstress in need of a position. I'm very proficient, and . . ."

"Do yer drink?"

"No."

"Do yer have a man?"

"N-no."

"Can yer start now?"

"Yes," she said, then timidly added, "but
first, what manner of place is this? I cannot
tell from this back alley."

That was when the man laughed, a
hearty sound that ended on a wheezing
cough. He held the door open and ges-
tured her to enter. "Now I say, that means
yer must be desperate-loike fer a job, eh?
If'n yer willin' ter work here and don't

know what we does. H'its a theater, missy, and *we* be in desperate need o' someone who can stitch a straight line with no airs, mind you, and no drinking! One whiff o' gin an' yer out."

A theater! Costumes! Amy squeezed past the man into a dark hallway. He shut the door with a slam and locked it, then took her arm and guided her down the Stygian dark corridor, past closed doors behind which stentorian voices declaimed in the bard's words, and high fluting voices practiced operatic runs and snatches of arias.

It was a kind of heaven for Amy, who had always loved the theater, amateur or professional, but had never been in the bowels of a *real* theater.

The man, who introduced himself as Jackson, pushed her into a dusty, grimy room and showed her where the supplies were and what needed to be done. She went to work immediately in the tiny closet of a room. She was not the wardrobe mistress or anything so very grand, but there were miles and miles of straight hems to be done, tedious eye-straining work. And yet she was happy at last, because there was room for Puss to lounge on a stack of loose fabric, and a kindly person brought her lunch, an eel pie which she shared with the cat and weak tea for herself.

The room darkened gradually, and she lit a stubby candle and kept working by its flickering light; silence fell in the back rooms as the theater filled and the actors moved to their positions in the wings. They were mounting a Restoration comedy, as well as presenting a popular actor who was offering Shakespeare soliloquies between acts and before the farce.

Amy worked on; she had no desire to go back to her boardinghouse that night or ever. She glanced around and wondered if anyone would notice if she made her bed there for the night.

Someone opened the door behind her and poked his head in. "Jackson back here?"

Amy looked toward the door to find a slim man of middle years in the doorway.

"No," she replied, shyly, of the man, Jackson, who was the one who had hired her and was apparently the backstage manager as well as being properties master. "I . . . I think he said he was checking on the gaslights; there was some problem, I believe."

"You're new, aren't you?" the man said, entering.

Amy nodded, but went back to her work,

not wishing to encourage the man if he was looking for something she was not willing to give. She was not as innocent as she had been just days before in the ways of the world and the position of women in it. She had learned that as difficult as her life had been so far, it had still been sheltered from some rough realities up to now.

Puss rose and stretched, sharpening her claws on the pile of fabric. She jumped down and twined herself around the man's legs, for all the world as if he had beckoned her. Amy glanced over and saw the man pick Puss up and the cat luxuriantly rubbed her face against his immaculate waistcoat, leaving gray fur as her mark.

"Is she yours?"

"Yes," Amy replied. She felt like holding her breath. Who was this man? Had he the authority to tell her to get the cat out of there? He was fastidiously groomed and well dressed. Perhaps he was a playwright, or manager. There were often superstitions about cats, and actors and theater people were notoriously superstitious.

"She's beautiful." He held her up and gazed into her eyes, then cradled her in his arms again. "I have a theory that cats were put on this earth to remind us that beauty and utility can sometimes be combined.

She is a lovely creature, but there is no more efficient mouser in the world than a female cat. I'm sorry, miss, but I don't know your name?"

"Miss Amy Corbett," she replied, keeping her eyes on her work.

"You know," he said, and then hesitated. He began again, "You know, the last woman, the one who was let go today, she made herself comfortable here. If you like . . . that is . . . If you care to, you may stay in this room as long as you like. Just tell Jackson."

Amy stared up at him in the flickering candlelight and stuttered, "Th-thank you . . . Mr. uh . . ."

He smiled a self-deprecating grin as he put Puss down and headed for the door. "Just tell Jackson that Mr. Lessington says you may stay in this room and make it comfortable. And have him tell the food mistress to bring you tea and food whenever you need it."

And he was gone, before she could stutter a thanks to the theater owner.

Twenty-one

Pierson put his head in his hands and groaned. Numbers danced before his eyes when he closed them, though, and so he opened them, rubbing the grit out of the corners. April had already passed, and so had May and June in a haze of work . . . long hours so he would not have to think of Lady Rowena and all he had lost.

He sat back wearily in his chair at the desk in the library of Delacorte. It was dark outside, and since it was past the middle of July that meant that it was very late indeed. And yet he had accomplished a great deal just that day. He had confirmed a buyer for a stand of timber that he was clearing in a far corner of his land with the intention of putting more land to crops. The money from the timber meant he could make needed improvements to the dairy and begin the apiary that he felt would increase profits. Research had shown him that there was no apiary for miles around and yet there was a local market for honey. It would take a few years to see any profit, but it would be a steady money-maker. He had thought at first it would mean hiring a beekeeper, but it turned out that the man his land steward had hired to manage the new orchards was also adept at the science of keeping bees. The hives would complement his orchard.

He had come so far in just three months. Life had changed in ways he had never fathomed when he retreated to Delacorte, hurt and angry, to bury himself in estate work. He supposed he should be grateful that the message that reached him that morning — the morning of Bainbridge and Lady Rowena's scandalous elopement — that Mr. Lincoln, his missing estate manager's whereabouts had been discovered. If he had not had to go to Delacorte immediately when he heard that the former manager had apparently died in another county, with no one knowing who he was, the tragic victim of robbers, who knows if he would ever have left London? After Bainbridge's perfidy and Rowena's desertion the temptation would have been strong to plunge himself back into the life he had formerly known, the life of drinking, gambling, and whoring.

The necessity to go home and handle things had immersed him, instead, in the work of recovering the estate. And he had found a joy in the work that he had never anticipated. Instead of the drudgery he had expected, there was gratification in the labor and a quiet satisfaction at the end of the exhausting days.

It occurred to him in that moment that Amy Corbett had been right. He had thought about her often over the months, especially as memories of Lady Rowena faded. Amy had been right when she told him once that if he just started, he would soon find himself wholly engrossed in his work, because he would see a return and would be spurred on to further improvement. His reformation had not been without setbacks, but he had steadily improved and now couldn't imagine any other life.

The housekeeper, Mrs. Manton, peeked in and seeing him awake, pushed in with her hip and put a tray bearing a late dinner down on the desk. "You mustn't go without something to eat, milord," she said, admonishment in her voice.

He grinned up at her as he leaned back in his chair, stretching and putting his hands behind his head. The first month he had resided at Delacorte, Mrs. Manton had barely acknowledged his existence.

The second month she had been starchy, but had slowly thawed, her manner becoming less rigid and more imperious. And now she treated him like the child she once knew, the one who, in his infrequent visits home from school, would haunt the kitchen demanding seed cake and milk at all hours.

The rest of the staff had followed her lead and now he could feel it; they *almost* trusted him. Almost, but not quite. True trust would take longer, years perhaps. He had generations of ill treatment to make up for, but had made a start.

He sat upright and uncovered the dish to find his favorite pigeon pie. "Thank you Mrs. M., and thank Cook, too. She doesn't have to cook for me these late hours, you know. I'll make do with a slice of bread and some jam. I wish to keep no one awake with me."

"She considers it an honor and a privilege," the woman said, with a sniff. "Don't complain. Before you came back she was on the point of leaving. She may be getting on in years but a good cook will always find a position. Now her only complaint is that it is high time you found a wife. The house has not had a viscountess for many, many years."

Pierson frowned down at the dish and stabbed it with his fork, the flaky crust breaking open to allow the fragrant steam out. He thought back to his intentions to marry and bring Lady Rowena here as his bride. That seemed so long ago now, and when he tried to imagine it, he couldn't. What would she have done? In truth, she likely would have complained constantly and been a burden on the staff, rather than the helpmeet he had pictured.

He remembered what Amy had said to him, that he could not marry virtue and expect it to rub off. Virtue was a habit, she said, and no one could instill that in him but himself.

How right she had been! It had taken much work to make new habits, ones of frugality, steadiness, and self-restraint. He had been tempted many times when the work had overwhelmed him, but always a soft voice in his mind had urged him on. Amy Corbett's voice. He looked up to find that the housekeeper had left and he dug into his dinner and ate steadily, remembering all of the conversations he and Amy had had, all of her wise words that he had not heeded then, but had since found to be true.

And his mind turned, as it often had, to

that last night, and the kiss.

The kiss. He had kissed her on an impulse, but impulses come from somewhere. He remembered gazing down at her in the moonlight, thinking he had never seen anyone quite so pretty, and then he had leaned in and kissed her lips. And he had wanted more, but had been shocked at his own thoughts; had disowned them, in fact, and backed off as if he had just faced the unthinkable.

The "unthinkable" being that he had made a terrible error in judgment in pinning all his hopes and amorous impulses on the wrong lady. He neatly sidestepped that thought once again and wondered instead, where was Amy? Had she stayed at the duke's residence . . . Well, no, of course she wouldn't do that, because with Rowena gone there would be no position for her. But surely she would have gotten another. Or she would have retreated to her aunt's in Kent. Possibly near him!

The thought that had begun as a random notion took hold. He had pictured Amy often over the months, her eyes, her face, her slim form. More than Lady Rowena, certainly; more than anyone. And after the initial shock, he realized that he had not grieved overmuch over Lady Rowena and

Bainbridge's perfidious behavior. In fact, he rather wished them well. If they loved each other so much they felt compelled to run away, then they surely belonged together. Why they had to do it in such a precipitate manner he still didn't understand, but it didn't touch his heart anymore.

But Amy: What had *she* done? Had the duke been angry that his daughter, supposedly in her care, had eloped?

He laid down his fork. Yes, knowing by reputation the difficult and demanding duke, he would have been furious and he would have let Amy go and he would have even spread across the *ton* that she was not to be trusted with precious daughters, and —

And he would not have given her a reference. Though Pierson didn't know much about the workings of chaperons and such, surely the duke's word would count heavily against her. And if she had been working as a chaperon and a governess before that, she clearly did not have any resources or money of her own. Or any place to go.

Pierson rose out of his chair as he pictured Amy Corbett's sweet, innocent face, turned up to his trustingly. Perhaps he ought to inquire about her. There was a woman in London whom she was friendly with, another chaperon . . . What was her name? *She* would know where Amy was.

It meant he would have to go back to London, and he felt a kind of dread of the place as the source of all evil in his life. He paced behind his chair and stopped, staring blankly at the empty fireplace. His long ten years haunting London hells and brothels felt like a prolonged nightmare now, a dream from which he had awoken, to find that there was so much more to life.

And it was all because of Miss Amy Corbett; she had given him the confidence in himself and the courage to do what he had to do. Just knowing she believed in him had made a world of difference. He had forged ahead in his new life and had made a success, so far, of everything he had had to do, learning the business of running an estate and farming with no prior knowledge.

She had believed in him and cared enough to talk to him about his estate, giving him solid advice, listening to his doubts, doing everything, in short, that a lady whom he would want to marry should do.

What was it that Bainbridge had asked him that last night? Who did he really love?

He slapped his forehead and sank down into his chair. It had been there in front of him the whole time and he had stupidly ignored it. Amy Corbett; she was the one, the ideal lady, the sweet, honest, worthy, lovely, decent, intelligent —

And was he doing the same idiotic thing he had done with Lady Rowena, attributing every virtue to her just because he cared for her? But no, she had demonstrated every day and in every way that she was all he could have imagined in a young lady.

It was true, he finally acknowledged; he loved her, but even if she didn't love him, even if she cared for him in no way other than a friend, he had to find out if she was all right, if she needed anything, or was in trouble in any way. Three months! He couldn't believe he had let three months go by without thinking of her safety, her comfort, and doing something to ensure it.

How could he have been so remiss?

He pushed aside his tray, his half-eaten dinner congealing greasily on the plate, and gathered some papers. He would need to write a note for his manager, telling him what he wanted done in his absence, and then he would head for London. And he would track down Amy Corbett and make sure she wanted for nothing.

And maybe, if he had the courage, he would tell her he loved her.

Maybe.

Amy pored over her sketches and opened a book to a well-thumbed page and shook her head. No, the costume would not do yet. The tiny airless room was sweltering hot and she pushed back one damp, errant curl as she made a few alterations to her sketch.

"How is my new wardrobe mistress?"

She looked up at the pleasant masculine voice and smiled. It was Mr. Lessington in the doorway. Puss leaped down from her perch to greet him and he affectionately reached down and petted her, scratching behind her ears just as she liked.

"Doing well, sir, but I just cannot get this Restoration costume quite right. If you are to have *She Stoops To Conquer* ready for the Little Season I will need to have the ladies' costumes done. The gentlemen's are right and the girls are working on them as we speak."

The theater owner sauntered into the room, looking cool and composed as always despite the July heat. Puss followed and twined around his legs. "I'm convinced you have been sent by an angel," he said, with a smile. "We have never had such wonderful costuming. Dress rehearsal for the Scottish play today. I'm looking forward to that. Will you join me in the wings to watch your costumes at work?"

He touched her shoulder lightly and she smiled at him and nodded. She had learned over time not to worry about his affectionate gestures. There was no man in the world from whom she had less to fear than her employer. She had been shocked when she learned his loosely kept "secret," but now it was simply a part of him, just as his immaculate dress and calm manner. He had no interest in ladies and it was rather freeing, she found; the actresses in his theater felt the same way, they had whispered to her as they told her about his private life. Mr. Lessington was a comforting gentleman to be around, the girls had told her, and one whom they could trust not to make demands of a sexual nature, unlike many theater owners and managers.

He put his arm over her shoulders and they both looked down at her sketch. "This looks wonderful. Whatever is wrong with it?"

"I cannot determine if this is accurate, this swooping part of the skirt." She pointed with her charcoal. "It is all so wonderfully different from the current mode of dress, so elaborate, and yet for this play the ladies' clothes especially must be simpler to achieve the right effect."

"You worry too much, Amy." He squeezed her shoulder and straightened. "You know our patrons aren't going to know the difference."

"I suppose. But it matters to me. Would you like a cup of tea, sir?" she asked, indicating the chipped pot on the table. She had, over the last three months, not only risen in stature from lowly seamstress to wardrobe mistress due solely to her hard work, imagination, and the ability of Mr. Lessington to recognize her learning and ability to design original costumes, but she had also made herself comfortable in the little room, making it her own, scrubbing and cleaning and organizing, and even furnishing to a degree. In the autumn she would need to find herself a place to stay that had a fireplace, but for now, she was quite comfortable. Over the months she and her employer had shared many a cup of dark black tea, both having a preference for a strong brew over the anemic one the food mistress offered from her urn.

"No, I don't think I have time." He

strolled to the doorway. "By the way," he said, casually. "There was a fellow here earlier asking about a Miss Corbett. I had Jackson deny you, since I didn't know . . . Well, you showed up with no money and nowhere to go and you have not been terribly forthcoming about your past. Not that I am prying for more information," he added, holding up one hand, "but I was afraid . . . You wouldn't be the first young lady to be trying to evade the, uh, attentions of a gentleman of aristocratic background."

Amy frowned. "Looking for me? A gentleman? What did he look like?"

"I didn't get a look at him. Jackson merely said 'aristocratic.' That could mean anything to him, you know, from a canary waistcoat to an accent."

"I'm not hiding from anyone, Mr. Lessington, I promise you that." Amy wondered if it was perhaps the duke at long last regretting his behavior, but if the duke had been to the theater there could be no doubt as to his aristocratic bearing. Could it be Lord Bainbridge then? "And I can't imagine who it would be," she added.

As her employer sauntered from the room after her firm negative, she shrugged it off and tried to forget it. She had worked hard to make a life for herself and felt more self-reliant than she ever had in her life. Her greatest fear had always been having to find work completely on her own, with no connections, no recommendations, no references. Well, she had had to do it, and she had done it. She had turned her one bit of luck — passing by the back of Mr. Lessington's theater when the seamstress was being ejected — into a position of respectability and if not wealth, at least a subsistence. Her wage would go up once the Little Season started and the plays were being mounted.

The day continued and finally it was time for the final dress rehearsal of Macbeth, "the Scottish play" as it would only ever be called in the theater. Amy stood off stage and watched, particularly paying attention to her costumes and how they moved, if they interfered, if they inhibited the actors and actresses at all.

Finally they came to one of the most haunting scenes, in Amy's estimation. Act Five, Scene One, and Lady Macbeth, candle in hand, wandered, sleepwalking and moaning, her nightclothes disarrayed. As the "Doctor" and the "Gentlewoman," as the play styled the two other players in the scene, watched and conferred, the actress wandered, giving her speeches, "*Out damned spot!*" and the rest. But Amy noted that as she rubbed her hands over and over, the frill on the edge of her nightclothes became tangled. That would never do!

As "Lady Macbeth" at the end of the scene exited, Amy called her over. "Dolly! Let me see that nightgown!"

The actress, one of the more obliging and less demanding, obediently approached. "What is it, Amy? It played well, don't you think?"

"Yes, except that the frill of this gown sleeve is going to give you trouble. Let me see it." As the actress held out her hand, Amy examined the cuff of the nightgown. "There's the problem," she said, turning up a seam and pinning it with a spare pin from her dress. "One of the girls did not take this up as I indicated."

Just then the actress pulled her hand away and Amy looked up. "What is it Dolly, what . . ."

Standing nearby, gazing at her with his mouth open, was the last person she expected to see there and then. It was Lord Pierson.

Pierson stared at Amy in disbelief. She was dressed as she always was, in a sober gray gown, but it was adorned in the oddest way, with rows of pins along the cuff and the collar. What was she doing backstage? He hadn't believed Mrs. Bower when that good woman had asserted that Amy, *his* Amy, as he had rapidly begun to think of her, was working at a theater in some sewing capacity. And earlier in the day they had been vague about the possibility that she was employed at the theater, enough so that he had come back to check again and pushed his way backstage. But this job, this position was hardly respectable for a gently raised young lady!

"Amy! What are you doing here?"

She stared at him and smiled. The actress in front of her glanced first at one and then at the other and then retreated, whispering to a rough looking man by the curtain rope.

"I'm working! I am wardrobe mistress here. Isn't it grand?"

"Grand? No! Good God, Amy, this is hardly a respectable position for one of your . . . for you." He moved toward her and took her hand. "Come, you must leave at once."

"Leave? Absolutely not! What are you talking about?" She jerked her hand out of his grasp.

"This is no place for you to be working. Come, we'll find you some place else to stay. Do you have lodgings? Shall we go there and get your bags?"

"My lord," she said, stiffly, evading his grasp when he would take her hand again. "This is my position and I like it. It is also my home. Mr. Lessington has been kind enough to allow me to stay here."

"Stay . . . here? Amy, of all the . . . a theater? This is not a fit place and you must know that!"

"Amy, do you need my help?"

Out of the gloom of the backstage area a very correctly dressed gentleman of middle years strolled into the dim light. He approached Amy and put one hand, proprietarily, on her shoulder.

She covered his hand with her own and smiled at him gratefully. "No, I'm all right. Lord Pierson was just leaving."

"I was not. Not without you, Amy."

"I believe the lady said you were just leaving," the man said. "Jackson?" he added, raising his voice slightly.

The rough-looking fellow the actress had spoken to moved forward. "Yerse, Mr. Lessington?"

"See this gentleman out."

"Here now," Pierson said, glaring at the

348

man and wondering what he was to Amy, with his hand so familiarly on her shoulder. "What's going on? Who are you and what are you to Amy?"

"Jackson?"

The tall fellow moved forward.

"No," Amy said. She gazed steadily at Pierson. "That's not necessary, is it, my lord? You will leave on your own without assistance."

"Amy," he said, and stretched out one hand. "I just . . . You must see that you cannot work here! It's . . . It's scandalous!"

Her chin went up. "As scandalous as your own life, my lord? Please leave."

"No! I'm not leaving without you," he said and took one step forward, grabbed her hand and pulled her into his arms. He had no idea what he was about to do until he kissed her, hard and thoroughly. His feelings were a tumult, but feeling her in his arms calmed him.

At first she was quiet in his arms, but then she pushed him away. "How . . . How dare you?" she cried, and turned, fleeing back into the gloom beyond the curtains.

He started to follow but found himself lifted, bodily, by the man named Jackson and another giant of a fellow in Elizabethan dress. And then he was outside in a back alley strewn with filth and inhabited by rats. He limped out of the alley and left, not sure where he was going, and not really caring.

Twenty-two

But that despairing mood only clung to him for a scant half hour. He did care. He cared too much to just let it go. And so he headed to a house he knew well, a mansion in the better section of London.

It was a chance, but one Pierson had to take, and he found that, indeed, the butler admitted that Lord and Lady Bainbridge were just returned from their continental voyage of the last three months. He demanded to see the marquess and was shown into the drawing room that he knew so well. Pacing up and down the carpet, he worried about his problem and wondered if he would ever find a solution.

How did a gentleman convince a lady he had ignored for three months or more that he truly cared for her?

Bainbridge soon joined him. "Pierson, I expected we would see you."

"You look fit, Bain. Congratulations . . . belatedly, of course."

The marquess looked sheepish, for once, and said, "Look, Pierson, I really have to apologize for how we left things, but I was desperate, and I knew it was the right thing to do, and I was right, for . . ."

"Bain, old man, I'm not angry," Pierson said, impatiently. "I have far more pressing things to think of, let me tell you."

"You do?"

"Of course. Good God, you didn't spend your whole wedding trip thinking I was here brooding over your idiotic behavior, did you?"

"Well, yes, I rather did."

"I was very angry at first, but I think my pride was hurt more than anything. No, look Bain, I have a problem and I may need your help."

Just then the new marchioness slipped in, saying, "Did I hear correctly? Is everything all right, Bain?"

"Yes, my dear," the marquess said, holding out one hand for his bride.

Pierson looked her over as she joined her husband, wondering what he had ever seen to love in her. She was still as lovely as ever, and with a new serenity that he knew she had never had before, but she stirred nothing within him. He was cured, it seemed, of that idiotic infatuation. Only to tumble headlong into a new one. But this time he knew it was not mere infatuation;

love had lain unrecognized within his heart, like a seed beneath the snow.

"Look, Bain, Amy is here, in London, but she won't come with me and I need her to, and there is this older fellow, well dressed, some sort of impresario, I suppose, but he seems to have some hold over her and . . ."

"Amy? You mean Miss Corbett? Pierson, what the devil are you talking about?"

Pierson collapsed on the sofa nearest him and buried his head in his hands. He needed to get a grip on his tumbling, wildly riotous emotions. This time the kiss he had shared with Amy had done more than upset his equilibrium and make him wonder what he truly felt. This time he knew he loved her; he was sure of it. All doubt had fled on the wings of a sweet delirium by which he was still possessed.

But calm; he must find calm.

He sighed, scrubbed his eyes and looked at the two. "I suppose I should start at the beginning."

And so he did. They canvassed, as a trio, what had happened, first, that day three months or so before when all of their lives had changed.

Bainbridge and his lady wife explained to Pierson how their antagonism toward each other had been the result of both of them trying to deny feelings that were growing, even though they both tried to disavow them. And Bainbridge had started trying to show Pierson how spoiled and impossible she was by sabotaging things and making her break out into the shrew he believed her to be underneath.

"That was you?" Pierson said, gazing at his old friend in wonder.

Bain shrugged. "Yes. I confessed and Rowena has forgiven me, so I can speak of it now. It was mean-spirited and I have long been ashamed of myself. I can't imagine what came over me to do such tricks." He looked troubled still, and sighed, finally. "I almost feel that was some other fellow, the one who would do something so despicable. But I knew she was not the little turtledove you believed her to be and I couldn't stand that you should woo her under a false banner."

"You were jealous, admit it Bain. You were *terribly* jealous," Lady Bainbridge said, tapping him on the shoulder. She then turned her gaze back to Pierson. "He just wanted me for himself, and wanted you to reject me as an unfit wife," she said, chuckling and squeezing her husband's hand.

Pierson gazed at her steadily, marveling at what marriage could do. He saw that now she was truly content as she never had been before. She had always been restless, he thought, searching for the next admirer, the next besotted suitor, and he had been one of them, more of a challenge perhaps because of his reputation.

But impatient, he said, "The same morning I got a message telling me that poor old Lincoln, my land manager, had been killed in another county by robbers. No one there knew him, for he had nothing left on his body to identify him. So I had to go to his sister — Lincoln was her sole support, I had already found out — and break the news to her. I have since found her a position as cook with a neighbor of mine, and so she is set. But before . . . that night you two eloped . . . I had . . . I kissed Amy . . . Miss Corbett, and . . ." He shook his head, trying to untangle his emotions along with his confused words. "What an idiot I have been," he groaned.

"Amy is working for the family she was with before, the Donegals, is she not?" Lady Bainbridge said. "In Ireland, correct? That is what my father said when I asked him."

"No, she's in London working at a theater," Pierson explained.

"In London . . . a theater?" Rowena appeared shocked and appalled. "I wrote and told my father to take care of her, to be good to her, and he told me just recently — he has forgiven all, now, of course, since he found out that Bain married me the same day we eloped — that he had sent her back to Ireland." She covered her face with her slim, white hands. "All that time . . . all the time we were roaming around Greece and Italy, poor Amy . . . and she was so good to me, and I never thanked her, and I was so wretchedly beastly to her . . ."

Bain pulled her hands away gently and said, as he sat down beside her, "My dear, it was more my fault than anyone's for convincing you to elope. We'll make it up to her and take her away from that wretched theater. She can stay with us, I promise you."

"You're so good, Bain," she said, her smile watery.

"But she won't come," Pierson broke in, before they began to bill and coo like lovebirds. "I spoke to her already, but there is some fellow there who had me thrown out. She says she is wardrobe mistress. I . . . I kissed her again. She must hate me; she pushed me away."

"Let me get this straight; you kissed her in front of others, and after just finding her again! Did you not think you might be taking the poor girl by surprise? After all, she doesn't know how you feel, does she?" The marquess was staring at him as if he was a lunatic.

"Well, no, but . . . I don't know!" A deep sigh shuddered through Pierson and he miserably felt his ineptitude. "I thought I was so proficient at lovemaking; I'm no amateur, anyway. But whenever I'm around her I act like the most absurd fool."

Bainbridge studied his face for a minute, and then said. "I think I'll go and talk to her myself."

"Would you? Only if I go with you, though. I will not stay away."

The marquess nodded. "It's the least I can do, after stealing my lady away from you."

"Amy, who was that gentleman?"

Mr. Lessington had left her alone for a couple of hours and she had retreated back to her cubbyhole, but she had known sooner or later she would owe him an explanation. He stood at her door now with a serious expression.

"Come in, please, sir. Come and sit for a few minutes, if you have time."

"I do. Dress rehearsal went smashingly, with one of the witches falling and spraining her ankle. Enough to prevent it being too perfect, you know, or I would worry."

She smiled over at him as he came in and closed the door behind him. He humored his actors, Amy knew, though he was notoriously not superstitious himself. A bad dress rehearsal meant a good first night, and with the Scottish play that was an especial necessity. "I'm glad it all went well. I wish I had seen the last part."

"You were . . . distracted. Now, who was that young man I had Jackson eject?" He came in and sat down, crossing one leg over the other. Puss deigned to scamper over to him and leap onto his knee, her habitual perch whenever he was near.

Amy sat down in a chair opposite him and gazed down at her hands. They had become work-worn over the last few months, with calluses where the needle pressed as she did the long hems and fine stitching necessary. She did little of the actual stitching herself, now that she had risen to wardrobe mistress and costume designer, but the calluses remained. "His name is Lord Pierson, a viscount, and . . ."

"I know who he is by reputation," Mr. Lessington said. "He's notorious. I believe he is one of those impulsive young men, always looking for a good time, always flirting with actresses and other ladies of their ilk and avoiding disaster by a hair. How is he connected to you? And why did he kiss you?"

Well, that was direct. Amy bit her lip. She supposed her employer had a right to know some of her story. She was secure in her position now and did not fear dismissal. She had worked terribly hard to come to this point and knew her story would not jeopardize that.

"I can't say why he kissed me, sir, as I am not privy to his thoughts. But . . . well, that was not the first time. I'll tell you the story, and it will lead up to the moment I met Mr. Jackson in the back alley of your theater. But I would appreciate it, sir, if you would keep this to yourself."

"Amy," he said, ruffling Puss's fur under her chin, the way she liked. "I am wounded you would think you even had to say that!"

She told him the story lightly skipping over certain areas, such as her own growing tender feelings toward the viscount, and emphasizing his reformation and growing devotion to Lady Rowena and how crushed he must have been when she eloped with the marquess.

At the end of the story Mr. Lessington said, "Hmm, I had heard the gossip, that Lord Bainbridge had eloped with the Duke of Sylverton's daughter. I have many friends in the aristocracy and they love a good scandal. Oddly enough it abated the moment it was learned that there was no terrible secret that made them elope. The girl was apparently not with child, nor was there some awful family secret. According to rumor it was a mad whim on their part, just a young couple wildly in love. They married the very day of their elopement. If there had been a necessity, it would have kept the scandal alive. But since they have come back . . ."

"They're back?" Amy asked. "Rowena and Bainbridge are back?"

"Yes, so I have heard, just days ago. They apparently traveled Europe, roaming over Italy and Greece, the Adriatic . . . The duke was reportedly beside himself. But then, you knew that part, didn't you? Poor girl; you must have been frantic with fear, with no place to go. What a dastard the man is!"

"I was terribly afraid," Amy admitted, reliving for a moment the few days she had spent not knowing how she was going to survive. "The duke is a hard man. I pleaded with him for time to find another position, for a reference so I would be able to find another job, but he was relentless and forced me to leave."

"Spoilt brat, that Lady Rowena, it seems to me."

There was silence for a long minute.

"But my dear," Lessington continued, rising and placing Puss on her throne of silk patchwork that Amy had made from scraps. He crossed to Amy and knelt at her knee, taking her hands in his and caressing them. "That does not explain why Lord Pierson — he is a very handsome young man, by the way — why he grasped you in such a terribly romantic way and kissed you so fiercely."

A tapping at the door interrupted them. Amy rose and opened the door, then backed away from it when the Marquess of Bainbridge, hat in hand, presented himself at the door.

Twenty-three

"Miss Corbett, I . . ." He stopped when he saw that she had company.

Lessington rose from being down on one knee and, when he saw the expression on the marquess' face, said, with a comical lift to his left eyebrow, "No, as much as I care for Miss Corbett, I was not, just now, asking for her hand in marriage. You are . . ." He paused and looked the other man over. "Yes, I believe you are the Marquess of Bainbridge. My lord, as much as I value Miss Corbett as a friend, I fear she and I should not suit. And I believe her heart is already claimed by another."

Amy glanced at him swiftly and felt her cheeks burn again. She had not thought she revealed so much, but then Mr. Lessington was a very perceptive man. Her employer bowed and left the room, saying, before he left, "Amy, dear, I will hear the rest later. Or perhaps . . ." He looked sad for a moment. "Why do I have the feeling you will be leaving us before the Little Season starts?"

"I won't, sir, I promise!"

"Don't promise, dear girl. You must do what is best for yourself and your heart. I care too much for you not to want the best for you." He exited.

As the door closed, Amy tried to still her thumping heart. It had been an upsetting day but she took a deep breath and gazed up at Lord Bainbridge. "Congratulations, sir, I wish you and Rowena all the best. I just wish I had been prepared for your flight." She tried to keep the edge of resentment from her voice, but it was there, just the same. She had thought she and the marquess were friends, but in the end he had not given her any inkling of his plans. In the normal course of things perhaps he didn't owe her that, but when his plans involved eloping with her charge . . . Well, it seemed the least he could have done.

"I suppose I should apologize to you for my precipitate action in taking Rowena away."

Her chin up, Amy said, "Yes, you should. You both placed me in a most awkward position."

Bainbridge stiffened slightly, but then relaxed. "I really am sorry, Miss Corbett. I . . . I was never the impulsive one, never one to do the impetuous deed. But . . .

Well, I knew His Grace would look favorably upon me as a husband for his daughter . . ."

"And that caused you to run away with her? Because her father would *favor* you? That's ludicrous." All the anger and turmoil she had been suppressing for months boiled up in Amy. "I cannot believe that while I thought Rowena and Lord Pierson were making a match of it, you were . . . were sneaking in and stealing her from him! Wasn't that your *true* reason for eloping? To evade the just indignation of your friend?"

He sighed heavily and sat down in a chair. "I can see my task is going to be much more difficult than I had anticipated."

"I didn't ask you to sit, my lord." Amy found that once the anger spilled out it would not be stuffed back down like a gown into a box. "The poor viscount must have been devastated."

Bainbridge chuckled, then put his head back and roared. "You idiotic girl!" he said, as he recovered. "Pierson told me he kissed you. Was that the action of a heartbroken swain still eating his heart out for Rowena?"

"Well, I . . ."

"Of course not! He never loved her! He became infatuated with some idealized version of her, some fantasy he had cooked up in his own addled brain. He wanted a lady to 'mold' into the perfect wife, for God's sake. You know Rowena better than that! They would have been miserable. I did you all a favor." He set his hat aside and crossed one leg over the other, much more at his ease.

Puss glared at him and stayed on her silken pillow.

"Not me! You did me no favor, my lord. I was cast out onto the street and . . ."

"I know! I know," he said. He jumped up and took her trembling hands in his, guiding her to her seat opposite him. He sighed as he sat down again. "Miss Corbett, if we had only known . . . but Rowena left a message for her father asking him to treat you well. She had no idea of what happened. In fact, the duke told her you had gone back to Ireland to work for the Donegals."

"Oh. She mentioned me in a letter to him? I saw it in her note to *me,* but I didn't know she had written one to her father. He never mentioned it."

"He wouldn't," the marquess said, dryly. "He has a resentful temper. But she did.

She pleaded with him not to take out his anger on you; she told him that she and she alone was responsible for her elopement."

"But why did you elope?" Amy came back to the part of his story that made no sense to her. "If you knew the duke would favor you . . ."

"I had heard how commanding the duke is. I didn't wanting him forcing Rowena to marry me. I love her. I wanted her to come to me, to dare for me, to upset all of her social reputation for me!"

"That is mad," Amy whispered.

"I know. I think I was in the clutch of a kind of insanity. My mother still has not forgiven me."

"And your sister? She visited me and was very angry."

"She has reverted now to her usual cynicism. There's another suitor in the offing, I understand, a gentleman just out of the army who is looking for a wife. Mother is not quite enamored of him, for he is merely a baron, but she's desperate. Harriet's opinion is unreadable, as always."

There was silence for a minute, but then Lord Bainbridge squeezed her hands and released them. "But Amy, I didn't come to talk about my sister or my mother nor even

Rowena and myself, though we hope you will forgive us and be friends with us again. I always did like you. No, what I have come to say," he said, holding up one hand against her reply, "is to talk to you about Pierson."

"He's infuriating! What did he mean by coming here and . . . and kissing me like that, in front of everyone?"

"Silly girl. He loves you."

Amy felt her heart thud in her breast and then stop; it just seemed to stop, and she could not breathe. It was as if she had received a blow to the chest. "L-loves me?" she gasped. "No, that's quite impossible."

"But he does."

"No! It's just . . . I know him, his gallantry." She rose and paced. "He saw me in the theater, found out I was a lowly seamstress and wanted to rescue me. But I don't need any knight on a white charger, and especially not after three months! I'm quite able to look after myself now."

"I can see that. I always knew you were a strong lady. But I think he was truly in love with you all along, he just refused to see it."

"No."

"Yes. Amy, he has been to see us and he poured his heart out to me. He's been working steadily on his estate and is making progress; that's what he has been doing for three months. I'm so proud of him. And he credits you with showing him the way, and with teaching him that he had it within himself all along. What is love, if not the ability to believe in another person against all odds? I think you love him. And I *know* he loves you. He's heartsick. I fear what he will do, that he may go back to his old ways if you don't . . ."

"No!" Amy held up her hands. "If you put that on me, I'll shake you. Lord Pierson must stand on his own, or not stand at all."

"You're right, Amy. I shouldn't have put that burden on you; I was being quite unfair. Honestly, I don't think he'll return to his own ways. He was ready to change, you just showed him that he didn't need anyone else to make him do it."

"Thank you. Give him more credit than that, Lord Bainbridge."

"But I still say he loves you. Look in your heart. Doesn't it feel like love to you?"

Amy stopped and sat back down. Did it feel like love? She knew she could stand on her own now. But still . . . A part of her longed for him and had for months. She had learned that she could survive on her own and be happy, but was there not a part of her heart that felt empty and ached for him?

"He's told me that he loves you, and you know he wouldn't lie about something like that," Bainbridge said, his voice gentle. "And do you really mean you would rather labor on in the theater, making your eyes weak and tired, than give your hand in marriage . . ."

"In marriage?"

The door burst open just then and Lord Pierson strode in. "I can't stand this anymore. Bain, get out; you're not saying this right. And I need no one to plead my case nor to propose for me."

Lord Bainbridge, with a mocking bow, exited and closed the door behind him. Amy stood facing the viscount. His golden brown eyes glittered in the increasingly dim light of late afternoon.

"Amy, I . . ." He surged forward to take her hands in his.

"No!" She backed away and clutched her hands behind her. "Stay back. Make your case, if you have one to make."

Pierson took a deep shuddering breath. "Do you mean I have a chance?"

"You may," she said, cautious in the face

of his presence. Her own feelings were no mystery to her. Seeing him again, she had known her love was no passing fancy, but solid and real. However, it didn't mean she would desert everything she had worked so hard to build, even though marriage — Her thoughts halted. Marriage, to Lord Pierson? How deliriously happy she would be! But only if he loved her too, and she wasn't convinced his love this time was any more real than that he had professed for Rowena. How could she believe him? And even if she were to trust him in this, why had it taken him three months to realize it?

Pierson could tell from her tight lips and doubtful expression that he only had one shot at telling her how he felt. He had better make it good. He had been such an idiot for so long; now he must mend his ways in this most important of all conversations.

"You know, I told Bain once that I thought that the perfect young lady was rather like a blank slate upon which a man wrote what he wanted, forming his wife into his perfect mate."

"And you thought Rowena was that blank slate?"

"I did. I thought all she needed to bring

to marriage was her own virtuous, pristine, amiable, mild mannered self and I would do the rest, writing upon the slate of her personality what I wanted. I thought it was her moral guidance I needed, rather than anything else."

She was silent; that wasn't encouraging. He wished he could reach out to her, take her into his arms. But he mustn't, not yet.

"I didn't realize that I should be whole, myself, before even thinking of a wife. I wanted a lady to fill in all the blanks in my character, to make me better by her example."

"And what do you think now?"

Now was his chance, his one opportunity. He took in a deep breath and let it out. It echoed in the highest reaches of the room, tall shelves to the ceiling piled with bolts of dimly glowing silks and satins. Puss, sitting in queenly peace on a silken cushion, regarded him with unblinking solemnity. "I have been working, at Delacorte, on bringing back my family's legacy. And . . . Amy, I'm good at it! I never thought I could be, but I am. So I don't *need* a wife, or her moral guidance. This is what I want to do now, for the rest of my life. And whether I ever marry or not, it's my life's work."

There was a long silence. "But?" she finally said.

He met her eyes, the blue-gray changing to deeper blue in the dimming light. "I've learned that women are not fragile, weak, and defenseless creatures. Nor dull-witted. And you taught me all that, even while I stupidly insisted on thinking I was in love with Rowena. All that time, all spring, I was falling in love. With you, Amy. With *you*."

Fear trembled in his stomach. Would she believe him? He couldn't tell by her expression, which was carefully blank.

"But three months!" she whispered. "Why did it take so long?"

How could he explain? "When I returned to Delacorte," he said, "I was hurt by Bain and Rowena's elopement, I suppose, but not like I thought I would be, or should be. It puzzled me, but I thought I must be numb. But more and more, as the months went by, I realized that I was glad. It freed me. Then I realized that I was often thinking of you, wishing you could see Delacorte, wondering if you would be proud of me. Wishing I could tell you everything I was doing, and asking what you thought of this improvement or that. And I realized that I was lonely, but not just for any company, for *yours*. For the conversations we had, and the way your beautiful eyes would light up when we talked. Did they light up just for me, I wondered? Or was I imagining things? I was so afraid of being wrong again that for a long time I didn't admit it; I don't think I even recognized it for what it was. But it's true. I love you."

"You . . . love me?"

"I do," he said, urgently, hoping that what he heard in her voice was longing. "I did all along. Amy, I love you so much. I see you everywhere, and I've held countless conversations with you as I walk at Delacorte. I want to show you everything. I want to see everything through your eyes. I . . ." He swallowed and took her hands, pulling her up to stand with him. "I want to touch you, to love you, and to *show* you how much I love you."

He wrapped her in his arms and pulled her against him, gazing down into her eyes. "Do you . . . can you ever love me, Amy?" But instead of giving her time to answer, he kissed her, gently, thoroughly, deeply.

Then he leaned his forehead against hers.

"I do," she whispered. "I love you, and I think I have from the first moment I saw you in that mud puddle, splashed with filth from the duke's carriage."

He gasped and drew back. "You saw me? You knew it was I? When? How?"

"That one evening . . . remember getting caught outside in the rain with Rowena? You came in and your hair was soaked and straggling down on your forehead. I saw you and I remembered that man, and knew why you seemed so familiar to me."

"Oh, Amy, you've seen me at my worst. Will you still marry me so I can show you myself at my best? Marry me and come to Delacorte with me. Please."

"I will," she whispered. "I will. And I'll love you forever."

"This is the part of the play when the romantic hero is reformed of his wicked ways and the heroine and he pledge their troth," he said, with a deep chuckle. "I guess we have fulfilled the play, and now we need only live happily ever after."

"Then I guess we can lower the curtain and bring up the house lights."

"I would rather dim them," he whispered and pulled her down to a pile of fabric. "Kiss me once more, before we find a vicar to marry us."

Amy sank into the material and heard a squawk erupt. Puss squirmed out of the cloth pile and then sat, elaborately performing her toilette as if she had never been almost squished. Pierson laughed, gustily, and Amy laughed too, only stopping when his mouth closed over hers once more and all thought was lost. But it did seem to her that Lord Pierson was perhaps not quite so reformed, for he still kissed deliciously like a rogue and a rake.

And that was perfectly fine with her.